Praise for
Mapping the Edge

"*Mapping the Edge* is a rivalry between two gripping stories, and each of them is a Rorschach test for the reader's own paranoia. Which do you believe? Which do you fear most?"

—MARY DORIA RUSSELL

"Two solid scenarios . . . There's a suspenseful rhythm to the writing as the story slips smoothly from one narrative to the other. . . . Dunant exerts complete control over her literary devices while adding insights on motherhood, relationships and lingering childhood traumas."

—*USA Today*

"A very smart book written by a woman who's mined her sex's most intimate, yet routine rituals . . . a riveting thriller. But on a deeper level, it's an intriguing examination of the devouring passion of motherhood and the difficult transition back to being a woman."

—Baltimore *Sun*

"Unnerving and elegantly written . . . and surely there's never been a more penetrating look throughout the suspense field at the ramifications of parenting for a gay man, a career-obsessed woman, or a single mother—nor a more trenchant study of one's core identity and needs."

—*Kirkus Reviews*

"Compelling psychological suspense."

—*Booklist*

"Tightly spun, edgy and faintly disturbing . . . [Dunant] gives this latest effort a nervy postmodern twist, spinning out two Borges-like alternative paths from the same unaccountable disappearance. . . . [An] astute psychological dissection of contemporary life . . . a compulsively gripping book."

—*Houston Chronicle*

"Sarah Dunant's unsettling, compulsive new novel grapples with several mysteries. The first involves the disappearance of the very model of a modern, capable woman, who has vanished while on holiday in Italy. But the second confronts an even greater mystery—how we never really know others, let alone ourselves . . . and how we always seem to be traveling along that perilous frontier which divides the obligations that bind us and the call of the wild. *Mapping the Edge* is that rare thing: a riveting read which also speaks volumes about the way we live—or fail to live—now."

—Douglas Kennedy

"A psychologically thrilling novel that never sacrifices character or verisimilitude yet plays convincingly with both. A compelling investigation of the dangerous menaces of contemporary life that resonates beautifully. A most satisfying experience, and one I highly recommend."

—Antonya Nelson

SARAH DUNANT is the *New York Times* bestselling author of *The Birth of Venus.* She has also written six suspense novels, three of which have been shortlisted for Britain's prestigious Golden Dagger award, including her most recent, *Transgressions.* Her third novel, *Fatlands,* won the Silver Dagger. As a journalist and critic she has worked extensively in print, radio, and television, and until recently hosted the leading BBC Radio arts program, *Night Waves.* She has also written two books of essays. Now a full-time writer, she is adapting her novels *Transgressions* and *Mapping the Edge* for the screen. Dunant has two children and lives in London and Florence.

Also by Sarah Dunant

Transgressions

Under My Skin

Fatlands

Birth Marks

Snow Storms in a Hot Climate

Mapping the Edge

RANDOM HOUSE TRADE PAPERBACKS
NEW YORK

Mapping the Edge

A NOVEL

Sarah Dunant

2004 Random House Trade Paperback Edition

Copyright © 1999 by Sarah Dunant

This work was originally published in Great Britain by Virago Press in 1999, and in the United States, in hardcover, by Random House, an imprint of The Random House Publishing Group, a division of Random House, Inc., in 2001.

Library of Congress Cataloging-in-Publication Data
Dunant, Sarah
Mapping the edge / Sarah Dunant.
p.   cm.
ISBN 0-375-75861-5
1. Mothers and daughters—Fiction.   2. British—Italy—Fiction.
3. Florence (Italy)—Fiction.   4. London (England)—Fiction.   5. Missing
persons—Fiction.   6. Single mothers—Fiction.   I. Title.

PR6054.U45756 M37 2001
823'.914—dc21   00-042533

Random House website address: www.atrandom.com
Printed in the United States of America
4689753
Book design by Meryl Levavi/Digitex

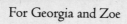

For Georgia and Zoe

Mapping the Edge

People go missing every day. They walk out of their front doors and out of their lives into the silence of cold statistics. For those left behind it is the cruelest of the long good-byes, because for them there is only pain and doubt. Did that person whom you loved so much—and thought you knew so well—did they simply choose to go and not come back? Or was it darker than that, and did someone do the choosing for them?

Missing rubs the soul raw. In place of answers all you have is your imagination. In place of reality, only fantasy. And the more you think about it, the more elaborate and the more consuming those fantasies become.

Stories from the edge.

Like this one.

Anna is leaving home. Bye-bye.

Part One

Transit—Monday P.M.

DEPARTURE LOUNGE, SOUTH TERMINAL, GATWICK AIRPORT. A shopper's paradise: two floors of superior retail space connected by gliding glass lifts and peopled by an endless stream of travelers, processed to have time on their hands and a permanent discount at the wave of a boarding card. If you are smart you come here with an empty case and do your packing as you walk: cosmetics, toiletries, clothes, shoes, books, perfumes, booze, cameras, films. For many the holiday starts here. You can see it in their faces. People shop differently, none of that suburban mall madness. Instead they stroll and browse, couples with their arms around each other, the beach saunter already in their stride, children dancing behind their parents in the hermetic safety of a controlled environment. When did you last read a horror story about a child abducted in a departure lounge?

Second floor, a cappuccino bar with tables out on the concourse, next to the Body Shop and Accessorize. A woman is sitting alone at a table, a small holdall by her side, her boarding card lying near to a plastic cup in front of her. She has no carrier bags, no duty free. She is not interested in shopping. Instead she is watching others and thinking about how it was twenty years before when she came to this airport as a teenager, on her first solo flight to Europe. None of this existed then. Before the invention of niche marketing, air travel had been a serious, more reverent affair. People wore their best clothes for flying then, and duty free meant two hundred Rothmans and a bottle of Elizabeth Arden perfume. It seems as far away as black-and-white photography. At that time her flight had been delayed for three hours. Too young for cheap booze and too poor for perfume, she had sat in a row of red bucket chairs nailed to the ground and read her guide-books, mapping a city she had only ever visited in her mind, trying to quieten the tumbling adrenaline inside her. The rest of her life had been waiting on the other side of Gate 3 and she had been aching to walk into it.

It is not the same now. Now, though there is adrenaline it has no playfulness within it. Instead it burns the insides of her stomach, feed-ing off apprehension and caffeine. There are moments when she wishes she hadn't come. Or that she had brought Lily with her. Lily would have loved the circus of it all; her chatter would have filled up the silence, her curiosity would have nudged the cynicism toward won-der. But this is not Lily's journey. Her absence is part of the point.

She pushes the coffee cup away from her and slips the boarding card back into her pocket. When she last looked at the monitor the Pisa flight was still waiting to board. Now it is flashing last call. Gate 37. She gets up and walks toward the glass lift.

Twenty years ago as she made this last walk there had been a Bea-tles track playing in her head. "She's Leaving Home." It was dated by then, already ironic. It had made her smile. Maybe that was her prob-lem. She was no longer comforted by irony.

Amsterdam—Friday P.M.

On Friday evenings I like to take drugs. I suppose you could call it a habit, though hardly a serious one. I see it, rather, as a way to relax; the end of work, the need to let go, welcome the weekend, that kind of thing. Sometimes it's dope, sometimes it's alcohol. Like most things in my life it has a routine. I come in, turn on the radio, roll a spliff, sit at the kitchen table, and wait for the world to uncurl. I like the way life becomes when I'm stoned: more malleable, softer at the edges. It feels familiar to me. Reassuring. I've been doing it a long time. I started smoking when I was in my teens. I got my first stash from the boyfriend of a friend: an early example of adolescent free enterprise. The first time I smoked there were other people around, but it didn't take me long to discover solitude. I used to sit upstairs and blow the smoke out of my bedroom window. If my father knew (and it seems impossible to me now that he didn't) he was smart enough not to call me on it. I was never into rebellion, only into solitude. And being stoned. And so it has continued throughout my life.

Though you probably wouldn't know it from meeting me. I don't look the type, you see. It has always been one of my greatest talents, that in the nine-to-five game I come over as the professional to my fingertips, brain like my clothes: sharp lines and no frills. Straight, in other words. One of life's good girls. The kind you can depend on. But everyone has to slip off their shoulder pads sometimes.

Other Fridays I vary the mood and go for alcohol instead. This has nothing to do with any queasiness about legality. Among its many splendors this adopted city of mine boasts a remarkable tolerance for dope and a system of distribution that suits even the most discreet members of the community. No. It's only that there are some Fridays when my brain yearns for another form of unzipping. On these occasions I indulge my appetite for frozen vodka. There is a singular pleasure to the way in which it flows out of the bottle, like heavy water, a thick viscous river of pure alcohol glugging its way over little chunks of ice. I keep a special glass for it; small, shot-sized, heavy—like the liquid. The sides go steamy with the cold as you pour, and when you drink, your fingers leave little wet prints on the glass.

The first hit is best taken on an empty stomach. I make sure that I lunch early that day so I'm already spacey with hunger by the time I arrive home. That way you can actually register the alcohol flowing into the blood, moving around your veins, making your hands tingle and your stomach burn. You mellow very fast. Then I start to cook. Timing is all here. Wait too long and you can lose the moment, find yourself too hungry to concentrate or too drunk to care. I put on music to focus me, and make something where the smell comes quickly, mingling the juices with the senses. Then I sit and eat in front of a movie previously selected from the video store. I don't watch television. A question not so much of language as of taste. Like the contemporary club scene, Friday TV schedules feel too young for me now, more like a waste of time than a passing of it.

I've become more aware of time passing recently. Not the day-to-dayness of it, but the bigger, structural stuff. Sometimes I have a sense of great chunks of my life floating, like space debris, in slow motion around me: three- or four-year bits that have got detached from the space station and can't be recovered. There goes twenty-two to twenty-six, passing so close I can almost touch it. Then a little further off I see my late twenties/early thirties turning over and over in zero gravity; glimpses of a job and a half-empty flat in a Scottish town where it never stopped raining and where anything decent was always a train ride away. Maybe I should reel it in and work a little revisionism on it—Scotland on the cusp of its style triumph. But then I think, Why bother? It's done already, over, all the possibilities hardened into choices, of no interest now except as history. And anyway life seems freer without it. I am, I realize, fortunate in this respect. Unlike others, I find myself growing less burdened with age.

Of course it helps to have been so bad at being young, though I had excuses enough at the time had I chosen to use them. While others were burning comet paths through the skies with their energy and ambition, I was standing underneath brushing their sparks from my clothing, afraid even to look up in case I got their fire in my eyes. In recent years, though, I have found myself passing an increasing amount of debris from the burnout of faster, more colorful lives. Negative equities, second wives or husbands, the beginnings of double chins, the drain of the psychotherapy bills. If they are coming unstuck this fast as they hit forty, imagine the dropout rate in another ten years' time.

But not me. I, against the odds, am doing okay. Maybe because I always asked for less, I have been rewarded with more. It's certainly the nearest I've ever got to contentment. I like this city. It has energy within its calm. Indeed, the whole country feels laid-back. Being underwater for so long seems to have imbued the land with an unholy sense of quiet, but since anyone who is anyone usually ends up in Amsterdam anyway you don't need to worry yourself too much about the waterland outside. I have a life here. I live in an apartment in one of the old merchant houses on the canal (the wealth of nations has been stored here at some time or another; scratch the wooden floors hard enough and you can still smell the spice); I have a job that I like and, most surprisingly of all, a man who likes me but doesn't need to live in my pocket (or my flat). I am satisfied. I could—and have—lived with less, and I have no wish for more.

It's usually when I'm in this mood that I know it's time to call Anna, if only to give her the pleasure of teasing me out of my complacency. In my more sentimental moments I think it's our friendship that's kept both of us from the fall. That while the married ones got bored and the single ones got bitter, good friends stayed alert to each other's needs. Of course Lily has helped. But this system of checks and balances was in place before she came along.

Friday is our phone night. Not that we do it every week—sometimes work or travel gets in the way—but as customs go it is an established one. And that particular Friday, I remember, I was looking forward to the call, because recently we had missed a few and I felt the need to catch up. And because, I suppose, yes, I did have an undercurrent of worry about her, a sense that there might be things happening in her life that I wasn't completely up-to-date with. But I was sure I would find out. Because in the end she would tell me. That's how it was with us.

We usually try to time the call for around 10:00 P.M. We wait till then because Lily is almost certain to be in bed and we can talk more freely. More often than not Paul is there, too, doing something inspiring with chow pak and sesame-seed oil, but he doesn't mind if she eats by the phone. So when the phone rang at 7:50 P.M. on that Friday night, the pan of finely chopped onions caramelizing on the stove, the second shot of vodka misting up the glass and my mind, I knew it was altogether too early to be her.

"Estella? Is that you?"

"Hello, Paul. How are you?"

"I'm fine. Listen, is Anna there by any chance?"

"Anna? No. Why?"

"Er . . . well, she's been away this week. We thought she might have visited you on her way home."

Out through the open windows the sky is beginning to bruise into a purple-blue twilight. From below I can hear the chug-chug of the first of the tourist barges starting off on the nightlife tour of the canals. "No. She's not here. Where's away?"

"Italy."

"Italy? What for?"

"I don't know, exactly. Have you heard from her recently?"

"No. We haven't spoken for a couple of weeks." I hold him snug to my ear as I carry the portable back to the stove and check the pan. "You sound worried, Paul. Is something wrong?" I ask quietly.

He doesn't answer immediately, as if he knows that the words, once spoken, cannot be taken back.

"Maybe, yes. She was due back yesterday evening. No one has heard anything from her. She seems to have gone missing."

Anna. Missing. I take another hit of vodka and turn off the flame under the onions. I will not eat dinner here tonight, after all.

Away—Thursday A.M.

THAT THURSDAY, ON HER LAST MORNING IN FLORENCE, ANNA returned to the souvenir shop near to the hotel.

It was one of those irrefutably Italian establishments, a mixture of Alessi chrome and upmarket kitsch: colored-glass perfume bottles topped in filigree silver, papier-mâché putti out of Fra Angelico via Disney, cunning CD holders in the shape of the Leaning Tower of Pisa—all with prices to match their sense of mischief.

The wooden horse, though, was different: less precious, more alive. It had caught Anna's eye on the first day she had gone walking. She had found herself returning later to check it out, though by then the sun had burnt the city into its afternoon siesta and she could only gaze at it through the window, trying to make out the price tag lying facedown on the glass shelf. It looked like sixty thousand lire, which at a good exchange rate—and it was—was still over twenty pounds. Too expensive a gift for a child, though Lily's obsession with horses already had an element of the adult in it, with any addition to her collection treated more as an object to be worshiped than a toy to be broken. Anna could already see the space on the shelf where this one would sit, pride of place, until it, along with the others, would be taken down for its daily exercise across the field of the bedroom carpet and out into the wilderness of the hall beyond.

Lily at play. Anna savored the image. It was one of many she carried inside her. Even now when she was supposed to be exploring time alone, Lily kept muscling in on her. Aren't I the most important thing in your life? How could you imagine the world without me? Her mental landscape was so colonized by her daughter that there were times when she wondered if there would ever be room for anything or anyone else. It was not that she was unhappy—life since Lily had been too vibrant for unhappiness—more that she was somehow impatient with herself. Which was partly what this trip to Florence had been about: the acting out of a serious whim, an instant strategy for revitalization.

And for much of the time she had reveled in it, the quiet intoxication of being alone. She had walked till she had blisters, writing the city on the soles of her feet, its beauty and its elegance made more intense by the pleasure of her own company. While Lily would have tugged at her hand and her soul, demanding food and entertainment, alone she could go for hours gorging on air and fantasy. She had always been a good traveler, and now she found herself to be the perfect single tourist. She had admired the dead through their art, the living through their style, and communicated with no one save the hotel clerk and the odd waiter. And if this last fact disappointed her she did not allow herself to feel it. It was too crude to suggest that she had come away from home for adventure (though of course she probably had). Nevertheless, it did occur to her that if this trip was in some way a pilgrimage to her past, then she had found precious little trace of the effervescent young woman who had walked these streets in her place twenty years ago. The memory of this different Anna, footloose, flirtatious, fancy-free, proved more painful than she expected. She couldn't decide if she was simply mourning youth or feeling something more profound. Just as when she thought about returning home, she didn't know if she felt relieved or saddened.

By that last morning in the shop she had stopped trying.

Going back, she found it crowded with a mixture of tourists and locals. She picked up the horse and checked the numbers written in a neat tiny hand on a tag attached to its hoof. The six turned out to be an eight, which made it nearer to thirty than twenty pounds. She put it back on the shelf and moved over to the counter to browse further—maybe she'd find something cheaper—but it was obvious there was nothing of interest and she soon gravitated back to the shelf, holding the horse in her hand, weighing it up, trying to convince herself that it was worth the money. Lily wouldn't know what it cost anyway; all she would know was the wrapping paper and the sense of expectation.

A few feet away she noticed a well-dressed man in his forties watching her. He was tall and stocky with dark thinning hair and he seemed strangely familiar. Maybe they had seen each other at the hotel, though if he was a guest he was Italian, of that she was sure; something about the suppleness of his skin, the way it kept its moisture under the sun, while English bodies reddened up and dried out, terrorized by the climate rather than nourished by it.

He smiled as their eyes met. She smiled back, because somehow it felt aggressive to refuse, then turned her attention back to the horse. She was imagining it gift-wrapped, Lily's little fingers poking and prodding, locating the sharp ridge of the legs, yelping with delight as she recognized what it was.

"Excuse me?"

She looked up.

"You are staying next door, yes? At the Hotel Corri?"

"Yes." The hotel then, that was where they had seen each other.

"You are English."

"Er—yes."

"You like this horse?" He pronounced the last word with a touch of the guttural, as if he expected to get it wrong and was compensating already. Oh, I see, she thought. He's a salesman. She gave a polite little nod, then looked back down at the figure.

"But this is a crazy price for such a thing."

"I'm sorry?"

"Eighty thousand lire. It is—how you call it?—stealing. They sell these in the market for under half the price."

"Do they?"

"Of course. They don't come from Italy. They are African. The boys from Senegal have them on their stalls. You don't see them?"

"No."

She had seen the boys, though. Beautiful young men, their skin gleaming like polished coal under the sun, startling in a city where the predominant color palette was burnt ocher and gold. Their presence was one of the many ways in which Florence had changed since she was first here so long ago. If now was then, would she have wanted to woo one of them rather than the olive-skinned young Romeo she had pursued through that teenage summer of Italian verbs and Dante? Maybe not. These tender young men seemed in more need of money than of love, their goods carefully laid out on brightly patterned lungis: soapstone figures and heavy carvings from the bush. She had seen elephants and the occasional wild cat but no horses. Surely she would have noticed.

"Of course," he said, "it is your choice. But you would save a lot of money."

His English was good, far better than her Italian, eroded by decades of neglect. She couldn't decide if she was flattered or irritated by his pinpointing her so clearly as a woman traveling on a budget. Maybe the hotel had given her away, the lower end of the scale, though—God knew—that didn't exactly make it cheap. "Actually I'm leaving Florence today. I probably won't have time to get to the market."

"Ah. You go back to England?"

"Yes."

"And from where do you fly? Florence airport or Pisa?"

"Pisa."

"At what time?"

She hesitated. "Er . . . around eight o'clock."

"Okay. The reason I ask is because of the trains. You must catch the six o'clock. It is direct to Pisa airport and will get you to the plane in good time. Also I make you a suggestion. You get to the station

early and there in front of the main entrance you will find some of
these boys with their horses. Very cheap. And then you will have a
good buy, an easy journey, and enough money for an espresso and a
pastry at the airport."

She laughed, charmed despite herself. "Thank you."

He shrugged. It was a gesture that on an Englishman would have
sat too theatrically. Here it seemed no more than what was called for.
"It is nothing. Just a—how you call it?—a tip for the day. Have a good
journey home."

She started to thank him again, but he was already turning away,
his attention on something else. She was sorry she had been so stand-
offish now. It struck her that this was part of her problem. She had
got so used to having her defenses up over the years that she had
started to read kindness as manipulation. She should learn to trust
people more, to take the time to enjoy them. She took one more look
at the horse, but her mind was made up and she left soon after, without having bought anything.

A few moments later the man went up to the cash desk and laid
down two fifty-thousand-lire notes. Next to them he placed the
wooden figure of the horse. As the sales assistant picked it up he
leaned over and said something to her. She reached underneath the
counter and took out a length of silver wrapping paper.

Away—Thursday A.M.

THAT THURSDAY, ON HER LAST MORNING IN FLORENCE, ANNA didn't leave the hotel at all. Instead she breakfasted upstairs, waiting for the telephone to ring.

The room was small and stuffy, with a window that looked out on a dingy inner courtyard and allowed for no wind, a place to sleep in rather than to live, cheap, although in high season it wasn't. She lay on the bed and watched the ceiling fan rotate lazily.

Eventually she got tired of waiting and fell asleep fully dressed on the bed. When she woke, bruised and confused from dreams she could barely remember but that she knew involved her in some vast and silent danger from which she couldn't save herself, she rang through to the switchboard in case she might have missed a call. But there had been none. Why hadn't he rung? Had something happened to stop him getting away? He was now two days late. It didn't make any sense.

To begin with she hadn't minded the silence. On the contrary, she had found herself grateful for the space. She had come out a couple of days early deliberately, needing to be calm when he arrived, so that she would know what to say and not allow herself to be blown off course by desire. She had used the city to center herself. She walked for hours, choosing routes away from the tourist haunts, to churches that only rated a sentence in the guidebooks, squares that history had largely passed by. In every place she could feel echoes of her younger self; eager, unformed, and in love with a city and her own sense of omnipotence within it. The idea of this earlier Anna was so powerful that once she thought she might even have seen herself, small and plump with funky look-at-me sunglasses and cropped punk hair—but it was only an illusion of fashion, evidence that the wheel was turning ever faster somersaults into retro.

It was one of the things she liked about the city: the way it vibrated with conflicting styles. Middle-aged Florentine women gilded and painted against age brushed shoulders with the latest breed of hippie travelers, the boys studded and tattooed, the girls with bare midriffs and backs the color of roasted chestnuts, their stick-thin bodies still clinging to childhood. It was holiday season and the surrounding countryside was full of local fiestas. A buskers' paradise. But they always came back to Florence. In the mid-morning heat you could find them at a pump by the side entrance of the Duomo, guys with dreadlocks thick as bead curtains stripped to the waist and washing themselves like puppies, water splashing everywhere.

She stood and watched them, mesmerized. They awoke a vivid memory in her of a night many years before, when she had been traveling and arrived back from Rome to find the hostel she had been staying in full. She had ended up sleeping on the steps of the Baptistery, then washing in the bathroom of a café nearby. It seemed inconceivable that she could do it now. Where had all those years gone? Places, people, lovers, jobs, Lily. The neck of the hourglass seemed to have widened since Lily, time gushing away more like liquid than sand. These Duomo kids were probably nearer in age to her daughter than to herself. How did that happen? It didn't seem possible.

Lily. She hadn't thought of her much in these last few days. In her guilt she realized that the connection between them was becoming fainter. She had called home the night she had arrived, but Lily had been engrossed in a video and didn't want to talk. She could hear her munching on potato chips, her attention elsewhere, still following the pictures on the screen. She was having a good time. She didn't need her.

Except, of course, she did. Before this thing with Samuel had threatened to blow her world apart, Lily's presence had vibrated inside her whenever they had been separated. She had imagined the bond between them as a kind of emotional chewing gum; the substance of love stretching out, malleable, tensile, pulling ever thinner until the moment when you choose to loop it all back into your mouth and chew it together again. But was there a chance that if you stretched it too far it might snap? Was that what the pursuit of this obsession was doing—weakening the thread?

In the hotel room the hours bled away. He wouldn't come now. A part of her felt almost relieved. Whatever his excuse, this would be the beginning of the end. If she were going to make the plane she would have to leave by mid-afternoon. She had had the desk clerk check the times. The trains to Pisa turned out to be erratic. Not all of them went directly to the airport. The five o'clock would be too early, the seven o'clock too late.

She had already packed, the clothes folded away, the wooden horse she had found in the market on the first day rolled carefully inside a T-shirt to protect its sharp edges from damage in the overhead locker of the plane. At least Lily would know that she had been thinking of her. She zipped up the holdall and got off the bed. He would not come now, and she needed to get out of there. Maybe it was for the best. She left her bag on the bed and went down to the hotel lounge to get something cold to drink.

Home—Friday P.M.

I AM GOOD IN A CRISIS. SOMETHING ABOUT MY DNA. I CAUGHT THE last shuttle by twenty minutes, but even with all the right connections the journey from Amsterdam to West London took three and a half hours. Still, I didn't allow the time to unravel me. No sir. Instead I spent the trip constructing scenarios of her homecoming. If Anna hadn't come back when she said she would, there had to be a reason. The most likely was that she had called to say she was delayed but that the answering machine hadn't taken the message. She was probably on her way even now. I pictured her getting out of a taxi, bursting through the front door, throwing down her bag as she ran upstairs to Lily's bedroom to wake her up to say good night . . . I did such a colorful job with the pictures that I had to call Paul from the Heathrow arrivals hall just to check I'd got it right. He answered on the first ring. He was still waiting.

I took a taxi. London was even warmer than Amsterdam. The grass on the motorway verges was dry as a bad perm and the air rotten with exhaust fumes: the sort of day where emergency departments would have been counting out the oxygen masks as the asthma patients checked in. Halfway to Chiswick the sky got so heavy that it cracked open and a wall of rain came down. The road steamed like a hot plate as the water hit and the windows of the cab instantly misted up.

England. I had forgotten how dramatic weather could be.

By the time we got to her road the shower had passed, soaking up the worst of the heat. Out through the window the air smelled of green. I hauled myself out of the cab. Paul must have heard the engine because he opened the door before I had time to reach the bell.

He beckoned me inside with a finger on his lips and a quick gesture upstairs. On the first landing Lily's door was ajar. I nodded and we moved quietly down to the kitchen. First things first. I rescued my London bottle of vodka from the freezer (a ship in every port) and poured us both a drink. He refused his. It made me look at him more closely. In his time I have seen Paul drop-dead gorgeous enough to turn every head in the room, but he was not at his best now. His skin had a tight, ironed-on quality to it—Christopher Walken in one too many psychotic roles—and his eyes were slightly bloodshot. He looked as if he wasn't sleeping well. But whether from sex or worry you can never tell with Paul.

"Still nothing?"

"Not a word."

"What have you told Lily?"

"That she missed the plane and she'd be back when she could get another one."

"Does she believe you?"

He shrugged. "What's not to believe? Why else would her mother not be home when she said she would?"

He sat down at the table and closed his eyes for a second, using his thumb and middle finger to massage into his eye sockets. No, I thought, not sex this time. "Have you been here all the time?"

He shook his head. "Patricia, the child minder, called me this morning. I pick Lily up most Fridays anyway, but Patricia had to go to Ireland today for her niece's wedding this weekend and obviously she was beside herself that Anna wasn't home."

"When exactly was she due back?"

"Yesterday evening."

"You called the airport?"

He nodded. "All the flights from Florence came in on time. No cancellations, no delays. They wouldn't give out passenger lists."

"Florence?"

"Yep. That's where she went."

"What was she doing there?"

He shrugged. "Search me. The last time I talked to her was last week. She didn't say anything about going away. Apparently she only asked Patricia to baby-sit two days before she went. Patricia thinks it was something to do with work, but when I called the paper this morning the features editor said she didn't know anything about it and neither did anyone else." He paused. "I thought she might have said something to you."

But she hadn't. The vodka slid from cold to hot down my throat. I wanted another one. I was trying to remember our last phone call, two—no, three—weeks before. She had been busy, something about an article she was working on but she didn't tell me what. She had sounded, well, a little distant, but I had put it down to work. She's always expended too much energy on such things. Unlike her best friend. But Florence? If she had known she would have told me. No question. Though it had happened before I met her, I knew all about Florence. Everybody has a story of being eighteen and the city which you finally grow up in, or at least that's what you'd like to believe happened. She hadn't been back for years. If she had been going to Florence she surely would have told me. "What about a contact number?"

"She left a number, but Patricia thinks she must have taken it down wrong. When I called this afternoon I got some woman running a dress shop."

"Still," I said. "It doesn't make sense. Why would she just not come back? She'd know Patricia was going away. You're sure she didn't leave any kind of message?"

"There's nothing on the machine."

"Maybe it didn't record."

"And maybe she didn't ring."

Neither of us spoke for a while. "I've been waiting till you got here. . . ." He paused. "I'm wondering if we should call the police."

"It's too soon," I said. Though I had no idea if it was or wasn't.

He shrugged. "If she's not here by tomorrow morning that makes two nights. I don't see how we can avoid it, do you?"

"Well, I don't see how we can avoid telling Lily if we do."

"So what do you suggest? Are you ready to move in here and field the questions till she turns up again?"

"Wait a minute, Paul. You're not saying you think this is deliberate?"

"No. I told you, I don't know any more than you do. I think it's suspicious, that's all. She doesn't say anything to anyone about going in the first place—I mean, not to you or me. She just walks onto a plane and doesn't come back. I think if we don't hear from her by tomorrow we have to assume something's happened to her."

"Like what?"

"Jesus, Estella, I don't know. Like . . . something."

Something. Take your pick. I read a statistic the other day that on average around the world 2,090 people die in traffic accidents every day. There must be another statistic about how many of those are in a foreign country at the time. But morgues have regulations whatever the culture, and where would her passport or credit cards be if not in her handbag? Forget it. Anna wasn't the kind of woman to die under a bus in a Florentine side street. That couldn't happen to her. Or to me. What do they say about lightning not striking twice in the same place? Or within the same family. My family. I felt myself oddly reassured by superstition.

Through the open kitchen door we both became aware of the guttural sound of a diesel engine in the street. I glanced down at my watch: 12:48 A.M. Last planes from Europe are usually in by 10:00 P.M. But not everybody flies. What if she had stayed on, then found that all the Friday planes were full and she had to go overland? I had a sudden ridiculous Vera Lynn image of her, standing full into the wind, looking out to sea as the ghost-gray shadows of the Dover cliffs loomed into view. Then from Dover to London on a slow train. Or even, if it was too late, a taxi. Outside, the engine was still turning over while someone paid their fare and got out their house keys. We heard a door slam, then another. After a while the taxi drew away. We deliberately didn't look at each other. How long could we wait?

He sighed. "How long can you stay?"

"As long as it takes," I said. "What about you?"

"Mike has tech rehearsals over the weekend. First preview on Tuesday."

It wasn't really an answer, but it helped to get away from it for a while. "How is he?"

How long had this one been? It had to be nearly a year now.

"Mike? Fine. Great. Busy. How about you? How's work?"

I shrugged. "You know the tax business. Moving A to B to avoid paying C. To my surprise, I appear to be rather adept at it."

"That's because it's not your money."

"Possibly," I said.

"Anyway, you're looking good on it."

I tapped the glass. "Must be the stimulants."

"She's probably got some dope somewhere if you want." Like many people he's amused to think of lawyers breaking the law. He doesn't seem to understand it's an occupational hazard. In fact, as gay men go Paul is in many ways really rather straight, which is one of the things that makes him so charming. I wondered if he was as diligent toward Lily now Mike was on the scene. In the past he always kept them separate, the boys and girls in his life, but from what I'd heard from Anna this one was different.

"Thanks, but I'll stick to what I've got."

We sat for a while longer, but it somehow made it worse, waiting together. He stood up from the table. "I'm going to go to bed."

"You sleeping in the spare room?"

"Yep."

That left Anna's bedroom. "Does Lily know I'm here?"

He nodded. "After I spoke to you I told her you'd be coming for the weekend."

"Do you think she'll mind if I sleep in Anna's bed?"

"If she does she probably won't tell you."

"No." She wouldn't. Some people say that only children are good at keeping their own counsel. I would know about that, of course, though I don't always feel like talking about it. Like Lily. But then that's a long story. . . .

He was standing by the table as if there was something more to say. I pulled the bottle toward me. His eyes followed the movement. I've seen you legless enough in your time, mate, I thought. I suggest you don't make a thing about it. "It's a tradition," I said. "Friday night. She wouldn't want her absence to spoil it."

He shrugged. "You know me. One man's abuse is another man's pleasure. Sleep well."

"I will. And, Paul," I said firmly, "don't worry. There'll be a reason why she hasn't called. She'll be back tomorrow, I'm sure of it."

"Yeah," he said. "I'm sure, too."

Away—Thursday P.M.

Anna took the stranger's advice and got to the Central Station with time to spare. But although there were a number of market stalls laced around the outer edge of the square, there was no sign of any Senegalese boys selling horses. The discovery annoyed her. She should have bought it when she had the opportunity. It was too late to go back to the shop now. She would have to risk finding something suitable at the airport.

She ran up the stairs into the entrance. The central hall, with its fake monumental architecture, was choked with people. Along the left-hand wall ran a set of ticket windows, all of them sporting queues three deep, the occasional Florentine lost in a mass of tourism, the seasonal crush of the long vacation. Thank God she had got here early. She joined the shortest line (which wasn't short at all) and checked the timetable board high above her. It told her that the last train to Pisa Central had left twenty-five minutes before. There was no 6:00 P.M. service listed. The next airport train was at 7:00 P.M., an hour and a quarter away and too late for her to make her flight. She looked around for an information window, but was concerned about losing her place in the queue, which was already stacking up behind her.

She was frantically thinking about buses when a voice behind her said: "Hello?"

She turned to see the man from the shop that morning standing before her, his jacket off and a worried look on his face.

"Oh, thanks God, it *is* you. I am so pleased to find you. I have been looking all over the station. You remember me, yes? From the shop this morning?"

"Yes. Hello. What——?"

"I am so sorry. There is a change with the trains. There is no more six o'clock service to Pisa airport now. They are running on——what is the words?——summer times. I did not realize."

"You came all this way to tell me that?"

He laughed. "No, no. A friend was going to Rome. I brought him to the train, but when I checked the board I remembered what I said to you."

"So I can't get to the airport from here?"

"Not in time for your plane, no. Your flight is——what——eight o'clock, you said?"

"Seven-forty-five. How about a bus?"

He made a clicking noise between his teeth. "No. There is a—— how you say?——a dispute. The drivers for the airport don't go. They want more money. There is a sign outside. You must have passed it. That's why there are all these people."

"Why don't they run more trains?"

He said nothing, confining himself to one of those gestures that tell, in any number of languages, of the unfathomable stupidity of the authorities. No trains or buses. If she missed this plane it would be a nightmare: The flights were packed, it had been a stroke of luck to get space on this charter as it was. But if she took a taxi from here it would cost a fortune. She would have nowhere near enough Italian currency to cover it. She looked around for an exchange office.

"Please . . ."

In her anxiety she had almost forgotten he was there.

"You must let me help. I have my car outside. The autostrada is quite fast and we can get there in one hour. Plenty of time, yes?"

She shook her head. "It's okay, I'll take a taxi. But I have to change some money first."

She was already moving away, but he stepped into her path. "Signora. Please. This is my fault. I give you the wrong information and now you are in trouble because of me. Let me help. I live near Pisa. I go that way now. The airport, it is not far from my home. Please. Let me help you."

It wasn't that she didn't think of refusing. On the contrary, the advice she had already drilled into Lily—never accept anything from anyone you don't know—she had taken instinctively. But there was another imperative at work here: the need, this time, to accept the kindness of strangers. After all, wasn't that partly why she had come back, to rediscover some spontaneity in herself, some sense of the possibility of life? "Only connect." Like many grand-tour teenagers she had first come to Italy with A-level E. M. Forster novels singing in her head, sporting his exhortation to life as a badge of romantic courage. Twenty years on, it might seem cheap to apply a literary aphorism to something as mundane as a lift to the airport. Nonetheless—

"Well," she said. "If you're sure it isn't out of your way . . ."

Away—Thursday P.M.

THE MESSAGE LIGHT WAS FLASHING AT THE BOTTOM OF THE PHONE, a small foggy yellow button, on/off...on/off, like a shallow-water warning to sailors coming too close to the land. She had seen it from the moment she opened the door, but she had been waiting so long that now it was here she suddenly couldn't bear to go near it. Instead she busied herself with last-minute packing. Even as she was in the bathroom gathering up her toothbrush and creams she could feel it pulsing on and off through the wall in between. It's too late, she thought. You've left it too late. The spell is broken. I'm going home now. I'm going back without meeting you. It's better for everyone this way.

She picked up her bag and walked to the door. She still had plenty of time. The flight didn't go till after seven. She could answer the message and still make it out of there. But somehow she knew that the temptation would be too great. She closed the door and walked down the corridor, the key clasped in a tight fist in her jacket pocket. The light would continue to flash as she took the lift downstairs to the desk, then out to the foyer and to the street to hail a taxi to the station. Soon after it would stop, as her checkout registered and the phone wiped itself clean in preparation for the next guest. The message would be lost. Gone. Over. No meeting. It was that simple.

As she stood waiting for the lift, it seemed to her that her life had become like a puzzle from a children's book: a figure—her—standing at the corner of the page with a set of different paths snaking out away from her, interweaving and overlapping until one emerged onto a cliff edge and a sheer drop, and the other to a green and pleasant land. Heidi has to take her grandfather's flock up to the summer pastures. Which path should she choose to avoid disaster?

The lift came. The doors opened. And closed again.

She turned back along the corridor, her fist uncurling from the key.

As the message activated in her ear she closed her eyes and listened as his voice scooped bits of her innards out. Then came an address. There was a notepad and pencil by the phone, but she made no move to use them. Forget this and it wasn't meant to happen, she thought, with one last careless nod to fate.

In the back of the taxi it was so hot that her skin stuck to the seat through the layer of linen. She hesitated for a moment when he asked her where she was going, then opened her mouth and heard the address sing out, clean and clear, word-perfect. When she inquired how far it was he told her it was in Fiesole, on the other side of the river. She looked at her watch. She would be cutting it fine to get to the airport in time. Maybe she'd have to take a taxi. He would have money. She would borrow from him and write him a check. She opened the window to let in some air, but it only served to funnel the heat back in. A few streets on they drove past the market where she had bargained for Lily's wooden horse on that first morning. It seemed so long ago. Her fingers closed over the holdall on her lap.

Home—Saturday early A.M.

PAUL'S FOOTSTEPS WENT UP THE STAIRS, THEN STOPPED NEXT TO Lily's room above. She must have been asleep, because almost immediately he climbed the next flight. After a while I heard the toilet flush and then a door close.

If I picked up the phone now might I hear him on the line to Michael? Anna says they keep night hours, regularly staying up till two or three. She says it's only a matter of time till they move in together. I thought it might make her feel strange, seeing Paul enjoy domesticity with someone else, but she likes Michael, says he's older than his years and that he doesn't let Paul get away with stuff. She approves of him. So does Lily, apparently. It seems he has the secret of not trying too hard, and that he knows how to make her laugh. Which in my experience means that she has decided to let him. So does this mean Paul is a man with two families now? Probably.

I sat and drank in the kitchen. Through the windows I could make out the shadows of the little garden; its patio stones, its borders, its colored climbing frame. It had been such a rubbish dump, a builder's scrapyard to judge from all the crap we had moved out of it the weekend after she moved in. It had been summer then, too, though nowhere near as hot as now. She had had no money to hire help, so she called in friends; free beer and food and all the pickaxes you could wield. We had filled two skips. Lily was slung in the hammock nailed between the clothesline and the elder tree at the back. Every time she cried whoever was nearest rocked her to and fro. We ate lunch standing up, hunks of bread and cheese and salami. Paul said it looked like a bad Italian movie: sweat, sunshine, and the rich pleasure of working the land. It was one of those days that everyone there would remember, something about the way it summed up a generation and an age.

Where and who were they now, all those people? Successful enough to have their own gardeners, no doubt. I had liked them well enough then, though they had been her friends rather than mine. Did she still see them? Did they exchange Christmas cards? She didn't talk about them, or not that I could remember. Come to think of it she didn't talk about anybody that much anymore, except for Lily of course, and Paul, and more recently Michael. Presumably I would find their numbers in her phone book if I needed them. At what point do you start checking with acquaintances rather than friends?

I was beginning to hear the vodka talking, the telltale signs of maudlin creeping in, like reaching the worm at the bottom of the mescal bottle. In Amsterdam it was nearly three o'clock in the morning and I would be a long time gone by now. Night shadows. I turned off the light and went upstairs.

Her bedroom was unnervingly tidy, the bed made and the cover unrumpled. It looked almost planned: the room of someone who had packed knowing that she was going to be away for a long time. Then I remembered that Patricia would have been here since, would have hoovered the floor, hung up the clothes, and generally cleared away the worst of the mess naturally associated with Anna's lifestyle. I opened up the cupboards to reassure myself. A great crush of clothes burst out at me, bringing with them the unmistakable scent of her, leftover perfume and body smell mixed together. A person's smell: it is such a powerful statement of them. I turned, almost expecting to find her standing behind me. But she wasn't there.

I went into her study next door. It was a mean little space, the famous "extra bedroom" of estate agents' jargon, in this case not helped by all its furniture: a desk, a filing cabinet, a computer terminal, and everywhere paper and books. Not even Patricia would or could penetrate this jungle.

I sat at the desk and switched on the light. If there was something to find it would surely be here somewhere. I sat back in the chair. On the notice board above the desk a group of photos was pinned at eye level. There was a picture of Lily in a playground, hands up above her head, caught in the split second of pure exhilaration before the descent down the slide. Then one of me looking younger and more serious with a baby, *the* baby, in my arms, and then Paul and an older Lily sitting opposite each other in some American fast-food diner, both in profile with their mouths open, teeth sunk into two gigantic hamburgers. The year before, Anna had done a freebie fly-drive travel piece for the paper, about Montana, and Paul had joined them on his way from L.A. and they had spent a week touring the Rockies. The last picture was of the three of them sitting on the bonnet of the car with the desert stretched out behind them, grinning into the lens in a delayed-action shot: happy family on vacation, seeing the sights, clocking up the miles, spending nights in motels where they slept three in the bed, curled around each other like the petals in the inside of a flower bud. Spot the difference between this and the perfect family. No sex please, the man's gay. Well, why not? Why should the hand that rocks the cradle always be attached to the penis that helped put it there? As surrogate fathers go Paul had turned out to be better than many originals. And anyway, I know enough couples who hardly bother to have sex anymore.

Just to prove the point, at the corner of the notice board, stuck at an angle as if it was only just clinging on, was a fading snapshot of Elsbeth and George in their garden in Yorkshire, the frost about to come in. They couldn't have been more than sixty-five when the picture was taken, but you could already sense the bony guy from *The Seventh Seal* lying in wait for them behind the shrubbery. By that time she had already taken to finishing off his sentences for him. They were sewn so tight together you couldn't get a breath between the stitches. Some might think it sweet. I thought it hell. But then I suppose I have a vested interest in not believing in happy families. He died the year after. As far as I could see it was his only strategy for getting away from her. To get her own back she followed him a year later. If she'd stuck it out a bit longer she would have seen her grandchild, though it occurred to me at the time that the lack of an identifiable father would probably have killed her anyway. Anna thought later that it was the loss of both parents that had made her want the child. That may be true, though I always felt it had more to do with Christopher and the affair from hell. But even within best friendships there are some places you learn to tread lightly. And once she'd made up her mind, the decision wasn't something that one could challenge.

I remember the day she told me. It was a Saturday morning and I was in the kitchen making my first cup of coffee. I was ten months into Amsterdam. I'd found a good dope source and a bicycle lock that worked. My apartment had pictures on the walls and I was beginning to feel that I might have a life here rather than just another job. It still didn't mean I was ready for anything. I didn't quite take it in when she first said it. I suppose it's a question of hearing what you want to hear. Or not.

"You still there, Estella?"

"Yeah. I'm still here. When did you find out?"

"I did the test last week." She didn't say anything for a moment. "But I think I've known for a while."

"Why didn't you tell me?"

"I suppose I didn't know what to say."

And the way she said it made my mouth go dry. I already knew who the father was, of course. That was the reason she hadn't told me. It had to be. "What happened? Did Christopher find he'd left a couple of videos at your place and come back to collect them?"

"It wasn't like that. He's going abroad. It was a way of saying good-bye, that's all."

And how many times does that make, I thought, but didn't say. I had disliked this man for so long by then that I could no longer work out if it was because he was a schmuck or because he had made Anna so unhappy. Every time she had stopped seeing him I celebrated; the last time must have been six months before, and because it had been such a dramatic and painful severance I had really come to believe it was the final one.

"What are you going to do?" I said at last, and the pause that followed had been so long that I remember I had had time to spoon in the sugar and stir it.

I also heard her take the breath before she spoke. "I'm going to keep it, Stella." She faltered. "Not because of him. I want a baby."

Four words. That's all it took. I want a baby. Anna would be thirty-three next birthday. I'd known her since she was nineteen, and in all that time I had never heard the slightest ticking of a biological clock. In the silence on the other end of the phone I knew that's what I was hearing then.

"And how about him? He's up for two families, is he?" And I know it was cruel, but I didn't like the fact it had taken her so long to tell me, and I needed her to know that.

"Don't be mad at me, Stella. This is hard enough as it is. It's got nothing to do with Chris."

I caved in immediately. "I'm sorry. What does he say? Have you told him?"

"No. And I'm not going to. He's not going to be here. He got the correspondent's job in Washington. That's what he came to tell me. They leave next week." And I remember thinking hallelujah. Now we wouldn't have to watch his mug on our nightly TV screens. Instead we'll just be spotting the jigsaw pieces of his features in his child. "I'm going to have the baby on my own. Though I was hoping you and Paul might want visiting rights."

"God, Anna," I said at last, because this was one of those times when you had no option but to tell the truth. "I'm not even sure I like children."

"That's because you've had no practice. You'll like this one. I promise."

. . .

And she was right. I did. We all did. Though when I thought about it later, even the glory of Lily couldn't take away from the fact that she had chosen to keep it from me for so long. However much you love someone it is only right that you should acknowledge their failings, and I suppose it was around this time that I accepted that Anna—who had always had a particular talent for telling the necessary lies of life, to tutors about exam papers, employers about deadlines, or lovers about endings—could also be economical with the truth when it came to me, her closest friend.

Six months later I came to London for the birth and Lily entered a world where she had a godmother who was closer than a blood relative, and a surrogate father who was better than the real one would have been.

As for my own biological clock, well, either I'm hard of hearing or it had stopped before it started. For as long as I can remember I have had no wish to have a child. Nothing personal, just a healthy form of self-absorption that allows for no competition. In fact, for years I didn't even think much of the idea of having a man—well, not in any serious way. As far as I'm concerned this was less to do with emotional damage than with the pleasure of my own company and the need for the toilet seat to be in the right place when I came to use it. There is a theory, of course, that children who lose their family early in life are frightened to make one of their own for fear of further loss. There is, however, another theory that says more or less the opposite. For myself, I have no time for theories, life being complicated enough without them. Whatever the reason, the lovers I specialized in were mostly short-term leases (Amsterdam was particularly good for this), boys on the move with passports stuffed with visas. If it lasted a month it was too long, after which they would set off for somewhere else and I would return to my old ways, happy in my aloneness.

In essence René has done nothing to disturb that, though in age and work he is at least my equal. The first time we met was before Lily was born. He was in town for a conference and we spent the night in his hotel, during which it did occur to me that I might be using him to compensate: a last-ditch attempt to get my own womb full to join hers. But when we got down to it, it didn't feel like that at all. Later when he put his head on my stomach to rest for a moment, I asked him if he could make out the sound of anything ticking in there, but only because I was absolutely certain there was nothing to hear. The next morning I cycled into work reveling in how beautiful the city was, and how much I loved my singular self within it.

I didn't see him again for six years. Then four months ago I picked up the phone to find him at the other end. He was living in Amsterdam now and wondered if I was free. So we picked up from where we left off: occasional sex, conversation, and a mutual need to lead separate lives. He spends much of his time traveling (aid consultancy is a mobile business), while work, Lily, and the need for my own space keep me occupied, too. If we tried to get any closer I suspect we would end up further apart. I count it as one of the success stories of my life. I also like its symmetry. So now Anna and I both have alternative families. I think the world needs more of them.

I turned my attention to her desk.

Away—Thursday P.M.

His car was astonishingly clean and sweet-smelling: no sweets wrappers, no sticky fingerprints, no split-open tape boxes, no bits of broken plastic from McDonald's toys, none of the detritus that came from small fingers and a rushed lifestyle. Instead there were wiped surfaces, shiny footmats, and a small paper tree swinging from the mirror, giving off a faint tang of chemical pine. Behind the driving seat there was even a coat hook for his jacket. A man without children, that was Anna's first thought.

He pulled away from the curb. Someone honked him. He flattened his hand on the horn back, then apologized. "I am a very safe driver, don't worry. We are maybe one hour away from the airport, though there will be worse traffic now because of this."

On their left they passed the market stalls. Scarves, posters, wallets, T-shirts. No horses. He glanced at her. "You must be angry, yes? First no horses, then no train. The Africans are usually here. I don't understand why they are not."

"It's all right," she said, letting her head fall back against the head-rest. "It's more important that I catch the plane."

"Of course. Oh, I forgot—you like cappuccino?"

"Er—yes."

"Good." He motioned to a brown paper bag sitting on the seat behind her. "You have sugar?"

"Yes—but . . ."

When she didn't take it, he lifted one hand off the wheel and reached back to get it himself, then handed it to her. "Please." He seemed slightly flustered, as if she was somehow not reading his behavior signals correctly. "It's still hot, I think. I got it for my friend to take on the train, but he didn't want it. It's a shame to waste it, no?"

As he said this it struck her that he might be gay. That would explain the spotless car, the classy clothes, and the almost exaggerated politeness. Anna thought about Paul and the way he had embraced her child-filled chaos. Maybe there was something about her that attracted gay men. No doubt a lack of predatory sexuality, she thought, almost ruefully.

"Please?"

He was proffering the drink, and it was clear that he might in some way be put out if she refused. In the hollow between the driver and passenger seats there was a shelf with cup holders. She dug out the polystyrene containers with their generous share of napkins, took the lid off the one without the letter "z" scratched on it, and slipped it into the hole for him. Then she opened the other and started to drink. She made a small face.

"You don't like it?" he said anxiously. "It has too much sugar?"

"I don't know. There's a funny taste. What is it?"

"Ah. The almond flavoring maybe. It is a syrup they use sometimes. Very popular now. Always we have America pushing at our feet. It is good, I think, no?"

"Yes," she said. In fact the flavor was a little strong for her, but in the stale heat of the car she was in need of the lift of caffeine. She drank it quickly.

"So." He had pulled up at a set of traffic lights. A phalanx of people surged across the road, office rush hour and the opening of the shops after siesta. Florence at its craziest. He smiled at her. "Now you can relax." He sounded like a host at a dinner party. "I will get you there in good time."

"It's very kind of you."

"Not kind. It is—how do you say?—the littlest I can do."

"The least."

"Least? Yes, yes of course. The least I can do," he said, pleased with himself, the word stretching out like a long smile.

They fell silent. After a while the congested medieval streets of the center gave way to wider, more relaxed boulevards, then to sprawling industrial outskirts. Italy was as new as it was old, as ugly as it was beautiful. Anna had always liked that about it, had found it reassuring. She tucked the empty container carefully back into the bag, observing the house rules of tidiness. He was still drinking, lifting the cup from the holder and taking a series of small sips, as if the liquid was still too hot to drink comfortably.

She glanced across at him. In the shop the face had seemed too broad to be that interesting, but in profile it took on more definition, the features etched rather than drawn, as if someone had dripped acid onto soft stone, the hand hesitating over certain key contours. Where she had first thought forties, now she was not so sure. He might be older; it was hard to tell. There was a quality of containment about him that made it difficult to determine what lay behind the politeness.

Maybe he wasn't gay after all. She thought of his life trailing out behind him, like smoke from a plane exhaust. She saw them intersecting, two silver trails in an empty sky. Merging, then passing. Except, wasn't it ships that passed in the night? She tried to re-form the image but realized that she had lost it. She felt suddenly rather weary, worn out by travel and the demands of politeness.

"So you like horses." They were almost onto the autostrada now, filtering into heavy traffic all moving at speed.

"Oh, it wasn't for me. It was for my daughter."

"Your daughter?" And he seemed surprised. "You have a daughter?"

"Yes."

"I . . . er . . ." And this time he went looking for words. "You don't look like a mother." It wasn't immediately evident that this was a compliment. Could this be some kind of elaborate pickup? she thought. If so, would she be annoyed or flattered? "How old is she?"

"Six. Nearly seven."

He drove for a bit. "You don't buy her guns?"

"Guns?"

"Isn't that what women do now? To make their children without . . . without sexism."

The sheer naïveté of the remark made her laugh. Someone had once bought Lily an electric car, all fast chrome and flashing lights. She had played with it twice, then left it to rot under the bushes where it had crashed in the garden. "She doesn't like guns. Or swords. They bore her. Some things you can't change."

He nodded, as if that idea pleased him. "And your husband? Does he agree?"

"I don't have a husband. I'm a single parent." She added the last sentence with a touch of defiance, just in case the listener might see fit to quarrel with this vision of the world.

"I see," he said. "That is all right for you?"

"Yes," she said. "Yes, it is."

"And your daughter, where is she now?"

"She's with a baby-sitter, a friend."

Talk of Lily made her want to be home. It was always worse on the return journey, as if she were a homing pigeon fixing on its spot, the emotional radar kicking in. She looked at her watch. Twenty to seven. There was a one-hour time difference. Lily would be home from school now, though Patricia and she would have probably stopped off at the park to play for a while first. In England it would be light for hours to come.

Not so here. Already there was the hint of twilight in the air. She would take off into a Mediterranean sunset, and arrive into northern light. It was over. No adventure, no change. So be it. It had been a romantic notion, anyway. Plane tickets don't alter your life; they just transport it somewhere else. For real change you need to be braver—or more foolish. She felt her eyes closing with an enveloping tiredness. She tried to rouse herself into conversation. They were in the middle lane of the freeway, both sides still heavy with traffic. She looked at her watch again. Almost 7:00 P.M. now. Her check-in time was already past.

"Don't worry," he said, in answer to the unasked question. "We are not far. See?"

In the distance she saw a set of signs coming up on the grass verge, one to the right bearing the symbol of an airport, a set of silver wings already airborne. She felt herself suddenly nauseated, as if the sight of it had given her a kind of instant vertigo. She fumbled with the door controls.

"I'm sorry, I have to open the window a little. I need some fresh air."

He glanced at her quickly. He pushed a button and her glass slid silently down. A wall of fume-clogged air hit her, worse than the recycled atmosphere in the car. She felt her eyes water with its toxicity. She tried to close the window. Again he did it for her.

"I'll turn up the air-conditioning. We'll be out of the traffic soon. Why don't you lie back and shut your eyes? We'll be at the departure terminal in ten minutes."

She wanted to tell him that she was okay, that it was just a touch of travel sickness and all she needed was to be out of the car, but then she began to feel decidedly worse, as if her brain were filling up with poisonous fog and she was drowning in it. She put her head in her hands; then, when that made her feel sicker, she did as she was told, leaning back against the seat rest and letting the darkness flow in. She closed her eyes. She might even have moaned. The last thing she heard was the click of his traffic indicator signaling their way right across the freeway toward the airport lane.

Away—Thursday P.M.

THE ROOM WAS GENEROUS, ITS PROPORTIONS DATING FROM A TIME when the wealthy saw fit to have a reminder of heaven above their heads. The ceiling would have been a fresco originally, baby-fat cherubim flitting around the Holy Trinity, rearranging their robes, punching exuberant little fist-holes into the cloud cover while a chariot of aspiring mortals—generals and nobles of the house—stood watching from the side. But fashion and time had long since wiped out such sensibilities; the ceiling was now a barreled expanse of grubby white, grubbier at the edges where decades of dust had coated the cornice gray.

The floor looked original: worn yellow ocher tiles with a geometric border, chipped in places. In contrast, the rest of the decor was jarringly modern: a scarlet sofa like Warhol's pouting lips, and across the room a table of white wood with a vase of wooden bird-of-paradise flowers from Peru. On the end wall two arched windows were taking the brunt of the late-afternoon sun, slatted blinds slicing prison bars of light across the tiled floor.

They stood with the stripes between them, the distance significant, uneasy. They seemed the perfect transient occupants for a room where no one lived, or at least left little evidence of living. His suitcase, black, executive, leaned against the sofa; her tatty holdall sat by the door like an old dog patiently waiting for its owner to leave.

"Where have you been? You told me you'd be here on Tuesday."

He clicked his tongue. "No, Anna, I said I'd let you know. I always knew I might not be able to get away that soon. I rang you in London on Monday to tell you, but you weren't there."

"I'd already left," she said quickly. "You didn't leave a message, did you?"

"No. We agreed I wouldn't do that. But I left one at the hotel on Tuesday. Didn't you get that?"

"No." She thought of the reception desk and the stream of ripe young girls who always looked as if they had something better to do. "It wasn't the world's most efficient hotel."

"You should have stayed somewhere better. I told you I'd pay."

"I thought we'd been through that one. I don't accept your money," she said quietly, glancing around. "What is this place, anyway?"

"It belongs to a friend. He works for one of the multinationals, but he travels most of the year. He doesn't spend much time here."

"Does he know?"

"That I use it occasionally? Yes. That I'm here with you now? No."

"Where are you supposed to be?"

"Away. Somewhere else. It's not important where."

"What about you?" he said after a while. "What did you say?"

"Oh, I made up some stuff about work. But I told them I'd be back tonight."

"Tonight?"

"Yeah, I know. But that was the plan, remember. You said Tuesday." And she gave a little shrug.

"Well, you can call them later. Have you changed your flight?"

She shook her head. "I can't."

"That's what they always say. We'll use my card. There won't be any problem."

"No, you didn't hear me, Samuel. I said I can't. I can't do it. That's what I came to tell you. I'm not staying; I'm going to go back tonight as I promised. I'd already decided that before you called."

He paused. "And is this decision about home or about us?"

She shrugged. "I don't know. Probably both."

"I see. So why are you here now?"

"You didn't leave a phone number on the message. I thought I should at least tell you myself."

He smiled as if to make it clear that he didn't believe her, but it didn't matter that much. "Well, so now you have. Thank you."

An unexpected breeze came through the half-open window and rippled across the blinds. The shadow stripes on the floor seemed to grow and shrink with the waves of light. She knew it was her turn to talk, but she didn't know what to say.

"I thought we'd worked all this through, Anna," he said gently. "I thought what was happening between us was okay."

"Yeah, well, so did I. But it isn't." And her voice was suddenly fierce. "I shouldn't be here. If I stay any longer I'll miss my plane."

"Listen," he said, so quietly she had to strain to hear him. "This isn't your fault. It's not anybody's fault. It just happened."

She shook her head. "That's not true. We made it happen." She made an angry noise in her throat. "Do you do this?" she said suddenly. "Is this what you do? In the past, is this what you do?"

He laughed out loud. "What—you want me to lie to you as well as her? Okay. Yes, I do this all the time. Start something casual and then push it till it gets out of hand." He stopped. "You're not the only one who thought about not coming, you know. This one has broken my rules too."

"I thought you said there were no rules. Wasn't that what you told me on that first night?"

"Yeah, well: you know first nights. . . . Come on, Anna, don't make me the bad guy in this. It's not how it is."

She closed her eyes. "Shit," she whispered.

She didn't move. What was she waiting for? For him to touch her? If he did, would that make her go or stay?

He shook his head. "I can't do it for you. Do you understand? That's not how it works. You have to make up your own mind."

Time passed. She took a step toward him. If she didn't get back that evening Patricia would take Lily home to stay with her. She would read her a bedtime story and take her to school next morning and Paul would pick her up, as usual. Lily would be fine. She was a happy little girl whose life was filled with people who loved her. She would make recompense later. To everyone. After all, it was only a night or two. And everybody deserves pleasure sometime, a chance to store up summer heat for winters ahead.

As they came into each other's physical orbit the heat of their skins burned off the remaining layer of conscience. The air relaxed. Her holdall remained where it was on the floor, the airline ticket tucked coyly into the side pocket.

Home—Saturday early A.M.

AMID THE SCATTERED PAPERS, LETTERS, BILLS, AND NEWSPAPER CUT-tings on her desk was her Filofax. Almost certainly Paul would have been here before me, looking for names and numbers. If he had found nothing, that was because there had been nothing to find. I picked it up and it fell open at the right page of the diary section, a paper clip marking the spot. The week was empty. There was no mention of any trip, no flight details, no hotel, not even the word "Florence." How could anything be so sudden or so secret as not to be recorded? I realized after a while that I didn't know what I was looking for.

Children can move as silently as animals when they want to. I heard the breath and found her at my side in the same instant. The shock sent a cold wash through my body. She in contrast was warm, nest-ripe with the milky perfume of sleep.

"Whoa . . . hello there. You made me jump."

"Stella," she said, bleary-eyed.

"Yeah. Paul told you I was coming, yes?" She gave a small nod. "You're up very late."

"Is it tomorrow yet?"

"No." I laughed gently. "It's still the middle of the night."

"Did you come on a plane with Mummy?"

"Oh, darling, no. I came from Amsterdam. Mummy isn't home yet." I put out my arms to her. She hesitated for a moment (I love watching her thoughts move) but stayed where she was. I wasn't offended. It takes time with Lily. It always has done. Nothing personal.

"Did you just wake up, Lil?"

She shook her head. "I heard a noise. I thought it was Mum."

"No. Only me. I was looking for something."

She gazed down at the desk, fingers prodding among the papers. Rushing her doesn't help. "Mummy went to Italy," she said after a while.

"Yes."

"Have you been to Italy?"

"Yes."

"Is it nice?"

"Yeah."

"Sometimes when you go somewhere that's really nice you don't want to come home."

"Oh, I don't think Italy is nice like that. She just couldn't get on a plane."

She frowned. It struck me that although Paul is not a bad liar she hadn't believed him.

"I know she'll be back soon; don't worry," I said, because that, as yet, was not a lie. "Shall I put you back to bed now?"

She shook her head quickly.

"You'll get cold."

She shook her head again, then climbed onto my lap and fitted herself into the curves of my body, inviting the hug. I pulled my arms tightly around her. Before she came along I hadn't even known how to look after a dog. It's amazing how children teach you what they need you to know. She was so warm. It was as if her blood was a higher temperature than mine. Do we lose heat as we grow older? I thought of death and its clammy coldness. Vodka. Once it's warmed the blood, it chills the soul.

"You have to put the light on."

"Which light?"

"The light in the porch. Mummy might come back and think there's nobody home."

"Okay," I said carefully. "I'll make sure I switch it on."

"Are you sleeping in her bed?"

"Yes, I am. Paul's in the other room."

"So where will Mummy sleep?"

"Oh, sweetheart, I'll move downstairs if she comes. I can always sleep on the sofa."

She considered it for a moment, then said, "She won't know. You'd better leave her a note on the stairs saying that you're in her bed. So she knows that she has to wake you."

I looked at her. Whatever your world picture, you still have to get it in order. The only difference is the size of the landscape.

"Good idea. Shall we write it together?"

I spelled out the words for her and she formed each of the big looping letters with great care. In the lamplight I watched her, entranced. Within the peach bloom of her cheeks I could read the outlines of Anna's sleeker face. She already had her hair, wild coal-black curls, almost too rich and voluptuous for such a little face. Her father was harder to find, but then I never knew him that well.

Lily was still laboring. "Hey, that's great. You're really learning fast."

She gave me a cool sidelong glance. "They're just letters, Estella. Everyone can do them."

I made sure I didn't laugh.

When we were finished I took her downstairs and tucked her in. The room was like a cocoon, the twirling silhouette figures of the night-light sending out wild shadows across the walls and ceiling. She slipped in between the covers and turned away from me, falling almost immediately asleep.

"Do you want a hug?" I whispered close to her ear, but there was no answer.

As I left I pulled the door behind me.

"Leave it open."

No, not asleep yet.

I did as I was told. I left the note in the middle of the carpet in the hall, in a place where neither Anna nor Lily could miss it. She would be up before either of us, and she had a memory like an elephant. Then, as promised, I switched on the light in the porch. The road outside was still and silent, the houses opposite dark.

I gave up for the night and put myself to bed.

I had to climb in over a pile of books and papers (this part of the jungle Patricia wouldn't touch). I went through them, just in case. The news went back weeks, left and right, tabloid and broadsheet; the theory being that if you write for newspapers, you should know what the rivals are saying. In practice there are too many words. Most of the papers hadn't even been opened. Mixed in with the news were well-thumbed children's books, a clutch of magazines, and a draft of something with pencil marks all over it. An article she was writing. I scanned it in the hope that it might explain everything: some major exposé of a Mafia ring set in Florence selling Italian choirboys into pedophile rings. But it was years since Anna's bylines had been so juicy, and it turned out to be a piece on the failure of nursery schools to comply with new government literacy targets for five-year-olds.

Yet another article she hadn't talked about. There had been a time before Lily when Anna's career had been on the fast track, but in the last few years she seemed to have lost the hunger for it. Single mothers can't be one of the boys, she had once explained to me. It only hurts if you fight it.

In the bedside drawers I found some pens, an old book of Auden poems, a chewed-up dummy—a relic from the era of sleepless nights and last resorts—and tucked away at the back a compilation of erotic stories. I flicked through them, but they were too literary for my taste, too many euphemisms and soft focus, not enough balls. Not quite Anna's taste either, from what I remembered. In the early days when I first moved to Amsterdam it used to be one of our regular Saturday-evening pastimes, watching the men watching the prostitutes in their rose-tinted shop windows, trying to work out who was exploiting whom, the different ways that power and pleasure plait together in people's sexual fantasies. We went there, I remember, one summer's night soon after Lily had been born. Anna had been carrying her strapped to her chest, Lily's eyes wide open and surprised in the way that babies often are, blinking in the sights.

I lay looking up at the ceiling. Anna had been missing for one day and almost two nights. It was unthinkable that she should simply have decided to stay away without getting in touch. Which meant that for some reason she couldn't. From one bed I imagined another: a room in an Italian hospital where a pale woman lay under a sheet, her nose and mouth filled with tubes, her body attached to a monitor, across which a wavy green curve was flattening out into a line, the bleep turning to a high whine as it registered the change. I blinked and the image changed: the same woman but without the screen this time, waking up into a profound silence, in her mind as well as in the room. The next time I looked she was sitting in a chair, her ankles and wrists tied to the legs and armrests, her face bled white by fear, the shadow of another figure projected across her body.

I sat up in the bed and shook the pictures away. Was Paul lying upstairs with his own slide show in progress or was I somehow more prone to this because of my own past? How soon after my mother went missing was she also dead? Two, three days? I couldn't remember anymore. I'm not sure I ever knew.

Impressive how the cancer cells of your imagination multiply even faster than the ones in the body. But if this is not about accident or crime, then what on earth is it, Anna? Don't you understand that people are going crazy with worry here?

Away—Thursday P.M.

HER BODY WAS LIKE A BALLOON BLOWN UP WITH HELIUM GAS. EACH time she tried to move her limbs she felt herself lifting off the ground, her whole torso rising and turning in a languid slow-motion dance that belied a heaving sense of panic underneath. She needed to see where she was falling, but her eyes kept opening onto darkness. Her breath hurt. The air was heavy, fat with moisture, filling up her nostrils and sucking at her skin. She tried to peel it off her, but the movement only caused her to lift farther off the ground again. She knew she wasn't properly conscious; she must be waking from some deep sleep or still embedded within it and only dreaming of being awake, but she could not hold on to that fact, nor work out what it was that felt so wrong.

This time as she slipped away, her body rising and rolling in a glorious defiance of gravity, she heard the crunch of gravel, and for a second she saw something—a snapshot of an evening sky, slashes of deep pink against a charcoal-blue wash, like swaths of bright cloth flung out from the bolt across the horizon. Her body felt like the colors, melting and wild. Someone grabbed hold of her arms and she felt herself being yanked back to earth. The velocity of her fall brought vomit to her throat and she knew she was going to be sick.

The darkness returned.

When she opened her eyes again she wasn't flying anymore. It took her a while to work it out. She was lying horizontal, fully dressed, her body leaden and flat, as if the air above were crushing her down. At least now her brain was functioning. The surface under her was soft, a couch or a bed, and the atmosphere was tame, inside rather than out. Gradually the darkness coalesced into a series of shapes, different densities of black. Directly in front of her she made out a bulky mass, some kind of cupboard or large piece of furniture, and to her right, near the ground, a thin slice of dirty yellow light from underneath what must be a door.

Her head hurt and she needed to urinate, badly. It was hard to think of anything else. She pulled herself off the bed, but her legs were like sponges soaked in water and she had to use the wall as a prop to get herself to the door.

Inside it, a ghostly night-light illuminated a cramped bathroom: tiled walls, a bath, and a marble top with a basin; a neat set of white towels and hotel shampoo and conditioner bottles nearby.

She fumbled with her trouser button to get herself undressed. The urine splashed fiercely into the bowl. She only just made it in time, like a child who waits too long at play, then has to rush to go. A child. Lily. Lily... The thought was like an electric shock. Lily. She saw traffic lights, a sign for an airport, a man's face glancing at her anxiously from the driver's seat. Then she remembered the flash of sunset, and the vomiting. She pulled herself up from the loo. I'm ill, she thought. I'm ill. But what? And how? And she felt a rush of fear in the bottom of her gut. Her mouth felt as if she had been chewing on gravel. She gulped down a handful of water straight from the tap, but it didn't help.

In the main room she searched for the light switch, only to be blinded when she found it. She blinked her way back into focus onto a spare, spotless hotel room: single bed, side table, wardrobe, chest of drawers and chair—inoffensive corporate furniture, not unlike the room she had left that morning. One wall was covered by heavy drapes. She yanked them back, half expecting to find a cityscape filled with lights, but instead there was only a window, considerably smaller than the width of the curtains, and blackness beyond. When she lifted the catch the window opened a few inches, then stopped. The air was unexpectedly cool, with a whisper running through it, like the sound of electricity singing through pylon cables. It was as if the world ended behind the glass.

When she turned back, the room appeared less benign. She noticed there was no telephone anywhere, no light by the bed, no leaflets or stationery on the desk. Not a thing, in fact, to identify this as a real hotel at all. Even the walls were bare. So was the back of the main door. No framed room charges or fire instructions. And when she turned the handle it didn't open. Whatever lock was in operation, it wasn't on the inside.

The discovery made her frantic. She sifted through the clogged debris of memory and came up with the syrupy coffee followed by sudden nausea and the need to sleep. She saw his face smiling across at her, reassuring, concerned. It couldn't be ... it wasn't possible. Her mind short-circuited to bizarre stories of kidnap, Italian-style; rich magnates or their children held in cellars and losing bits of their anatomy to prod their relatives into vast ransoms. It didn't make any sense. Why would anyone in their right mind want to kidnap her, an anonymous tourist and single mother with no family and no money? It was all some grotesque mistake.

She threw herself at the door, smashing on the wood with the palms of her hands and shouting at the top of her voice. How long had she been unconscious? She felt sick again and she was sweating heavily. She stopped to look at her watch, but the face was splintered and the time behind it was forever ten to nine. Now it was the middle of the night. But which night? How long had she been there?

She went back to the door with renewed panic, using her fists this time and carrying on until the pain in her head forced her to stop. No one was listening, or if they were, they were choosing not to hear. She was suddenly greedily thirsty. She went into the bathroom and drank more water. She grabbed one of the plastic bottles sitting on the side. Green shower gel, "made in Milan," bottled by the thousand for any number of hotel chains. Where was she? She felt dizzy. She moved back to the bed and sat heaving, staring at the door, taking deep breaths.

Around her the silence was profound, deeper than the room, deeper than the building. She felt sick and clammy. She lay back and pulled the covers over her. From a vent in the room the air-conditioning kicked in, a low mechanical hum, like a hotel. Like a hotel. At least it wasn't a cellar. This was the last thing she remembered before she fell back to sleep.

Away—Friday A.M.

ANNA WAS SITTING BY THE WINDOW IN A LARGE CHAIR, SO DEEP
that its wings seemed to envelop her, cutting her off from the rest of
the room, its arms wide enough to use as a table. A glass was balanced
on one of them, the liquid alive with bubbles, and there was a towel
thrown on the floor nearby.

She was naked, her legs curled up under her, her hair wet, pushed
back from her face. Her skin was clear, no makeup, washed clean and
shiny like a child's. She looked tired but composed. She seemed to be
staring out at something through the half-open window, but there
was nothing to see. In the middle of the night even the city was still.
Florence lay below them in the valley, its night-lights like a constella-
tion of stars in distant space. She moved her right leg slightly and her
skin made a small sucking sound as the thigh pulled away from the
back of her calf. She slid her fingers down the inside of her leg, feeling the sweat that had gathered there. The surface of her skin was
alive to the touch. She couldn't remember the last time she had been

so aware of her body. No, that wasn't true. She could remember quite clearly.

Anna saw herself five weeks earlier, returning home to Lily after their first encounter. They had said good-bye to each other in the hotel room in Central London and she had driven back across the Westway in the silence of an early morning, much like tonight's, hers one of a handful of cars still on the road. She had come into the house quietly: Patricia was asleep upstairs in the spare room, Lily was in her bed. She had been desperate to see her daughter again. Not to assuage any sense of betrayal or guilt, but from the need to hold her in her arms and know that nothing had changed. She would have liked to have a bath—his smell was all over her—but the pipes ran next to Patricia's room and would have made discordant music in the middle of the night. She stripped off her clothes, brushed her teeth, and crept into bed, for that second the subterfuge making her feel like an unfaithful lover.

Lily, like a heat-seeking missile, had located her body and moved into it. The cotton nightgown was rumpled up around her waist, and her flesh was warm and soft. Child after adult, female after male, the contrast was profound and delicious. I love you, she thought. What happened tonight doesn't make any difference. She wanted to wake her up and tell her that. She moved her grip and Lily started to cough, once, twice, then enough to wake herself.

"Mum?"

"Yes, darling?"

"Hello." And the voice was richly croaky, like dark wood splintered along the seam.

"Hello. You got a cough?"

"Mmn." She was still half-asleep. But when she coughed again it was more like a bark, the throat angry.

"You okay?"

"I want some water."

Anna slid out of bed and filled her a glass from the bathroom tap.

Lily was sitting up now, eyes blinking open, solemn. She grasped the glass with both hands and gulped it down noisily; Anna could hear the liquid traveling down her throat.

"You smell funny," Lily said, wrinkling up her nose as she handed back the glass.

"Do I?" Anna had replied, marveling at the radar detection. "It's hot out. I've been sweating."

"Where have you been?"

"Working."

"Did you have a nice time?"

"It was all right," she said as she slid herself in next to her. "Come on now, get back down under the covers."

"I cried at bedtime, you know."

"Did you? Why?"

"I missed you."

"Oh, you silly duck. Patricia was here."

"Mmmn. She called me a silly duck, too. But she said I could sleep in your bed."

"And that made you feel better?"

"Yes."

"I see."

"But that's not why I cried."

"Of course not. Now, come on, let's go back to sleep."

"It's like cigarettes."

"What is?"

"Your smelliness. Eleanor's dad smells like that. Eleanor told him that he's going to die, but she says he doesn't care." She was wide awake and cooking now, enjoying the transgression of being awake in the night.

"Hmmn. Well, we're all going to die sooner or later. I bet Eleanor's dad doesn't smoke that much, anyway."

"He does. She gets the packets out of the bin."

"Little snitch."

"What's a snitch?"

"Nothing. Hey, it's the middle of the night. Aren't you tired?"

Anna said, but not with any real passion. She loved Lily's noise and curiosity, enjoyed these illicit night communions as much as her daughter did.

Lily lay quiet for a moment. Then: "Mum. Paul is sort of my dad, isn't he?"

"Yeah, darling. Sort of."

Pause. "So will Michael be like another dad now?"

"No, Michael's just a friend. You do like him?"

"Oh yeah, he's really funny. But I don't want another dad. One's enough."

In the darkness Anna pulled her daughter to her closely. "Yes, one's enough. How about mothers, though? Do you want another one of those?"

"No, silly," she chirruped, curling her arms and legs around Anna's body like a monkey.

Afterward Anna had lain awake reflecting on how easily she had moved back from him to her, the lover and mother separating out like oil and water. The next morning she had come back from taking Lily to school to hear the phone ringing through the front door. She knew it would be he. He had asked for her phone number rather than offering his own. She also knew what she was going to say. The one-night stand had given her everything she needed, even down to what she suspected had been their mutual lies.

"Morning." His voice was already familiar, the cadence around a single word recognizable. She was surprised by how tender it made her feel. "How do you feel?"

"Tired."

"Me too." He paused, and the silence was suddenly full of his fingers, slipping inside her skirt, tracing a line down over her stomach. "Do you have to work today?"

"Yeah, I'm just on my way out."

"Shame. Listen. I discover that I have to be in London again on Monday week. Can you get free?"

Thanks but no thanks, remember? But it was already too late. Along with the other things the night had given her had come a sudden taste for more. She would justify it to herself later. She tried to make it sound tough. "Okay. But now I have some rules. No promises, no bullshit. We don't meet each other's family and we can stop it anytime either of us wants, all right?"

"Absolutely." He had sounded amused. "Anything else?"

"Yes. The restaurant has got to be cheaper. I don't have that kind of money and it's not all right if you pay."

"Fine. You want to change anything about the sex, or did we get one thing right?"

"I'm thinking about it. For now we can leave it as it is."

"Thank God for that." Pause. "We picked well, didn't we?"

"It's early days," she said. "Don't push it."

But of course, they had.

From behind her in the apartment she registered the sound of a shower turning off. She closed her eyes. A moment later she heard his footfalls on the tiles. He came and squatted down in front of her. She didn't move. He was dressed in a dark bathrobe, water still clinging to the hair on his arms and legs. He smiled and with his right hand he pushed back a strand of damp hair that had fallen from behind her ear. Still she didn't react. In the darkness she could barely make out his eyes. He kissed her gently, playing with her lips, suggesting she play back. She followed, then broke away. She put her head back against the chair and closed her eyes.

He leaned forward and kissed her again, this time on the forehead. She frowned, as if the gesture were in some way painful to her. She opened her eyes and looked up at him. He took her hand and guided it underneath his robe to his half-erect penis. She left it there for a moment. They smiled. Both his invitation and her touch felt more about comfort than passion.

"You look cool," she said.

"It won't last. You're already hot again."

"Mmm..." She let out a long exhalation, half breath, half sigh.
"Are you all right?"

She took her time. "I don't know."

"Why don't you come and lie down?"

"I should have called."

He traced her face with his finger. "It's okay. She'll be fine. You said so yourself. We'll do it in the morning."

"You shouldn't have let me fall asleep."

He smiled. "It was only for an hour or so. You were tired."

She brushed this aside. "I feel bad about her."

He looked at her seriously for a moment. "You know what I think, Anna?" he said, as he ran a slow finger down her arm. "I think you feel bad because if you're really honest you don't mind that she's not here."

"Well..." She sat with it for a while, acknowledging the hit. It was a measure of their closeness that she didn't feel the need to deny it. "If you get any smarter I'll probably have to be frightened of you."

He smiled. "What's the problem? Not used to the competition, eh?"

"Don't flatter yourself."

She looked around the room. In the darkness the tiled floor was like a skating rink, an expanse of ice with a pale mist lying on top of it. It looks so cool, she thought, so inviting. But it isn't. This is how people drown. They mistake exhilaration for safety.

He stood up and made a move to walk away.

"No." She put out a hand to stop him. "Don't go."

"I'm tired, Anna," he said softly. "I want to sleep and I want you to come and sleep next to me."

When was the last time she had lain next to a man she wanted to wake up with? A lifetime ago. Certainly too long ago to remember. "I can't come yet. I don't know how to cross the floor."

If he found the remark oblique he didn't show it. Maybe he understood it. He sat down at her feet again, this time laying his head on her lap, his hair cold and wet against the heat of her legs and stomach. She put a hand on the top of his head and stroked him slowly; then she leaned forward, draping her body over his. They stayed like that for a long time. The air around them began to change, the darkness breaking up with the first hint of a summer dawn. She slid her hands under the back of the bathrobe, massaging, caressing downward until she reached the cleft in his buttocks. She pushed further, sliding a finger across the crack of his anus. He moaned at her touch, then twisted himself up and around to meet her. As they met he pushed his bathrobe open and pulled her to him inside.

"Come to bed."

"Okay. But we mustn't sleep."

He laughed. "I think there's very little chance of that. I tell you what. We'll be like an old married couple. I'll put on an alarm."

Afterward, they slept curled away from each other, their bodies disentangling in search of more familiar spaces alone. Or maybe it was the heat.

At dawn he got up quietly and closed the outer shutters to keep out the sun. The room descended into black. She slept on. At 6:37 A.M. too many Florentines got up at once and the local generating station hiccuped into a moment's power cut. The radio alarm by the bed flashed off, then on again, all previous instructions wiped from memory, the numbers randomly rearranged. It beeped a sad electronic apology. There was no one awake to hear it.

Home—Saturday A.M.

I'VE ALWAYS FOUND IT EASY TO MOCK THE POLICE. WHEN YOU'RE young they reek of authority, upholding laws that you're breaking, breaking ones that you uphold; then, as you grow older, they get younger and you mistrust them for that, too. But when something bad happens in your life, when you need help and there is no one else, the chances are that the policemen you get will not be the corrupt ones they make the TV documentaries about, but the other, everyday lot: job, life, troubles, and venial sins, just like your own. Like the two smooth-faced young men who came to Anna's door that morning, sweating slightly in their heavy uniforms, their helmets tucked under their arms and a halo of community policing around their heads.

Paul wasn't at his best by then, and neither was I. We had both begun the day on too little sleep. I had heard so many cars pulling up during the night that I could no longer tell which were dreams and which reality, but when I woke with a start to hear sounds in the kitchen I was careful not to be disappointed to find that it was only Paul. Against the odds Lily was still asleep.

He was sitting at the table with a pot of coffee and the telephone directory in front of him, and I could feel a new tension about him, as if somewhere in the night fear had overwhelmed hope, and he was worried now that we had done the wrong thing in waiting. It's possible that he saw the same thing in me, because his hand moved toward the phone as soon as our eyes met. Before he could get to it, it rang under his fingers. We both started with the sound. He grabbed the receiver and I heard what sounded like a female voice in his ear. It's over, I thought. She's back. I knew she would be. He shook his head at me immediately.

"Oh, Patricia, hello. How was your journey? Good, good. No, no, nothing." He paused. "No, she's fine. She's still asleep. Yes, I know, we've already discussed it and I think we'll have to do that. Yeah, she got here last night. Do you want to talk to her?"

He handed it on to me.

She has the nicest voice, Patricia, soft, as I imagine the Irish countryside after the rain (a sentimental idea, I know, and one that I would never dare to admit to her), and somehow patient. She was calling from her sister's on the outskirts of Dublin; in the background you could hear the house waking up to the swish of wedding dresses and the smell of hair spray.

She felt the need to tell me everything she had already told Paul. It was clear she was afraid that all of this was somehow her fault. Anna's trip had been so last-minute she was worried that she had got the days or the times wrong. She had been certain Anna had told her Thursday night, but when she didn't turn up she wondered if maybe she had meant Friday. If only she had called Paul earlier or had checked the hotel number . . . fear like a petrol line of fire was running through us all now.

I did my best to reassure her. I saw her standing by the phone, a small energetic woman in her early fifties. She'd probably already be dressed for the day. Would she wear a hat to church? Presumably. Catholic wedding, Catholic customs. She didn't seem the type for hats—too down-to-earth. She never really cared that much about her appearance.

Patricia was the mother we all used to have before feminism arrived to split the nuclear atom. The woman who knew how to get rust stains out of a colored dress, but who would never fill out her own tax form because that was man's work. She had three grown-up children of her own and had agreed to take on Lily because she couldn't get out of the habit of mothering. She had been part of this unorthodox family since Lily was six months old, first full-time, now as child care after school and in the holidays. The love affair was mutual. She would have done anything for them, and what hurt most was that there was nothing she could do now.

I told her that if we decided to call the police they might need to check some details with her; would it be all right if I gave them her sister's number? She said yes, but that nobody would be back until late tonight. And had we remembered that Lily had a swimming lesson at 11:00? And that her friend Kylie's mum would be picking her up at 10:30 and that her swimsuit was on the hook by the washing machine? I lied and told her that we had and that she was to forget all about this now and we would see her—all of us—when she got back on Monday afternoon. And to wish her niece all the best for the day. And then I put down the phone and told Paul I thought we should call the police now.

I made tea while he did it. I heard him getting through. This is someone's job, I thought. They deal with this kind of thing every day of the week. He walked to the other end of the room so he didn't have to look at me and when it came to the relevant bit he described himself as a close friend of the family. He was saying something else when Lily appeared in the doorway.

"Hi, Lil," I said loudly, because he hadn't seen her. "You look hungry."

He turned and gave her a wave, moving out into the garden. She watched him go, then padded in and sat herself at the table.

"Breakfast?" I said. "How about pancakes? I'll do the flour if you crack the eggs."

"It's Saturday," she announced. "I've got my swimming lesson this morning. Mum said she'd be home for that."

"Well, sweetheart, she's not going to be able to make it. Kylie and her mum are going to go with you instead."

Lily scowled. "But she promised." I waited for her to make a thing about it, but instead she said: "Why can't you or Paul take me?"

Outside I heard Paul's voice—"Yep, yep. That's fine. We'll be here. Thank you."

"Lily says can we make swimming at eleven?" I said as he came back in.

He clicked back the receiver. "Sorry, squirt. Estella and I have got work to do. But I think we could probably manage McDonald's afterward."

She shook her head. "I'm fed up with Chicken McNuggets." I raised an eyebrow. "You're lucky, Estella," she said. "In your country the cows haven't gone mad."

They arrived ten minutes after the swimming party left. It was so warm we sat out in the garden around the slatted wood table, self-assembly Ikea, circa 1995. I remembered it well. I had got a blood blister from jamming my thumb in between the slats. Lily had put on her doctor's uniform to deal with it.

Their very presence made her absence more sinister, and I found myself feeling sick again, the kind of nausea you sometimes get in important meetings when you have to talk for too long. Paul was more settled, but then he is better at playacting than I am. What would they think of us; father and friend? And would what they thought mean anything?

I have to say they were good at it, thorough and sensitive, trained to deal with jagged nerves. Name, age, height, weight, coloring, clothes. All those little boxes to fill in. Anna formed like some verbal hologram in front of our eyes.

Missing person, Anna Franklin, Ms.: age thirty-nine, height five seven. Striking—"pretty" was always too tame a word for her—good build (a little heavier since Lily, but she could carry it), with thick black hair cut in a wedge, open face, broad forehead, and full lips in a slight Cupid's bow.

Identifying marks: pierced ears, no body rings, but a small blue elephant tattoo on her ankle. (No bluebirds or panthers, she had insisted, too New Age. Why not have it full-sized?, I had suggested, as I sat with her in a seafront shop in Brighton watching the needle buzz.)

Clothes: in general, stylish, probably more expensive than she could afford; in particular, no idea, though Paul claimed she had a yellow linen jacket that she hadn't left the house without for the last two months and that wasn't on the hat stand now, and who was I to contradict him?

Character: clever, funny, intense, loving.

There was a pause when we came to the end of the list. Anna? Was that it? I thought about her. There were other things, but I didn't know how to put them into words. At least, not for strangers.

"Any history of depression, mental illness, that kind of thing?"

"None." Two voices on a single thought.

"Does she often spend time away?"

"The odd night here and there for work," said Paul briskly.

"And who looks after the little girl then?"

"If it's in the week, Patricia, the child minder, stays. At weekends I'm usually around."

"But you're not the child's father?"

"No. Not biologically, that is. But I see a lot of them."

"So could you tell us what the nature of your relationship with Ms. Franklin is?"

Paul smiled. "We're just good friends, Officer," he said prettily.

"I see." Though it was clear he didn't. "So if there was someone else, I mean if she was seeing another man, you wouldn't necessarily know that? She wouldn't tell you?"

"*Au contraire*—she most certainly would." He had been so good up till now, not a hint of camp in his performance, and you could see how this one had been irresistible. It came so out of left field that I'm not sure they recognized it anyway. Sweet boys. "But she hasn't. Told me, that is."

How about me?, I thought, I'm her best friend. Who would know if I didn't? They must have heard me thinking and looked in my direction.

I shook my head. "She didn't have a lover. She would have told me if she did."

There was a small silence. I got the impression they were checking their list, making sure all their little boxes were properly annotated.

You could see how from their point of view this wasn't unfolding like your average nuclear family. I wondered how much it mattered. Surely most policemen must have waded through enough dirty washing to realize that the dynamics of contemporary life are more complex than current political rhetoric would have you believe.

"So she's never gone missing like this before?"

It wasn't what you'd call a long pause, but there was a definite charge to it. Since it was inevitable that they would, at some point, ask the question, it made it even stranger that we had chosen not to discuss it before they came. Across the table they were looking expectantly. First we should have decided which one of us was going to answer it.

I took a breath. "A few years ago she went off for a bit without telling anyone. But it wasn't for long, and it was before Lily was born. She wouldn't do that now."

Nevertheless, they were interested. How could they not be? It was on the form.

"Did you contact the police then?"

"No. It wasn't serious."

"Could you give the circumstances?"

Could I? "It was a bad time in her life, that's all. There was some personal trouble; her mother was ill, and I think that really affected her. Everything just got too much. Er . . . she just packed a suitcase and took a train somewhere. To get away from it."

"Where did she go?"

"To the Lake District. A hotel there."

"And how long was she out of contact?"

"Not long. Five or six days."

"But she didn't tell anyone she was going."

"No."

"How did you find her?"

"She called me. And I went up to see her."

I saw Paul look away toward something on the table. He picked up a water jug and refilled their glasses.

"Have you checked that hotel this time?"

"It never occurred to me."

"You don't remember what it was called?"

"Yes. It was the Windermere. After the lake." He wrote it down. "But that was completely different from now."

"You mean she's not under any kind of strain now?"

"I mean she has Lily now."

"And she's not under any strain," he repeated, doing his best to make the statement sound less like the question.

"No," I said. I waited for Paul to back me up. When he didn't, I glanced at him. He was still looking at the table.

"And you'd agree with that, would you, sir?"

"Yes, I would."

The officer gave a little smile. "You don't sound so sure." And he was right. Paul didn't.

Paul shrugged. "She's like everybody else. She's too busy. She's got a job and a young kid. She gets tired. Sometimes she gets stressed. Still . . . I don't think . . . well, I don't think that's got anything to do with this."

"But if she did go off she'd know that you would be here to look after Lily?"

"Yeah, but . . ." Paul trailed off.

"What will you do to find her?" I said, because I didn't feel like answering any more questions.

"Well, this report will go in when we get back to the station and from there an officer will make contact with Florence, and check the airlines in and out of Florence and Pisa for the particular dates, see if she left the city and if so when and where she went. If it turns out that she's still there we'll put out descriptions through Interpol." He paused. "You know, ninety percent of people who are reported missing to the police make contact or are found within seven days."

Simple as that. We were in the once-upon-a-time land of police training statistics, where bad guys broke the law and the good guys made them stop doing it. I could read it to Lily as her bedtime story, except even at her tender age she was starting to ask questions about the gap between what if and what is.

They had a few final requests: a photo and any further help on what clothes she might have taken with her.

Upstairs I did the clothes first, checking the wardrobe more carefully. I fumbled through the rack. I thought I remembered a pair of black crepe trousers that she had bought in Amsterdam earlier in the spring and that weren't there now. And Paul was right, there was no yellow jacket in the cupboard either. In the bathroom I checked her jewelry. Anna was an earring junkie, the longer the trip the more of them would be missing, but who was I to know how many had been there in the first place? I looked in the mirror and saw her staring out at me; black trousers, yellow jacket, airline boarding card in her hand.

God, Anna, wherever you are, why don't you pick up the phone? One call is all it takes. I thought of myself mellowing into last night's alcohol. What if I hadn't been there to answer the phone? René and I might have decided to meet somewhere for the weekend. We might have been sitting in some medieval square in Amiens or Bruges sipping coffee and eating pastries while in my mind Anna was safe and well, standing in the shallow end of a swimming pool in London, arms outstretched as Lily splashed her way toward her. When my mother died it took me months to accept that she hadn't just gone away on a trip somewhere and forgotten to write. But this wasn't the time to think about that.

I moved into the study in search of a decent photo. The three of them on holiday in Montana wasn't clear enough and anyway I didn't want to take it down from the wall. I went through her desk drawers in search of something more suitable. The bottom right was a set of old *Guardian* weekly Guides (why?) and a jumble of photo envelopes underneath. I was about to select from memories of last Christmas when I came across another set, one that I'd never seen before: bigger prints, maybe six inches by four; Anna with a half-smile staring straight into the camera. The lighting was professional; this was a portrait rather than a photo, the kind of thing that mothers of missing models give to the police just before their lovely daughters are found with their throats slit on a patch of wasteland in the Hackney marshes. What Anna could be doing with such a set of shots I couldn't imagine.

"How's it going up there, Estella?" Paul's voice rose up through the stairwell. I had been daydreaming too long. The officers had moved to the door now, eager to be on their way.

I picked two of the photos and shoved the rest back in the drawer.

"Well?" I said as we closed the door on them. "What do you think?"

He shrugged. "The dark-haired one is straight, the other could go either way but doesn't know it yet."

I didn't laugh.

He sighed. "I don't know. Presumably they know what they're doing."

"If they take it seriously."

"Why shouldn't they?"

"Because you told them she was in a disturbed state, that's why."

"No, Stella. That's not what I said."

"Yes it was."

"I said she was stressed. That's not the same as disturbed. I hardly think they're going to stick her in the pending tray because one of us says she might have been under a bit of strain."

"I don't think we should have given them any excuse, that's all."

"Which is why you lied to them about the Lakes, presumably."

"I didn't lie."

"Oh, please, Stella, give me a break. She contacted you? I was around, too, if you remember. She never rang anyone. You found the number of the hotel on a piece of paper in her flat and called. Or did I just make that up, too?"

There was a time after Anna got pregnant when Paul and I didn't get on that well. It didn't take a genius to work out why. Since we'd always liked each other before, I reckoned that we would grow to like each other again. And so we have. But our relationship has always been funneled through other people, first Anna and now Lily. When we're on our own there is always the risk of a shadow falling between us.

"Okay, so I lied," I said. "If I'd told them the truth they'd just have assumed this was like the last time and not bothered to look for her."

"Yeah, I know." He nodded and rubbed his forehead. "Jesus, I've been thinking about it all night. Why would she be late? Where could she be? Between Lily and Mike and work, everything's so damn busy these days there's no time to talk properly anymore." He paused. "But I do think she's been different recently. I don't know—cut off, distracted. I can't put it any clearer than that. I thought it might be connected to a man. But if it was serious she would have told you."

What did I think? I hadn't seen her since Easter. Over two months ago. She and Lily had visited for a week. She was researching a story on Amsterdam's soft-drugs policy. Lily and I had played for three days while she frequented my favorite brown cafés and politicians' waiting rooms. A good time had been had by all. Since then it had been business as usual on most of the Friday nights . . . me a little high, her a little . . . A little what? Busy? Tired? Offhand? Had there been something I hadn't noticed? Something that got lost between the vodka and the dope fumes? What could there be that Anna wouldn't tell me?

"This couldn't have anything to do with Chris Menzies, could it?" I said, because, of course, he would have to come up eventually.

"The TV-star sperm donor?" For a man who makes his money out of things you can do on small screens Paul has always had a healthy mistrust of television. "Coarsening the nation's culture" is his line. I know enough of the nation who might accuse him of doing the same thing. But at least we had always agreed on Menzies. "No, I don't think so. She never mentions him."

"Where did he go after Washington?"

He shrugged. "I dunno. Somewhere in Europe, I think. Paris, maybe?"

Not a million miles from Florence. I shook my head. He was right. It couldn't be Menzies, not after all this time.

Paul looked at his watch. "I told Kylie's mum I'd pick them up at the swimming pool and take Lily to lunch. You going to come with me?"

"I think somebody should stay here," I said. "In case she rings." Though as I said it I already knew there were no guarantees.

Away—Friday A.M.

THE SUNLIGHT WAS CRASHING IN THROUGH THE WINDOW AND there was a rapping, the sound of someone knocking on the door, then unlocking it. Anna was up and out of the bed before he got into the room, snapping herself into a standing position, tense, ready to shout or to run.

"You are awake?" he said with a smile. "Good." The door swung back of its own accord, slamming shut behind him. "How do you feel?" He stood awkwardly, a tray in his hands: coffeepot, milk, cup and saucer. It was all she could do not to send it crashing on her way to the door.

"You've made a terrible mistake," she said, her voice flying out of her like a missile. "I don't know who you think I am, but I have no money, none at all. No one will pay for me, do you understand?"

The smile hovered, but didn't break. It was clear he didn't have a clue what she was talking about. Slow down, she thought. Try again.

"Where am I? What happened? What did you do to me?"

"Please. Don't be upset. You are very all right. You were ill in the car. You don't remember this? I called a doctor for you. She said you are going to be fine."

"Where am I?"

"In my house. I bring you here last night after you got sick. You don't remember getting out of the car? You spoke to me, I told you what was happening. The doctor made an examination of you and she said maybe you have—I don't know the word—epilepsia? Or a reaction to something, but I couldn't tell her what you have eaten."

Her mouth was too dry, but she couldn't work out if it was fear or the remnants of sleep. "It wasn't anything I ate. It was the drink. The coffee."

"The coffee? But how . . . ? I drank a cup, too. Except for the syrup . . . You are not having a reaction to almonds? I didn't think . . ."

She jerked her head in denial. He gave a little shrug, as if the whole thing was simply one of life's mysteries that couldn't be explained. She thought of the locked room and the darkness. He was lying. Even his English was splintering under the strain of deception. As he put the tray down on the table she rushed past him and made for the door.

He made no effort to stop her. It was unlocked. She found herself staring out onto a corridor and then a staircase at the end. She ran to the landing. The stairs led down to a hall. As she leaned over she could see a front door. Where to now? She stood for a moment, unsure of what to do, then walked back, but didn't go all the way in, standing instead in the doorway. He hadn't moved from the spot. The coffee tray was still on the table waiting. He looked concerned, a well-dressed man with a troubled houseguest; not a hint of the mob or the gangster about him. She felt suddenly wrong-footed.

"Didn't you hear me shouting in the night? I yelled and screamed for someone to come. The door was locked."

"You woke up in the night?" And he sounded genuinely upset. "I am so sorry. I sleep downstairs at the other end of the house. I locked the door because the house woman comes early to clean. I didn't want her to disturb you. You didn't read the note?"

"Note?" She glanced around the room. "What note?"

"I left it by the bed."

He moved rapidly over to the bedside table, bent down, and straightened up, holding something in his hand. "Here. It fell down the side."

Still she didn't budge. He came to her, holding it out at arm's length so she wouldn't feel threatened. She grabbed it from him. On a piece of paper ripped from a notebook were five lines in small, neat writing:

Don't be worried. You are quite safe. A doctor has checked you. She gave you something to help you sleep. I called the number for your home, which I found in a book in your handbag, and left a message. I told them you were delayed. I will wake you in the morning.

So polite, so solicitous, such grammatical English. She felt another collision of panic and confusion. He had even called her home . . . Lily . . .

"What time is it?" she said quickly.

"I think eleven o'clock."

"Eleven? I have to call my daughter."

"But I told you," he said gently. "I did this. I left a message on an answering machine. I said you are delayed, and that you will be home when you could. I told them not to worry. I hope that was okay. Your daughter, she will be at school by now, yes?"

Eleven o'clock here, ten o'clock there. Yes, she'd be at school. And Patricia would already have left for Dublin. She would have taken Lily back to her house for the night and left the answering machine on in its place. She could try Paul's mobile, but he wasn't always connected. He picked up Lily anyway on Friday after school, took her out for tea or to a movie. If she caught an afternoon flight she'd be back home almost the same time as they would.

She looked up and found him still watching her intently. He seemed different from yesterday, but she couldn't work out how.

You're making all this up, she thought suddenly. The note, the story, it's all made up to reassure me.

At the same time the thought was ridiculous. Why shouldn't he be telling the truth? After all, things do happen to people. Once last autumn, Lily had fainted at a friend's house. One minute she was upright in the garden, the next crumpled on the grass. They had spent three hours at the hospital waiting to have her checked over. The doctor had said she was fine, that these things sometimes happen. Like now. But it still didn't feel okay. Maybe it never would until she had got out of there and was sitting safely in her own house again.

"I made a booking for you," he said, as if reading her thoughts. "The planes are very full now, but there is an Air Italia flight to London this afternoon that had one seat free on it, so I reserve it. I hope that is all right? You will have to pay. It is not a charter." He paused. "You don't mind that I did this? I found your ticket in your bag with the book."

"No." She gave a short laugh, the sense of relief palpable. "I don't mind. Thank you."

"So you have time now, yes? The airport is not far from my house. I booked a taxi for four P.M. Why don't you have a shower and come downstairs for some breakfast? You will feel better when you have eaten something."

And sensing her discomfort, he turned and left the room, closing the door behind him. When she tried it quietly afterward it was open.

The water woke her up, but it didn't wash the panic out of her. No doubt he was right and it would take food to untie the knots in her stomach, fill up the empty space that had been taken over by fear.

She changed her clothes and dried her hair. As she rolled up the shirt she had discarded, a faint smell of vomit came off it. She smelled it more closely, then studied the material. There was a stain around the left breast, as if someone had scrubbed that bit with a soapy cloth. She remembered how nauseated she had felt in the car and then again later in the darkness. It wasn't a doctor's job to clean up a patient's vomit. Which meant he would have done that too.

That was the problem, of course; she couldn't stand the idea of his intimacy with her unconscious body: the carrying from the car, the laying out, the cleaning, the watching and waiting while someone examined her. All of it was too much like violation to be able to forgive or forget.

She slipped a hand between her legs. If you were unconscious, how would you know? Of course you would know. Surely. She remembered a wild story glimpsed at the bottom of a front page about a woman in a New York hospital who had given birth to a baby even though she had been in a coma for three years. It was one of those apocalyptic tales that seemed like myth even before it happened. No, it wasn't possible. She would know. He hadn't touched her.

Once she was out of there she would feel better. On the plane she might even write him a letter apologizing for her lack of gratitude. He seemed a decent enough man. He would understand. By the time she had got home, the events of the last twenty-four hours would have become her own urban legend, one of life's more colorful party pieces.

The room was less forbidding in the daytime, though the décor was still too corporate. Maybe it was Italian style to make the guest bedroom like a hotel. She checked it more carefully: the chest of drawers and the wardrobe were both locked. She went back to the window. A wilderness greeted her. Where an unkempt garden ended a forest began, a mass of closely packed pine trees, tall and regimented, like some silent army waiting for the signal to move. It explained the hissing blackness of the night.

As she opened the window a rush of outside air hit her, cooler than the stale fist of city heat and sweet with the scent of pine. It made her realize how, despite the shower, her head still had traces of fog inside it. Could she really have been allergic to something? She knew children, friends of Lily's, who were allergic to nuts; it was so serious that their parents rang to warn you before they came round, just in case you might be careless enough to offer them the wrong chocolate bar. But you didn't just develop that out of nowhere. On the other hand, she couldn't even remember the last time she had eaten almonds.

She packed up her suitcase and took it with her as she went. She looked back into the room one more time, imprinting it on her memory: somewhere she wouldn't want to forget—as long as she didn't ever have to see it again. She left the door ajar behind her and made her way quietly downstairs.

Her footsteps echoed on the wooden treads. It was a spacious house, old, halfway between a farmhouse and something more pretentious. Beautiful, calm. There was no sign of anyone else living there. The sense of isolation made her nervous all over again.

She left her suitcase at the bottom of the stairs. To each side of her there were a number of closed doors and one, at the end of the hall, open. Another time she might have been curious enough to pry a little, but it somehow didn't feel right. She made for the light.

It was an extraordinary room, large and open with a stone floor and two long high windows through which the morning sun was pouring. There was hardly any furniture, just an old sofa near an open fireplace, a chair, and a table laid for breakfast, at which he was sitting. The space seemed too big for him, except he wasn't alone in it. On the walls all around him were photographs, dozens of them, blown up and framed like paintings, every one a study of the same woman.

She was young and attractive, with full black hair like an ink cloud against almost translucently pale skin. In some of them she was talking, animated, busy, apparently ignorant of the camera, in others staring or smiling almost coquettishly straight into it. A good-looking, stylish woman, radiant with life. For the photographer who took them, creating such a gallery had obviously been a labor of love. This couldn't be him, could it? she thought. At the same time as absolutely knowing that it was.

He rose to greet her. He had changed too: a cotton sweater over a pair of jeans with a pronounced center crease in them and his hair brushed back from his forehead. His eyes looked smaller, and the morning sun picked out a network of lines on his face, two furrows along his brow as deep as the trouser press, making him older than she had thought. He reminded her strangely of Dirk Bogarde after he had given up on the matinee idol in search of roles more complex and more sinister. Something unnatural about the way he held himself . . . She thought of the stain on her shirt, and all those little bottles of hotel glup in the bathroom, and her mind lit up with warning flares again. Even if I'm wrong I have to get out of here quickly, she thought.

On the table was a basket of fresh croissants and pastries with half a dozen kinds of jams and honey, a parody of a perfect breakfast. He guided her to her seat, pulling the chair out for her in a gesture of old-fashioned courtesy.

"You feel better?"

"Yes, thank you."

"Good."

She refused the coffee in favor of plain water, but ate the bread and jams. He watched her, smiling, enjoying her appetite, but saying nothing, as if waiting for her to guide the conversation.

"This is an amazing room," she said at last as the silence started to draw attention to itself.

"Yes. It was a part of a . . . ah, I have forgotten the word—a religious house, for women—how do you call it?"

"A nunnery?"

"Yes, yes, a nunnery. But in modern Italy, of course, there are not enough such women."

"Where is it, exactly?"

"As I told you—near Pisa, but more up. In the hills. That's why it is more cool." Pisa was near the coast. She couldn't remember any hills nearby, but Tuscany was full of them and after so many years her geography was decidedly shaky. "My wife and I came here seven years ago." He gestured around the room. "It is she who make these changes."

His wife. Once again it was not what she expected. "Is that her in the photos?"

"Yes."

"I'd like to meet her."

He shook his head, putting his cup down carefully on the saucer. Oh God, she thought suddenly. She's dead, and that's what this is all about. His wife's dead and he's still in trouble about it.

"She . . . she is not here. She died one year ago."

Of course. It explained it all, the pictures, the exaggerated gallantry, the weird intensity . . . "I'm sorry, I—"

He frowned. "You didn't know. She had a—what do you call it?—a lump. On her brain." He paused, as if waiting for her to supply the word. She didn't say anything. "It was very sudden. She was in the garden one afternoon and she fell over. They said she does not suffer. It is like she has gone to sleep."

Just as she had done in the car last night; one moment there, the next slipping into a crack as deep as death. The familiarity of it must have chilled him. Had he been thinking of his wife as he carried her into the house? Was he still thinking about her now, and did that explain the tension in his posture, the strain around his eyes? Repressed grief can be its own kind of poison, a thick vein of rage running underneath silence. Could that explain all this? Maybe, maybe not . . .

"Why didn't you take me to a hospital?" she said suddenly.

"What?"

"Last night, when I was ill in the car, why didn't you take me to a hospital? Why did you bring me here instead?"

He shrugged. "The hospital of Pisa, she is on the other side of the city. Also, I don't know if you have insurance. It is expensive. I thought it would be better to bring you here. My own doctor is very good." She frowned. He poured some water into her glass. "You must have been worried, no? Last night—waking up in a locked room. I didn't mean to scare you."

"It's fine," she said quickly. Then, as if aware of her bad manners: "I'm sorry about your wife."

There was an uncomfortable silence. She glanced down at her watch, remembering too late its shattered face. "What time is my fli—"

"Five o'clock. There is plenty of time. Have something more to eat, please."

But the food was doing nothing for her nerves. She sipped at her water. The house was so quiet. It was hard to believe a major airport was only a few miles away.

"No more? Okay. Shall we go and sit in the garden? It is not so looked after now, but there is a place in the shade where it is very pleasant. Or would you prefer to rest some more?"

She had a sudden picture of a seat under a tree, and a woman falling backward into death. She pushed her own chair back and stood up from the table, the two images clashing fiercely in her mind. "Actually, if you don't mind, I think I'd like to go to the airport straightaway." He said nothing. The silence grew. It was almost as if he hadn't heard her. "I need to sort out the ticket," she added lamely.

"The ticket is ready," he said quietly. "I asked them when I called."

"Yes, but I . . . well, I'd like to get there early."

In a world where good deeds hadn't been squeezed out by suspicion his care might have been read as kindness. She risked being rude, she knew that, but she needed to be out of there.

"I see. Very well." And his voice was mild.

He got up and moved to the other side of the room, to a sideboard with a phone on it. He turned to her as he picked up the receiver. "You are sure you can't stay longer? You don't look so well yet. You could lie in the sun, go for a swim in the lake. I still have some of her things. Her costume would fit you, I am sure." He paused. "I would be happy to have you as my guest."

He's a man on the edge of middle age who misses his wife too much, who yearns for company and doesn't know how to get it. It didn't have to be sinister. It could simply be sad. The world is full of sadness. Be polite, Anna thought to herself. Be polite and don't let him know how much he scares you.

"I'd love to. Next time," she said evenly. "Next time I'd love to stay."

He went back to the phone. He said hello a couple of times, then sighed and started punching the buttons in an irritated kind of way. He turned to her. "I'm sorry. The telephone. It is not working. It happens sometimes at this time of day. Not enough people to pay the workmen the right bribe. I will try later. If not, the taxi I booked this morning will be here at four."

Only this time there was something in his voice that sounded different. The lie seemed to leak like a spreading stain across the stone floor. She felt panic like a swarm of fireflies in her stomach. She thought about walking out of the front door. Without her holdall she could move as fast as he could. Probably faster. There must be a road somewhere. And where there was a road there would be cars, drivers . . . But she had forgotten he still had her handbag. Tickets, passport, money. She wouldn't get anywhere without them. He was saying something . . .

". . . the car."

"What?"

"I said, if it is so important for you to get there now I will take you in the car. But I have to get it out from the garage."

"Er . . . well, thank you, I mean—" She fumbled, caught again between his solicitude and his creepiness. "That's very kind. I—"

"It's not a problem." He cut across her, definitely cooler this time. "You get ready. I will get the car."

"If I could have my bag?"

He frowned. "Your bag?"

"Yes, my handbag. You took it last night. It had my address book in it. To call my home?"

"Yes, but I put it with you in your room."

"Where?"

"Under the bed," he said rather impatiently. "I saw it this morning there when I picked up the note. You didn't find it?"

She hadn't. But then she hadn't looked that well, had simply pulled the covers over and left it at that, assuming he still had it in his care. She felt her legs go weak. She didn't want to go back into that room again. She stood for a moment, not knowing what to do.

He walked past her toward the door. For a moment she thought he might offer. "I'll get the car and meet you outside in five minutes." And he turned on his heel and left.

She waited till she had heard the front door open and slam closed, then made her move quickly, out into the corridor, up the stairs and into the room. She tried to find a way to wedge the door open, but there was nothing she could use. She went to the bed and flung back the covers to expose the space underneath, keeping one eye on the door and using her hand to try to locate the bag. Nothing. She ducked her head down and looked deeper. Sure enough the bag was there, pushed way back in the dark. She had to get down on her hands and knees and crawl to reach it.

She had got it out and was opening it up when she suddenly heard him. He must have come up the stairs silently. How could he do that? In the split second before it happened, she saw that her ticket and passport were gone and was on her feet moving toward the open door. He got to it first. As he slammed it closed she caught a glimpse of his face. This time he wasn't smiling.

Away—Friday A.M.

SHE STOPPED TALKING AND PUT THE RECEIVER DOWN. IN AN INNER courtyard below the kitchen window, a woman was hanging out washing, using a pulley system to push the clothes farther out into the sunshine. The image echoed a film she had seen somewhere; Italian, black-and-white, fifties or sixties, she couldn't remember the title.

"All right?" he called from the other room.

"There's no answer from Patricia's. I got through to Paul's mobile and left a message."

"What about your daughter?"

"I left one for her there, too. She's crazy about phones. Especially the mobile. Loves all the buttons."

"Good. So now we can have breakfast."

"Patricia must have left for Ireland already. I should have talked to her before she went. She'll be worried."

"You should have warned them you'd be late." He stood in the doorway dressed to go out, linen trousers and a soft cotton shirt; casual, deliberately. If she went up to him now and put her hands on the material she would feel money. And behind the money, flesh. A part of her would have liked to go back to bed with him now, but along with the missed alarm the morning had brought with it a renewed fear of her own desire and the damage it could do to both their lives. He took pity on her. "Didn't you tell me that this guy—what's his name?—"

"Paul."

"Didn't you say that Paul picked Lily up from school on Friday anyway?"

"Yes."

"So—by then he'll have got your message and will tell your baby-sitter himself when she calls. What did you say?"

"That I'd missed the plane and I'd be back sometime over the weekend, whenever I could get another one."

"There you go. Crisis over. Come on, I'm starving, let's go eat."

"First I have to book a return flight."

"Anna!" He laughed. "Our relationship may be almost exclusively carnal, but if there's one thing you must have learned about me it's that I can't function on an empty stomach. It makes me irrational and difficult."

It had, right from the first phone call, been his humor that had been one of the attractions. She liked the way it earthed the tension in her. "Don't tell me. You have to go to football matches too."

He shrugged. "Why do you think I suggested Florence?"

"See. And all this time I've been thinking it was about infidelity."

The café was on the main square. She had powerful memories of Fiesole from twenty years before. She had liked it best in the winter, when the tourists cleared away and the mists rolled in. There was a monastery she used to visit, no longer used by the Church. You could go and sit in the cells, stone bare and cramped, thin windows cut into thick walls with just a cot bed and wooden table as furniture, all pre-served exactly as it had been for centuries. She had liked imagining the monks living there in prayer year after year with only God to keep out the cold, until at last their souls flew free through the keyhole window. What at eighteen had seemed romantic now felt rather cruel. But then since Lily, even acts of kindness could make her cry. Add it to the list of ways that children undermine you.

Across the table he was concentrating on his stomach. She studied him studying the menu, as he had done on that first evening when they met. He had warned her then about his obsession with food. She had found it annoying, then funny. Now she simply found it familiar, which was somehow more disturbing. How quickly it happens. They had both been so sure of themselves that night, riding the wave of each other's confidence. Where he saw a good lay, she saw a good story. Nothing more. A no-risk venture. Easy. What had changed?

Somehow, without her realizing it, this man had walked through the KEEP OUT notices with which she had decorated her life. In the six and three-quarter years since Lily had been born she had got used to accepting that she would never feel this way again. It wasn't that she was an obsessive mother. On the contrary, she had both the appetite and the capacity to enjoy being free of her daughter sometimes, to play as an adult in a grown-up world. But not this world. Not like this. She had come to believe that the sweet/savage energy of sexual passion had all been torn out of her at the birth, torn out or rechanneled into the deeper passions of mothering. The few men she had slept with since then had been deliberately second-rate, picked more for their availability than their charisma; a way of keeping one's hand in, checking that the machinery hadn't gone rusty through underuse. They scratched the itch, and she went back to Lily renewed. She didn't want for more. She didn't have the energy for it. Of course there had been times when she had found herself mourning the loss of intensity, but then Lily would walk back inside her head and there would be no room for such nostalgia. How could she have been on guard against something she didn't expect to feel again? As he had said, it was no one's fault. What you felt was one thing. It was what you did with it that mattered.

"So, let me tell you about my plan for the weekend," he said, sub-merging a hunk of bread into olive oil as an impromptu first course while they waited for the food to arrive. "After we've visited your monastery I think we should get out of the city. Drive up into the hills, away from the heat and the crowds."

"Where?"

"Casentino? . . . To the east. Forest and mountains, I gather. My friend—the one who owns the apartment—says it's one of the less visited regions. Do you know it?"

"The name is familiar. But it's been a long time."

"According to the guidebook there's a ribbon of Romanesque churches that runs along the valley beside it. And up in the hills there is a monastery built on the spot where St. Francis got his stigmata. A kind of cave grotto. The church has got a number of Della Robbias in it. One of the most impressive collections anywhere, by all accounts."

"You wouldn't be trying to slide in a bit of work on the side, would you?"

He shrugged. "We can't fuck all the time, and I thought you said you liked art."

"I do."

"Well, then. I've already hired a car and booked us into a hotel in a town called Bibbiena. There's a picture of it in the book. It looks quite unspoiled."

She paused. "You were very sure I'd agree to stay on, weren't you?"

"I was very sure I wanted you to. I don't know if that's the same thing. What is it, Anna? In London you were up for this. What's happened?"

She saw last night's mist like a vaporous quicksand lying across the floor. By the time you realized you were sinking it was too late.

"Maybe I just had time to think." He had a wife; she had a child and a job. Neither of them had told the other the whole truth about either. Surely the lies would be protection enough. She sat back in the chair and felt the sun run a hot caress over the skin of her left arm. It was all there for the taking. Maybe it didn't need to be a compromise.

It might even be another kind of independence. "What about the flight home?"

"I've already done it. You're booked on the first plane out of Pisa on Monday morning. We can drive straight there and leave the car. You'll be back in time to pick up your daughter from school. You can leave a message with your friend giving him the flight details before we go."

"And you?"

"I've got to go to Geneva for work. I'll catch a later flight."

"Is that where your wife thinks you are now?"

He hesitated, as if the question had surprised him. "Somewhere like that, yes. I told you, those aren't the kinds of questions that we ask each other. Anyway, I thought this conversation was out of bounds. No families, remember? Your rules?"

When she had first met Chris all those years ago he hadn't told her about his wife. They had spent the best part of two weeks working together, minds and chairs inching ever closer, with never a word about nappies or prior commitments. When he had finally got around to telling her, he was so apologetic and upset she felt she almost had to comfort him. Her reaction surprised her. She ought to have read the warning signs then: Emotional riptides at play, only strong swimmers should proceed. Except, she had thought that she was. But then most people do—until they drown. She wondered how often he had played that card since. Christopher. She hadn't thought of him for the longest time. Strange that he should pop up now, when the air was so full of threat and promise.

The restaurant was busy, and the waiter's English nowhere near good enough to read a tense moment when he walked into it. They sat quietly as he bustled about them. The pasta, the salad, gradually filled up the space between them. He refilled their glasses and sped away.

"Look at it this way," he said. "Three days is a long time. We'll probably get tired of each other. We might even quarrel and go home early." And he smiled.

She smiled back. And as she did so she recognized the way that guilt bled into desire and made it taste even sharper. For years this had been her regular spice. She had assumed that after Lily the taste for it had gone forever. Apparently not.

"Okay," she said. "When do we set off?"

In the end they didn't leave the city till next morning. The monks' cells on the top of the Fiesole hill were pleasantly cool in the midday scorch, but the stones told stories of centuries of celibacy and isolation and the lack of human heat sent them spinning back into each other's arms. It was as if they had been waiting for an excuse. Rejecting self-sacrifice in favor of greed they played through the rest of the day and into the night and then got up while it was still dark and drove out east into a misty sunrise and the long winding climb up from the valley floor.

Halfway up, the snaking road and the lack of sleep made her carsick, and to keep her mind off her stomach she recounted some half-remembered stories about the countryside. Twenty years before, as part of her Italian journey, she had au paired for a doctor's family in Florence for two months. The children had had a book she remembered now, handed down from their grandmother: witches and demon tales set in the Casentino forests and full of unlikely conjunctions of fate and furies. There had been one about a young girl who, refusing to go to church, lost her soul down a cleft in the rock face and had to climb down into the center of the earth to find it. Valeria, the six-year-old, had made her read it endlessly, captivated by the mix of disobedience and punishment.

She hadn't thought of it for years, but the way the road bit into the rock and the land dropped away, sheer and deep as if a meat cleaver had sliced through it, brought it back to her. She couldn't remember if the story had had a happy ending.

Home—Saturday A.M.

Before we go back to the photos, I need to talk about Anna and Chris. It's only that he kept coming back into my mind, which probably isn't surprising given that the only other time Anna went AWOL was after they had finished and she was carrying him around like a fishhook in her soul. In retrospect, he didn't seem worth the pain. But then, in my opinion, they never are.

She had met him the year before I went to Amsterdam when she was working on an exposé about abuse in a local children's home. He'd been the star reporter on some flash TV documentary that wanted to blow the gaff on the whole thing, but she was the journalist who had done the legwork so they decided to pool the resources and share the credits. A good liberal bleeding heart was Christopher, a man who cared about the state of the world and claimed to adore her, but who could only return her phone calls when his wife wasn't in the room. Anna thought she was in love. I thought she was in obsession. It was about the only serious disagreement we ever had.

The affair lasted eighteen months. During that time she was the wildest I have ever known her, yo-yoing up and down, happy, sad, happy, sad, desperate. It was almost as if she needed the pain it brought her. Her father had died the year before and I always thought that in some way she was looking for a man to take his place, but that since she couldn't bear the idea of the betrayal involved she chose one who wouldn't stay either. She knew it was doing her head in. She broke up with him so often I almost lost count. He only had to snap his fingers and she was back again, waiting in pubs for the evening news to finish, taking rooms in strange hotels in strange places at the deadest times of the week. Still, on balance it could have been worse. He could have left his wife and kids for her and then she would have been stuck with the guilt as well as the wanker. And I think we both know that would have been unbearable, much worse than anything that subsequently happened.

In the end it was left to him to do the right thing the wrong way. One day she rang up his office and his PA (people in the media don't have secretaries, they only have personal assistants) told her he was too busy to speak to her. No last good-bye, no "Thanks for the memory" or "Sorry it didn't work out," just the sound of the line going dead. Maybe God had spoken to him in the night. Or perhaps somebody else spoke to his wife first. Whatever the reason, he became a face on television, and she, rough, tough Anna, who had once had the capacity to eat men for breakfast, became a bit of a basket case.

Because I hadn't anticipated it, I didn't notice it straightaway. I had recently moved and was still living out of packing cases, so I wasn't as sharp as I should have been. Also, I had never felt what she felt. Having watched her go through it, I can't say I regret that. Between one visit and the next she seemed to have stopped sleeping, stopped eating, stopped doing most of anything except watching the television at around the time the evening news came on. Back in my new house on the canal I would call her at the same time every night just to get her away from the flickering set. "How's life. Whatcha doing?"

"Oh, nothing," she would say.

And then you'd hear his voice in the background, droning on about some impending catastrophe in Burundi, or the latest figures on health care funding and a government spokesman's reaction to it. Like he knew it all. I rang up the TV company once complaining about him, saying they needed more women reporting the news, but what is one voice amid consumer apathy?

And still she kept on pining. Two weeks later she took off. I had taken to calling two or three times a day by then, just to check. But one morning she wasn't there. No one knew where she was. Not work, not home, not Paul. In the end I got so worried I came back to look for her. When I finally found the hotel name written on a scrap of paper in her desk and rang the number, they told me she was out for the day walking. She called that evening. She sounded almost relieved. I think she was frightened that with him and her father gone nobody could ever love her enough anymore, and this was a way of testing me. What is it with us women? We are new and brave and clever and wild, but we still feed our hearts into the meat mincer of love and then weep and wail when they come out all broken and bloody. Not me, though. If I ever had that potential (which I doubt), then watching over Anna during those times cured me of it forever. It is one of many unexpected things I find myself grateful to her for.

When she came back to London a few days later, she seemed, miraculously, to have made up her mind that life was worth living without him. Whatever flame it was that she had passed through it had successfully cauterized the nerve endings. She even regained some of her old fuck-you jollity, though there were times when I fancied it was bravado rather than fact. To the best of my knowledge there was no further communication between them until that final meeting when he, ostensibly, sought her out to say good-bye and when she, at least, got something permanent out of him. Of course, I wondered afterward if that too had been planned. What is that old saying from the world before political correctness? "There's no such thing as an accidental pregnancy." Still, there was something about the fervor with which Anna embraced the accident that meant I never quite had the courage to ask. And then, after Lily was born, the question became irrelevant, as if the answer must have been yes, because once she was there, it was obvious that Lily was always meant to exist, that there had been a space in the world waiting for her and all the two of them could do was bow to the imperative of filling it.

And so Christopher was finally eclipsed by his own offspring—a fitting conclusion for a man of such narcissism—and Anna was released from the jaws of the wolf. In the years since then, I have often wondered what it would be like if or when she met someone else who proved important. But it has always seemed to me that she has turned her face against that possibility, too much in love with Lily to bother falling in love with anyone else.

I sat at her desk in her study and tried to imagine myself into her shoes. Sometime last weekend she had made the decision to go to Florence. I went through her desk again, this time with more care. Such work suited my talents well. Slow, steady, methodical. I found bills and notes and paper clippings, some so old that they were fading at the edges. The chaos of Anna's life was as personal as the smell of her clothes. During the years we lived together there had been firm demarcation lines between her space and mine. I had always envied her ability to operate in the middle of the whirlwind.

Finally, on the back of an envelope in the middle of a set of papers, I found jottings of flight details and prices, the kind of thing you scribble when someone is talking to you over the phone. There was a travel agent she used for Amsterdam, a guy who got her good deals and had managed over the years to fiddle some frequent-flier miles. I found his number, but when I got through he hadn't heard from her in a couple of months, which meant she must have booked elsewhere. I flicked through her contact book. Maybe there was a connection in Florence I didn't know about. It was strange to come across my own name there, an address written hurriedly in pencil years ago with phone and later fax numbers added. A sudden thought struck me. If she were in some kind of trouble and for whatever reason felt she couldn't call home, wouldn't mine be the first number she'd dial? But when I called my answering machine there were only two mes-

sages, one from a colleague inviting me to a barge party for his forti-
eth birthday and the other from René telling me he was still in Stockholm and would call when he got back.

I returned to my search and in the end came back to that drawer
with the Guides and the photos. I laid the pictures out on the desk,
like a magazine editor looking for a cover shot. Half a dozen smiling
Annas stared out at me, confident, poised. By their side I put the stack
of *Guardian* weekly Guides. There were three or four of them and they
dated back over two months. Since everything in them would be out
of date the day after they finished why bother to keep them? I flicked
through the most recent. It fell open over a rack of staples; I was staring at a densely printed page of what looked like personal adverts di-
vided into columns, with three or four of the entries ringed with black
felt-tip. I checked the masthead: SOULMATES. Soulmates? Then I read
the marked entries:

Professional man, likes culture, music and life WLTM lively
female 35–45 GSOH, to talk and maybe more. ML 32657.

Sorted, straight, but thinking there must be more to life than
this. If you are over 30 and can still walk on the wild side call
me on ML 457911.

Solvent successful romantic wants soulmate to watch *ER* with.
If you are same, and under 40, GSOH, I'd like to hear from
you. ML 75964.

I checked the other magazines. Each had a couple of ads ringed,
and all of them had one thing in common—they were in search of a
lively, willing woman under forty. I couldn't believe it. Anna looking
for lovers in a newspaper? It didn't make sense. I knew about my
friend's love life, didn't I? Since Lily's birth there had been a couple of
flings, both while she was abroad for work and more recently a one-
night stand when Paul had taken Lily to Brighton for the weekend, the
last encounter so forgettable that she claimed not to remember a
name. We had laughed about her amnesia. But sex through the want

ads? It wasn't the same thing. Even the words smelled of loneliness. Imagine being so needy that you couldn't watch *ER* alone. Imagine ringing a newspaper for help. I wouldn't do it. Maybe that was why she hadn't told me about it.

A man. Could this really be what all this was about?

Away—Friday P.M.

AT FIRST THE FEAR HAD BEEN PHYSICAL, THE SLAMMING OF THE door registering like a punch right through the middle of her body. She felt herself double up under its force. Snake muscles of panic pulsated around her chest, crushing the air out of her. Even if she'd wanted to she couldn't have cried out. She couldn't breathe properly. She could barely swallow. It took all her energy to get herself upright again.

As her body recovered so her mind started to disintegrate, flashing up instant horror scenarios: incarceration, mutilation, slow death, the stuff of a hundred teen-scream movies. But even as she careered toward the edge she knew she couldn't let herself be undone by secondhand terror, knew that it was imperative that she keep her wits about her if she was going to survive.

She forced herself into the bathroom and put her face under the cold tap, holding it there until the shock of the water had sluiced the panic out of her. She wasn't dead yet. She held on to that fact like a piece of wood in a tumbling sea. She wasn't dead yet. She had just had the grotesque bad luck to walk into the fantasies of some nutter who had turned marital grief into a pathology of kidnap. It wasn't her fault. So now she had two clean thoughts to put against the avalanche of pain. Not dead, and not her fault. She still had some agency here. Once you understood that, you could fight back.

She sat on the loo seat and started to piece together what little information she had. First where, then how. From her shoddy geography she constructed a kind of chronology of the night before. The last thing she clearly remembered was the sign to Pisa airport just before seven o'clock. Then came the end of a sunset as someone pulled her out of a car, either to be sick or more likely because the journey was ended.

At this time of year the light finally died sometime after nine, which meant that between the Pisa autostrada and the house there had been two or three hours' driving. But in which direction? The only clue was the landscape. The window, which opened enough for ventilation but not for escape, gave out onto further pine forests. Since it seemed safe to disbelieve everything he had told her, his insistence on the coast made her think inland. There was an area, less touristy, to the east of Florence; she remembered visiting it in the height of summer, but she couldn't remember what it was called. It had been high and forested, a kind of nature reserve that stretched for miles and miles, the nearest thing to a Tuscan wilderness. It had been beautiful there, the altitude and the forests sweetening the air, rejuvenating after the greenhouse heat of the city. Just as now. She remembered someone telling her that the whole region had once been virtually inaccessible, its economy as primitive as its road system, but that with transport improving more adventurous Florentines had started developing summer houses there. By now there must be hundreds of semi-isolated dwellings where holiday populations came and went and where another couple more or less could be easily overlooked.

The act of detection gave her a sense of control, but it also increased her despair. Even if she managed to get out of the house, how would she get herself to an airport and out of the country without money or passport? Step by step. First she had to negotiate the extent of his madness, and how it might be mitigated or assuaged.

Him. Since the panic of the door slam, she had kept him buried. Now she made herself look at him closely. She studied his face, his rigid body posture, his solicitous manner, his endless, restrained politeness. Observing him gave her a sense of distance and proportion. As madness went, his seemed rather ordinary, the weight of repression almost mundane. How crazy could he be? She couldn't believe herself to be so out of touch that she would have got into a car with a total psychopath without registering something amiss. Maybe his was the madness of suffering rather than violence. That was something she would have to find out.

It was late afternoon (the sun had dipped below the line of the window and the light was losing its glare) when he came back.

Again he must have climbed the stairs silently because the first thing she heard was the knock on the door, gentle, almost tentative, like a hotel employee checking to see if the guest was there before coming in to turn down the bed linen. She started up from the bed, her eyes racing around for something with which to defend herself, realizing too late why the room had no bedside light or ornaments— nothing, in fact, that could be used as a weapon.

"You are hungry?" The voice, dimmed through the wood, seemed almost genial. "If you stand away from the door I will bring some food in."

But at the sound of him the calm she had so carefully cultivated deserted her. She had a sudden longing to rush at the door, beat her fists against it, and scream abuse at him like some mad wife in the attic. At the same time she knew that fury would do her no good. It was imperative that she didn't lose her sense of self, whatever that meant.

If not fire then ice. "I refuse to eat anything until you let me out of here," she said, impressed by the cold stone in her voice. "Do you understand?"

His answer was silence, a long flat expanse of it, and then, slowly, his steps moving away down the corridor. Thrown by his retreat, Anna tried to pretend that she wasn't. See, she thought to herself. Our first encounter and I'm still alive. He can't intimidate me. What next? He wouldn't starve her to death, surely. There'd be no point in that. She would just have to wait till he came again. Then I'll be ready for you, she thought fiercely, I know I will.

Since Lily's birth, Anna had grown used to accepting limitations: things she could no longer do; places she could no longer go; levels of success she no longer had the time or tunnel vision to reach. In many ways it had not been such a loss. She had already begun to feel some-what dissatisfied with her life, as if the inexorable march of feminism demanded that she always be better or braver than she actually was, not allowing her to rest or take pleasure from what had been achieved. Lily's arrival had changed all that. The very fact of her daughter's ex-istence was such a miracle that it seemed to release Anna from any fur-ther need to rule the world. She was almost relieved to feel the compulsion gone, the wildness tamed. Now, she felt, she wouldn't have to try so hard anymore. And that had been true. But nothing lasts forever, and over the last year or so she had slowly come to realize that something inside her was shifting again. Lily would be seven next birthday. Next year she would be in junior school. She already knew how to read, and some nights chose to do it alone, rather than want-ing a story. She had friends she visited for the night, a few chosen lit-tle girls who giggled and closed the door when you came too close to their games. Of course, when things went wrong—illness or acci-dents, tears or disappointments—she was still a child, but there was no mistaking the gradual metamorphosis that was taking place under-neath. Recently Anna had begun to contemplate a time when Lily would no longer be small.

With it had come a shadowy sense of unease as to who she would be without her daughter's dependency to define her. The world had not stayed still either. Friends and colleagues had moved on. Paul had Michael; and Stella—well, even Stella had René now. Anna didn't want a man (at least she didn't think she did), but she didn't know if that meant she wanted to be alone forever. She tried work again, started offering features and chasing ideas rather than just taking on what was given. It didn't work. A story was just that; absorbing enough while she told it but soon gone. Quietly she began to realize that she wasn't satisfied.

Thus, when she had opened the paper that Saturday and her eye had fallen on the half-page ad for last-minute cheap flights to Europe, she had picked up the phone before she even thought about it. Three days away on the spur of the moment. What on earth had she been hoping for? A shot of memory, some time alone, an adventure? Well, she had got them all now, and more. The question was how would she get out of it.

The first day turned to dusk and eventually to dark. Hunger nudged a place next to apprehension. She drank bathroom water from a plastic tooth mug which she kept by the bed, small sips of it like morsels of food. He didn't return. Though she was exhausted by an excess of emotion and the remains of last night's drug, still she forced herself to stay awake into the night. His unpredictability undermined her. At the same time as she accepted that he might indeed be taking her at her word and leaving her to starve, she became equally terrified of what would happen if he came back when she was asleep. She got up and pushed the armchair across the room until its back was wedged under the door handle. It wouldn't stop him, but it would give her time.

Not till I'm ready, she thought, though she had no idea when that might be.

Away—Saturday A.M.

THE CHURCH, THE THIRD THEY HAD VISITED THAT MORNING AND the hardest to find, was tucked away behind half a dozen houses at the end of the village. The exterior was austere, its simple stone façade dating from a time when Christianity was still young enough to be modest. It had been locked when they arrived in the late morning, but the sign by the door told of a custodian who lived at the nearby house and could be summoned at any time.

"He's probably taking an early siesta. Should we wake him?"

She glanced at him. "I didn't think you could read Italian."

He shrugged. "Only a few words. Nothing that I would risk out loud," he said. "You can do the talking."

When they finally roused him, the custodian appeared almost as ancient as the church itself, back bent like a Gothic arch and eyes as milky as old glass. His mind was active enough though, and once inside the building it was clear he knew his history. It was years since she had heard such a thick Tuscan dialect and she found it difficult to keep up with him. Still, she got the broad bones of it, translating as well as she could as they stood together in the central aisle.

"He says this is one of a series of churches that were built in the eleventh and twelfth centuries as part of the Pilgrims' Way, but that there have been people living in this area since the Romans. The men who worked on these churches were all local, the craftsmen as well."

"They still had pagan imaginations by the looks of it. Check out those figures on the pulpit."

The stone relief was crude but gripping: a man seated above a woman, his head in the jaws of a serpent's mouth and his body distorted, legs splayed so wide apart that his feet reached to his ears and his pubic hair and penis almost touched the wild waves of hair on the woman's head underneath. Her legs, too, were splayed, curving up toward her body and transforming into fish tails as they went, fins like barbs running down each side.

The old man was talking rapidly.

"He says no one knows what it means. Some say it's a . . . a field symbol? I think that means fertility. . . . Others think it's God's punishment for . . . for something or other—I can't make out the word."

"Sin, I expect," he said dryly, but his attention was already elsewhere. He had walked down toward the nave of the church and was studying the altar. On the wall behind, it was possible to make out some faint patches of color. "Can you ask him about the altar?" But the old man had already spotted him and had shuffled off to join him at the rail, gesticulating and nodding.

"He says there was some question of a fresco on the back wall. So last year they took everything down and that is what they found."

"Hmmn. The tabernacle's pretty good too."

"Tabernacle?"

"The marble box at the back of the altar. It's where they keep the host. It's got a rather classy piece on the door. Painted straight onto the wood, do you see? A pietà. The Virgin and the dead Christ."

"Sì, sì, la Pietà." The old man nodded quickly and launched into another river of words. She struggled to keep up.

"He says . . . at least I think he says . . . that when they took the . . . the altar down someone thought the painting—the tabernacle painting—was maybe important. Botteno, Bottinno—some name like that? He—" The old man butted in, even faster this time. She shrugged. "I really can't catch all of this. Something about a daughter, a nun? And a present to the church. He says he always thought it was a great painting. But that when it was . . . restored, yes? When it was restored they found it wasn't by this guy—whoever he was—after all."

"Hmm. Shame. Well, whoever did it, it's a nice piece." He grinned at the old man. *"È bella, la figura de la Madonna."*

"Sì, sì, bellissima."

Spurred on by what he recognized as genuine interest, the custodian embarked on what was evidently the deluxe tour: a lecture on the wooden cross at the side altar, fashioned from Casentino chestnut, a torch-beam study of the rest of the faded fourteenth-century frescoes, and the story of some noble bones underneath the stone floor: a local aristocrat apparently, someone mentioned by Dante in the *Inferno.* He ended standing on the gravestone, declaiming what sounded like the relevant part of the original poem.

It was, he explained after he had locked up and they were walking slowly back to his house in the grinding heat, a Tuscan tradition, the learning and reciting of the *Divine Comedy* by heart. In the past there had been many local people who knew the whole work, but now he was one of the few left. It was clear he rated the loss of this tradition at the same level of perfidy as the inadequate upkeep of the churches.

They shook hands at his door. He held hers only a little too long.

"It was the way you talked Italian." They laughed about it on their way back to the car. "It was so sexy."

"Oh, sure. And you, meanwhile, are a fraud. You didn't need me at all. You understood most of what he said perfectly."

"Not really. I just happen to know the word for sin. Anyway, if it had been me doing the translating we wouldn't have got him out of his house." He slipped an arm round her waist. "You should have seen his face. When he was talking to you his eyes shone as brightly as when he was reciting his beloved poet."

"No." She laughed. "Not quite as bright as that."

He had parked cleverly in the lee of a large chestnut tree, its full leaf like a gigantic parasol. They took out the map and spread it over the shaded bonnet, plotting the remainder of the day's route.

Half of her stood next to him, checking roads and the contours, while the other half flirted with the idea of his hands upon her body again. She studied his face, the way his jawbone tightened and shifted as he concentrated. What is it about sex? she thought. What switch does it throw in your head as well as in your body? Six weeks ago she would have walked past this man in the street and not noticed him. Now just the curve of his fingers splayed out across a road map made her fat with desire. It was as if it had nothing to do with him, as if it were her juice lubricating them both. But she also knew that wasn't true, that somewhere there were two appetites at work here. And in many ways his was the stronger, not just for sex, but for a whole number of things.

They had known each other so little time. If one added it all together—the meals, the phone calls, the grabbed hours in hotel rooms—they had probably spent less than two whole days in each other's company. What do I really know about you, she thought, save for the fact that you have been married seven years, sell art for a living, enjoy food, and like oral sex as a digestive rather than a main course? For all she knew he might even be lying about the first two. It was easily enough done, as she was well aware. If she found out more, would she like less? Maybe the detritus of everyday detail would muddy the flow of the current.

"What is it?" He looked up, feeling her attention on him rather than the map.

"Nothing." She shrugged. "Just daydreaming. Tell me ... did you recognize that painting? The one in the church, on the tabernacle?"

He frowned. "No. What makes you ask?"

"I dunno. The way you looked at it, I suppose. It was like the way you look at a menu when you're hungry. You obviously thought there was something about it. I wondered what you saw."

"Probably the same as whoever thought it might be a Bottoni. It had good lines. The composition was very strong, which is important for such a small piece. And the Virgin was beautifully painted, didn't you think?"

She shrugged. "I couldn't tell. I wouldn't know what to compare it with. Who was Bottoni, anyway?"

"Oh, I don't know much about him. Not my period. Let's see. Italian, eighteenth century. Painted a lot of portraits, I think. He's not known for his religious art."

"So would that have made it more or less valuable—I mean if it had been by him?"

"More, probably. Certainly more unusual."

"But it's not the kind of thing that you'd buy for your work?"

He shook his head. "No. Bottoni is more a collector's painter. And even if he wasn't, and the painting had turned out to be by him, you can't really buy this kind of stuff anyway. It belongs to the Church and it never goes on the market, or very rarely. No—my work is more in the mainstream."

"Tell me how it works."

"Like any business. A company comes to me, tells me how much they've got to spend. I advise them on what's coming up for sale, usually through auctions, private collections, death duty sales, that kind of thing."

"Which is why you're in London so often?"

"Yes."

"So why do you live in Paris?"

"Because it's convenient for all the markets." There was a second's hesitation. "And because my wife is French."

"Ah. I see." She paused. "Is there a lot of money in it?"

"For me or for them?"

"You I know about. I can read it in your labels. What about them?"

"Well, they wouldn't be in it if there wasn't. Yes, there's money. It's a growing market. Pension funds, mostly. You've probably invested in some of this stuff without knowing it. It makes business sense. Low risk, high profit. Tiger economies can turn into sick cats, shares can rise and fall, but with the exception of a slight dip at the end of the eighties art just keeps on coming. All you've got to do is invest wisely."

"Which is where you come in?"

"Yep."

"So if that work in the church had been a Bottoni—was that his name?—and you had been able to get hold of it, how much would it have been worth? To you, I mean."

He shrugged. "I don't really know. It's not my field. But an eighteenth-century minor Italian master, unusual work? On the open market, to the right collector . . . two, maybe three hundred thousand."

"And to you?"

"Depends what I'd done. Maybe twenty percent of that. Though price is also about who's buying and how badly they might want it. As I say, the Church isn't usually interested in selling. Anyway in this case they've nothing to sell. I doubt there's much of a market for an almost-Bottoni."

"Still, you'd think they'd have better protection. I mean, anyone could walk in and carry that off under their arm."

He smiled. "I would think the security is more sophisticated than it looks. Anyway, I wouldn't rate the chances of anything getting past Ol' Rheumy Eyes. So, what do you say? Is art consultancy more interesting than teaching?"

She laughed. "I don't know. Certainly more financially rewarding. How far do you think it is to the town now?" she added quickly, eager not to get caught in a reciprocal conversation for fear of running out of make-believe. If she had foreseen this that first night in the bar would she have lied more wisely? What would he say if she were to tell him now? No doubt that would depend on what she was going to do with it. And she still wasn't ready to think about that.

Bibbiena, when they finally arrived, had its eyes tightly closed against the sun, the shops and houses all shuttered up and the main square virtually deserted.

In the hotel she went straight up to the room while he registered them at the desk. The journey had taken longer than they thought, and with the lack of sleep the night before they were both ragged. She put a call through to London but the desk hadn't connected the phone yet and when they did the number was engaged. She stepped out of her clothes and into the shower.

Out through the bathroom window she could see a piece of a clock tower and a ceramic-blue sky. I want to sleep for a week, she thought. Maybe I'm even too tired to make love. When she got back into the room he was lying on the bed, fully clothed, his eyes closed. She pulled the towel around her and went looking for her holdall. It wasn't there.

Three bags were standing by the wardrobe; his briefcase, his overnight bag—equally smart, equally anonymous—and next to it a large Victorian-style doctor's bag made out of the most exquisite Italian leather; supple, elegant, expensive, the kind of luggage one imagined going down on the top deck of the *Titanic*. It looked full. She crouched by it and fiddled with its central clasp. It sprang open. Inside was her old holdall. She looked up.

"So? What do you think?" He hadn't opened his eyes.

"Where does it come from?"

"Florence. A shop I know. It's handmade. I was going to transfer your things directly into it, but, well, I thought it might annoy you."

"What do you mean? You didn't buy this for me?" She turned to him. He was feigning sleep again. "Hey, Samuel. Stop playing coy and talk to me."

He sighed, grudgingly lifting himself up onto one elbow. "It goes particularly well with the towel. You should wear them together."

"What is this?"

"It's a present. You know—as in something that one person gives to another to tell them how much they like them."

She shook her head. "I can't accept it."

"Why not?" And he sounded genuinely surprised.

"Because it cost too much money."

"How do you know how much it cost? You didn't pay for it."

"That's the point. Listen—I—"

"No, Anna, for once you listen," he said and this time his voice was more serious. "I sell art, you teach kids. I earn a lot of money, you earn a little. When this thing started between us you made the rules and I agreed to them. We eat in your restaurants because you can't afford my taste and won't let me pay for you. When you flew to Florence you stayed in some third-rate hotel because you didn't have the money for the one I suggested. So instead I decided to buy you a present. I thought about it long and hard. What it could be. I figured you'd probably be offended by clothes, and anyway I'm useless with women's sizes. You'd never accept jewelry or anything so frivolous. But you arrive with a battered suitcase that's falling apart and you're obviously not interested in doing anything about it. So—it seemed a good idea. Don't worry. It doesn't change anything between us. You don't even have to say thank you. All you have to do is use it. And if possible like it." He paused. "The one thing you can't do is give it back. Because I had your initials put on it."

She went back to the case and found them near the clasp, "AR" in long, elegantly engraved Gothic script. How ironic, she thought. The most beautiful thing I've ever received and it's addressed to someone else. Serves me right for my deceit. She ran her fingers across the leather. The surface felt almost as soft as human skin. What did you have to do to a pig to make it feel so good? But there was something else. Something that didn't make sense.

"Where did you keep it? I don't remember seeing it in the apartment."

"I had it in the car. Under a rug, so you wouldn't spot it."

"When did you pick it up?"

"Thursday afternoon."

"You ordered it before you got here? But . . . but you hadn't even seen my suitcase then. For all you knew it might have been brand-new."

He smiled. "It wasn't, though, was it? I told you, I gave it some thought. Maybe I know you better than you realize."

She stared back at the case. She imagined it moving toward her on a slow conveyor belt in the Heathrow arrivals hall, preening itself, so much classier than its companions. Look at me. I'm here now. Let's go home together. It was indeed a clever present. He was right. Not only would she never have bought it for herself, but it meant that whatever happened between them he would continue to travel with her, to be with her on planes and in hotel bedrooms all over the world, regardless of who else she might be sharing them with. She played further with the image of the carousel, this time with half a dozen identical cases juddering their elegant way around the long bend and half a dozen separate women walking dreamily toward them, then stopping and noticing each other with a dawning horror in their eyes. The cynicism behind the image shocked her. That wasn't really what she thought of him, was it? Maybe she was just not used to being given presents. Or not such expensive ones. Different styles . . . She decided to give in gracefully.

"Well, it's beautiful. . . . Thank you. I don't know what to say."

"I told you, you don't need to say anything. I'm just glad you like it."

She got up to come over to him and as she did so misjudged the distance between her and the open wardrobe door. The crack to the side of her forehead was hard enough for them both to hear it.

"Jesus. You all right?" he said, clambering off the bed to get to her.

"Oh, God." She blinked back the tears, more of shock than of pain. "Yeah. Fine. Well, almost fine."

He held her head gently in his two hands and ran a light finger over the reddening skin on the eyebrow ridge of her right eye. "Nasty crack. You're going to have a black eye. We'd better be careful with the hotel staff. People are going to think I beat you."

She smiled. "And do you?"

"What?"

"Beat women?"

He grinned. "Only if they ask me to. Do you want me to go and get some ice?"

She shook her head. "I'm fine, really."

"Well, you better come and lie down, just for a bit."

As he took her to the bed the towel fell off her. He didn't bother to pick it up again.

Home—Saturday P.M.

I WENT BACK TO THE FIRST MAGAZINE AND NOTED DOWN THE advertisement numbers carefully. On the front page of the section there were instructions as to how to use the service. I dialed the number. It connected immediately. A woman's voice, disjointed, as if she had some developing neurological disease, welcomed me to the main menu and gave me instructions as to which button to pick for which service. I chose men. The voice came back again. "Thank you. Enter the number of the advertisement you wish to listen to." I punched in the details of "Sorted, straight, looking for a woman to walk on the wild side."

"Message Line. ML 457911," the woman said, her vocal disability further advanced as each number was plucked out from the computer bank. A soft, rather apologetic male voice jumped into my ear. Straight, no doubt, but not that sorted. I tried to imagine Anna sitting in my place listening.

"Hello. It's hard to know what to say really. Right. Well, my name is Frank. I'm forty-two years old. Divorced, with one child, whom I see at weekends and I'm very attached to. I work in business, an export manager for an overseas company, so I spend a fair amount of time away from home. I'm fit, active—gym, swimming, that kind of thing. I like all the usual things: music, football, cinema. And I'm learning to scuba dive. I want to go to the Red Sea in the autumn. I keep myself very busy, and I like my work, but I want to be able to make time for a different kind of life. I suppose the woman I'm looking for would be attractive; no preference for blond or brunette, but I'd like her to be slim, have a sense of humor and be intelligent. Be nice if you shared some of my interests. My politics are, well, I suppose center left, but I don't have much truck with politicians. I don't know what else to say. I'm a caring kind of bloke, who's looking for a caring kind of woman. I'm not frightened of commitment—at least I don't think I am. Anyway, I want to meet you if you think you fit the bill. So please leave me a message and I'll call you back. And if you don't want to leave a message, then good luck with your search anyway. Thanks for calling."

The metallic lady cut back in, asking if I would like to hear the message again or leave a reply or hear another selection of messages. I scrabbled for another number. The professional looking for GSOH. GSOH?

The voice was gruffer, tougher, but still in need: "Hi, I'm Graham. I'm thirty-nine years old. I work in the City. I've never been married, I own my own house, and I have a wide circle of friends. I'm five foot nine, weigh one hundred and sixty pounds and belong to a gym. I like football, music—all kinds, particular fondness for country and western—and traveling. I've just come back from a safari in Tanzania. The woman I would like to meet will be thirty to forty, small, curvy, and blond with a love of life, an optimistic disposition, and a good sense of humor. Does that sound like you? If so, leave your message and I'll call you back."

I could almost hear the crinkle of paper as he folded away the script. GSOH = Good Sense Of Humor. WLTM = Would Like To Meet. The codes weren't exactly taxing. I wondered what Graham would be doing on this Saturday morning. In bed with a curvaceous blond optimist, or bent double over the latest Guide to see if any of the new women's ads might fit the bill?

I pushed another number. The *ER* watcher turned out not to have left a message. But you could still record one for him. Why would you do that? Talk to somebody who hadn't talked to you? But then why would you pick up the phone in the first place? Because you wanted something that life couldn't give. Was that really what Anna was feeling? I dialed another number. Then another. There was a muddy compulsion to the whole process, like eavesdropping on someone's therapy session. "I'm not afraid to say I'm looking for a long-term relationship, that I feel ready for that now" . . . "I'm looking for a woman who isn't too judgmental, and who would be willing to take risks." Did that mean sexual risks? Surely not. Sex was one thing that nobody mentioned.

The more I heard the more cruel it made me feel. Frank was too apologetic, Graham too pushy, Dan too boring, Ron too earnest . . . The list went on. Why would Anna be interested in any of them? I picked up one of her photos. Was this the next stage? You rang someone up, exchanged pictures, then met under the clock at Waterloo Station?

My eye was drawn to a small box on the page with a set of warning instructions under the heading SAFETY FIRST. It told you to meet in public places, not give your home address to anyone until you were sure, to trust your instincts, and to let your family or friends know when you were meeting someone for the first time.

I rolled back the voices in my head. One might use a lot of adjectives to describe them, but dangerous wouldn't be on the list. What marked them out was how ordinary they sounded; nervous, casual, sometimes embarrassed, as if they wouldn't need to be doing this if life had treated them a little better. Sad even, but hardly psychotic. Though no doubt any psychopath would at least make an attempt to disguise it. Nevertheless Anna had picked out their names in black pen, she'd listened to their stories, and if she had met any of them then she certainly didn't seem to have taken the last piece of advice. But did this have anything to do with her absence? I didn't have a clue.

On the desk in front of me the phone rang. It nearly plucked my heart out of my chest. "Anna," I said out loud. "At last. What's been keeping you?" Then I picked up the receiver.

In the background there was a wall of noise, people and music. I shouted hello a couple of times; then a small high voice came through against the chatter.

"Mum?"

"Oh, hi, Lily. It's not Mum, it's Stella. How was swimming?"

"Fine. Is Mum there?"

"No. She's not back yet, darling."

"Oh."

She hesitated. "What are you doing?" I said to cover up the gap.

"Er . . . there's a fair on at the green. We drove past it. Paul says we can go." She stopped again; someone was saying something in the background. "Do you want to come too?"

"I'd love to. But— Listen, why don't you let me have a word with him. Is he there?" I said as the phone started to beep frantically, then went dead. It rang again less than thirty seconds later.

"No news," I said before he asked. "What happened to your mobile? Lily drop it in the bath again?"

"How do you know about that?" How did I know? Anna must have told me. The warp and weave of life recounted through another Friday-night phone call. Where had she been for the last one? "No, I lost it yesterday on the tube. Bloody annoying. It's the second one I've had nicked within three months."

"In Amsterdam they replace them within the hour."

"I know. But they also speak Dutch. Listen, our chicken-burger-eater is a little wobbly here."

"Tears or temper?"

"A bit of both."

"About Anna?"

"Maybe. Though right at the moment it's about how many rides she can go on at the fair."

Bribery. If it's good enough for the real parents it's good enough for the surrogates. "Give in," I said. "It's not a battle worth fighting. Where do I fit in?"

"I thought she might appreciate a woman's touch for a while. Do you want to jump in a cab and join us?"

"What if she comes back or rings while we're out?"

"Leave a note and switch on the answering machine. It'll only be a couple of hours at most."

As I put the phone down it struck me that Anna would surely have had Paul's mobile number in case of emergencies. What if for some reason she couldn't get through on the others and had called him and left a message? The line would be canceled now and life doesn't throw up many thieves with hearts big enough to reroute stolen messages.

I had a sudden image of Anna in the middle of a sun-soaked Tuscan landscape with a man from the small ads, someone looking for love and growing violent when he couldn't find it. There was no way of knowing. That was what hurt the most.

Away—Saturday A.M.

SHE FOUND THE KEY TO THE WARDROBE IN THE AFTERNOON, IN the place where she was always meant to find it, the place where he must have put it that first night when she was unconscious: buried at the bottom of her handbag. It was inevitable she would go back and look there, not with the same panic she'd felt when she first searched for passport or tickets, but in a calmer, more methodical way, on the lookout for anything that might help her to get out of there, anything that he might possibly have overlooked.

The wardrobe was the only lock it could fit, and as she opened the door and saw it all hanging there in front of her—a life spread out along a line of hangers—she understood more clearly what was being asked of her and why it had been necessary to take away her clothes as well as her liberty. At least it gave her something to fight with.

It had been a bad morning. She had woken early with the sun, plucked out of an intense, enclosing dream of Lily: the two of them sitting in a bath full of bubbles, Lily ducking her head under the water, then coming up for air with a halo of foam and blinking eyes. Everything about it had been real. She could see the chipped soap dish in the shape of a frog, behind her daughter's head. She could feel the warmth of the water around them, could hear Lily's giggles before she plunged under again. It was happening. They were actually there. She had come home. She could taste relief like a flood of flavor in her mouth, a kind of salivating. When she woke into the still-locked room, shafts of dappled sunlight playing across the floor and her stomach growling for food, the cheap trick of the dream sent a shock wave through her, the courage of the night before lost in the wave of despair.

Lily. She had curled up on herself in the bed, trying to contain the pain of the disappointment. Lily. She heard herself groan quietly. Oh, Lily. What would happen to her now? Don't think about this, she told herself urgently; there is nothing you can do and the horror of it will make you mad and hopeless. But once started it was impossible to stop. She could feel the mental whirling take over, yanking her mind out of her control; constructing pictures, spinning bleak facts into bleaker fantasy, colder than fear, so cold and clear that you couldn't believe it wasn't real.

Two nights gone, and her missing would have brought the gathering of the clans. She saw Paul and Estella standing together outside the school gates waiting for Lily to come out. She watched her daughter's face, solemn and questioning, her right hand flicking her hair behind her ears as she always did when she wasn't sure of something, as she asked where Mummy was. Once again they would deflect the question, making light of her absence, blaming flights and work, then take her back home to dinner, TV, or the park.

In the days to come, while the police followed a trail that disappeared into thin air in a foreign city, they would continue the pretense. (In this scenario she was already dead, her body buried somewhere in a garden wilderness, her suitcase and belongings all ashes on the wind—though, of course, they wouldn't know that yet.) They would give her friends to play with and videos to watch, filling up the time so there would be no space for worry. Lily would not be fooled. She would go on as usual for the first couple of days, a little distant, but amiable, obedient, going to bed without fuss, curling up on herself and pulling the bedclothes close around her.

But soon enough it would start to break through. She would wake in the night, getting up and going to sit on the top landing, arms around her knees peering out into the darkness, as she did when something was worrying her. Would Estella know she was there? Would she be awakened by the difference in the night silence, detect her presence on the stairs? And when she did, what horrors would they unlock together, sitting in the darkness where lies burn as bright as fireflies? It would be on such a night that Lily would ask the question that could not be deflected, or, more likely, would say something which proved that she had known all along, and only then would Estella really understand how all of their lives had been changed forever. Poor Lily. Poor Estella. Because she would find herself fighting her own demons on that staircase. Fate could not have played a crueler trick on all of them. Its very symmetry was breathtaking.

She sat behind them on the staircase and tried to put her arms around them both. But she couldn't help them. They were alone now, that was the point. How long would it take for the missing to turn into the dead? And what would become of Lily then? Would it be better for her to stay at home, even though it wasn't home anymore, or to go with Stella abroad to a place where forgetting might be easier? They would give her help, no doubt: an army of compassionate therapists with their dolls and paintboxes, teasing out the pain until it was spread thin enough to be absorbed, like oil on ocean waters. Until, eventually, Lily would start to forget her . . .

It was the violence of that thought that had finally forced her back into life. Lily would not forget her, because she was not dead. Yet. She was not dead. Not dead yet. She used the old mantra to get herself moving. When she checked the room she found the chair was as she had left it, but that next to it on the floor lay a folded piece of paper, ripped no doubt from the same exercise book as before. On it were written just two words: "Dinner tonight."

• • •

She flicked through the wardrobe. The woman who had worn these clothes would have been taller than she, but otherwise there were clear similarities. Their build was similar, as were their hair and their complexion. Of course they didn't really look alike—or at least, not from what she could remember of the photographs—but that would depend on what you were wanting to see.

She remembered the way she had caught him staring at her that morning in the shop, as if he already knew her. Of course they had seen each other before. He must have been following her. What did he do? Roam the city in search of look-alikes? Is that how he had known she took sugar in her coffee? She had sat in enough cafés over the last three days. He could have been in any one of them with her. Was it just look-alikes or talk-alikes that he needed? It occurred to her that this wife of his might also have been English. Despite the occasional mistake, his grasp of the language was confident and colloquial. Chances were he had learned it from a native speaker. And someone with whom he had had a lot of practice.

She had died a year ago, he had said. Was it seasonal, then, this pilgrimage for the dead? Did that make her the first? How much worse would it be if she wasn't? Whatever it was, she would cope. If she was going to get herself home to Lily she would have to. At least now she had something to negotiate with. She felt almost excited. It would be important, however, not to show it.

When he came back for her, he, too, had changed for dinner. She could hear bright shoes chipping their way along the flagstone corridor, her ears acute now to the smallest breaking of the silence. The lock disconnected and the door opened a fraction until it met with the obstruction. She had already moved the chair enough so that with a little effort he could get in. He pushed harder and the door shifted. Another push would do it. She stood up to meet him.

The sight of her seemed to poleax him. He couldn't take his eyes off her, or rather the dress on her. It wasn't her style, its elegance too traditional, too devoid of any wit, but the color suited: the deep red silk standing out against black hair and pale, almost ghostly skin. Striking. As she remembered from one of the photographs. As he remembered, too. He stood staring at her, eyes shining, no game-playing now, no pretenses of politeness to get in the way. What do you want? she thought. A wife? A substitute? Dream on.

"Where the hell have you been?" And her voice was huge, fear turning to aggression like winter breath into smoke. "I've been starving in here."

He appeared to be taken aback, as if this was not what he expected from the woman wearing the dress. "I brought food to you this morning. I couldn't get in." He gestured to the chair. Bullshit, she thought, if you had tried to move the door I would have heard you.

"Bullshit," she said, standing her ground.

He took a step toward her.

"Stay where you are."

He stopped immediately.

She caught a whiff of a smell about him, strong, chemical almost, familiar and weird at the same time. What was it?

"I already told you," he said quietly. "You don't need to be frightened of me."

"What do you want from me?"

"Why—"

"What do you want?" And this time she sounded almost out of control.

He frowned, as if her outburst were somehow irrational as well as unhelpful to their unfolding relationship. "I told you already. I want you to be my guest."

"Your guest! What does that mean?"

He hesitated. "It means . . . it means you stay here with me for a few days."

"A few days?"

"Yes."

"How many days?"

"Three."

"Three days. Till Tuesday?"

"Yes."

"And then?"

"Then you can go home."

"On Tuesday you let me go?"

"Yes, I let you go."

"Just like that?"

He nodded.

"And what happens here?"

He frowned again, as if he didn't entirely understand the question. "What happens? You spend time with me."

There was a pause. "Spend time with you. That's it? Nothing more?"

"Nothing more."

"I won't sleep with you, you know that," she said, making it into a flat, almost surly statement. "And if you so much as touch me I'll kill you. You understand?"

He shrugged, as if the idea bored him. "I'm not going to hurt you," he said patiently. "If I wanted to hurt you, I will have done this already."

There was a silence. "And if I don't agree to stay. If I say no?"

He said nothing. He didn't need to. No passport, no money, no ticket. A house in the middle of nowhere, with the doors and windows locked. He was right. It wasn't worth discussing.

Three days. Three days . . . until when? Some painful anniversary was over, maybe? Could it be true? He had lied so much before there was no reason to believe him now. It didn't matter. It was what came next that was important.

"Okay," she said coldly. "That's what *you* want. Now I'll tell you what *I* want. I want to call my daughter. I want to speak to her over the phone to tell her I'm safe. Understand? I won't say anything else, I promise, but if you don't let me do this now then I shall stay in this room and refuse to come out, whatever you do to me, and however long you keep me here. And then I will be no company at all. Do you understand me?"

He stared at her for a moment, then looked away, and there was, she thought, almost a smile about him. "If you do this, then you will stay?"

She took a breath. "Yes, I will stay," she said, because one good lie deserves another and no one would ever condemn her for it later.

He stepped aside to let her walk in front of him out of the room.

Away—Saturday P.M.

FROM SEX THEY HAD MOVED FURTHER INTO LOVERS' GAMES, THE verbal kind, exploring each other's past as if it were their bodies, each revelation slipping off another layer of clothes, every question the trigger for another confession or surrender. All in all, a pastime more dangerous than fucking, because it is harder to know at which point you should stop to make sure you are protected.

"And so you never told him?"

"No."

"You didn't think it was his right to know?"

"I told you, he was going away. He and I had finished. He would have wanted me to have an abortion."

"You're sure of that?"

"Yes, I'm sure."

"How would you feel if he found out now?"

"How could he?"

"I don't know—a hundred different ways. You and she are walking across a park one Sunday afternoon and he comes toward you on the path, him and his family. As you pass, pretending not to recognize each other, he glances at you, then at her, and there she is—the daughter he didn't know he had."

"Unh-unh. She doesn't look anything like him. And he was never that observant."

She rolled over onto her back and stared up at the ceiling. The shutters were still drawn, though the sun had dropped beneath the axis of worst damage. The bed was a ghostly raft in the middle of a sea of charcoal air. She felt an extraordinary sense of physical comfort, lying there, as if she were being held suspended in the palm of a huge hand in midair.

"Was it sex? Was that the pull between you?"

"I suppose so. It was very sexual."

"Like this?"

"No. Not like this. Different."

"How?"

"I think it was something to do with anticipation. The fact that we never knew when we were going to see each other. When we actually made love it wasn't always that great. But I'd been waiting for so long it didn't matter."

"Do you think you were obsessed by him?"

She imagined the fingers of the hand unfolding slowly, one by one. It was like flying. Everything would be fine as long as she didn't look down. She could do or say anything here. Even the most painful memories would hold no terrors.

"Obsessed? I don't know what the word means. I know there were times when I couldn't think of anything else. I used to stay in every weeknight in the hope that he might get free and call me. It felt like I had a disease I didn't want to get rid of. I suppose that's a definition of obsession, yes."

"Did it scare you, when it was happening?"

"Sometimes. Sometimes I didn't even like him very much. Or myself. But I also enjoyed it. I liked the feeling of being—I don't know—out of control. It hadn't happened to me before. It made me feel very alive."

Of course, for all her feeling of security she knew she could still fall. Anyone can always fall. But then that, too, was part of the excitement. For so many years now she'd been more worried about Lily than about herself. Now, suspended here in time and space, she had become a lover rather than a mother. She had crossed over, and the pleasure was partly in the risk. This was absolutely why she had come. She knew it now. Welcome back, Anna, she thought. Welcome back.

"So what happened between you? In the end."

"Ah, that's a good question. I used to think that he finished it and I got mangled. But now I'm not sure anymore. In a way I think we both ran out of energy. Or rather the energy that we had went sour. I felt very . . . I don't know the word—soiled for a while afterward. As if I'd bought counterfeit goods, squandered a part of myself on something that wasn't worthwhile. It made me kind of crazy. But I got over it. Eventually."

"What about him, what did he feel?"

"I don't have a clue. When I saw him again nine months later he said he'd been gutted. He told me that he'd missed me every day of every week. But he had a talent for telling people what they wanted to hear. It comes with the business. I think he was probably too busy to care. Two kids, wife, big job, public life, and so many people wanting him. I can't believe he noticed one less."

"Yet you still slept with him again."

"Only because it was over and I knew I wouldn't feel anything."

"And did you?"

"No, not a thing. It was rather weird. I remember that after he left I sat up in bed and read a book. I got quite into it."

"And then there was Lily."

"Yes. Then there was Lily."

"Was that deliberate?"

She paused. "I didn't think I'd get pregnant," she said carefully, knowing that this was not an answer, but also knowing it was the only one she could or would give, to herself as well as to other people.

"And you didn't mind that she'd been conceived that way? With you not feeling anything?"

"No. Not at all. On the contrary, it felt quite proper. As if it had been about her and me, rather than me and him."

"So you don't think of him now?"

"Hardly ever. It's funny, I'm not sure I can remember him very well. It's so long ago, as if I were another person."

"Sounds like you came out the victor in the end."

"You think so? I don't see it as a battle anymore."

"That's how you know you've won."

"Aaah. Well, I'll remember that for the future."

She shifted her body on the bed and her hand came into contact with his upper arm. She let it lie there for a moment, registering the damp warmth of his skin, half-anticipating the move he would make toward her. When it didn't come, she let her fingers travel along the underside of his arm, up into the armpit and the tangled growth of hair. She tugged at it gently. She imagined him turning over toward her in playful revenge, pulling himself on top of her, his weight pinning her to the bed. It was almost cool enough now to make love again. They would lie there, their bodies sticking together, then sucking apart. Still he didn't react.

She moved her face close into the hair, breathing in the tangy scent of his sweat. The strands were long and surprisingly silky, like a child's, not at all the same as the wiry tight curls of his crotch. She ran her tongue through them, licking and probing, imagining in turn the pleasures of his mouth as it made its way down through her hair. The thought aroused her further. She continued her journey, marking out a pencil trail of saliva down along the inside of his chest. His skin felt softer here—younger, almost. She thought of Lily's tender flawless surface, so delicate underneath the arms that you felt it was not properly formed yet. She thought of the way they would lie together when Lily was falling asleep; she using her finger like a feather, playing across her daughter's back, tracing the chicken wing outline of her shoulder blade and on into the armpit underneath. She heard her giggle sleepily, then demand a replay.

For six years Anna had been perfecting the skills of how to touch skin. And all the time the line between the sensual and the sexual had been thin as a thought and as thick as desire. She couldn't understand how anyone could ever confuse the two.

Yet crossing back into adult flesh now she was amazed to realize how much she had learned. How much more she could feel and the particular pleasure that comes from being the one doing the feeling. There was, she had discovered, a powerful eroticism in generosity that she couldn't remember from affairs before Lily.

His continued refusal to respond made her more excited. She slid her hand down over his stomach toward his prick. It stiffened slightly at the anticipation of her touch. She thought about pursuing it. It was one of his attractions as a lover, allowing himself to be seduced, not afraid or nervous of her lust. Maybe that was a change in him too, a product of age and marriage. Probably if they'd met twenty years ago they wouldn't have found each other nearly so intoxicating. But the pull was more than sex. It was also about the power of secrecy; things that were hidden, truths only half told, the potent intimacy of strangers. In the quiet light of the encroaching evening what they said to each other continued to be as erotic as what they did.

"So, let's move on to you," she said, shifting herself onto one elbow to look down at his face while her fingers continued walking. "What grubby little secrets have you got that you need redemption from?" She poked him gently in the ribs. "Come on, let's hear it."

The eyelids flicked open. "Hey." Then: "Don't stop. I like it."

"Well then, answer my question."

"Why should I?"

"Because it's your turn in the witness box. I want to see you under cross-examination."

He shook his head, smiling. "I warn you, I'm devious. Under pressure I'll plead the Fifth Amendment."

"If you don't answer I'll stop touching you."

"Okay, okay. I give in." He opened his eyes and looked directly up at her. "You already know all there is to know about me, Anna. I'm a married man who shouldn't be here, but who can't keep away." He smiled. "Maybe it's your fault. First—what was his name?—Chris; now me. Maybe you're the kind of woman who lures married men onto the rocks with your siren song?"

She laughed. But they both knew it wasn't true. To be a genuine siren you have to be deaf to all other songs but your own. And Anna already had too many voices playing in her head. "Bullshit. You're just trying to shift the conversation back to me again."

"Okay. So you start. Tell me what *you* see."

She thought about it. "I see a man who is easily bored, someone who is used to getting what he wants, and who therefore wants what he can't have."

He made a face. "Hmm. Do you want to go on to the criticism now, or shall we stay with the flattery?"

She smiled, but kept going. "I suppose what interests me most is what you do with the guilt."

He shook his head. "I'm no good at guilt. I told you that the first night we met. I never have been, even when I was a kid. There's no point in guilt unless you believe in contrition, and I never did."

"And it's that simple?"

"Probably not, but at least it's honest."

"Honest. You know you use that word a lot."

"Yeah? Well, I think I am."

"Honest? With whom? Yourself? Me? Her?"

He gave a small shrug, as if there was an answer to her question but she wouldn't believe it, so what was the point in giving it.

She tried again. "Tell me one thing. When you go back to her from being with me—you're what? Not guilty? Just the same as ever?"

He thought about it. "No. Not the same. I think I'm more attentive to her."

"Sounds like guilt to me."

"That's because you haven't done it. It's more complex than guilt. Being with you makes her more foreign to me. She feels different, and I like that."

"So making love to other women makes her more sexually interesting. You get turned on by it?"

"It's not necessarily about sex," he said quietly. She was silent for a moment, watching, waiting for more. But it didn't come. It was hard to know if that was because it wasn't there or because he didn't want to give it. "What happened to your hand?" he said lightly. "You stopped seducing me."

She laughed and her fingers fluttered on his chest but stayed where they were. Somewhere in the last minutes they had crossed a kind of line. In their own separate ways both of them knew that.

"What about her? She knows that you fuck around."

"Is that a statement or a question?"

"Take it whichever way you want."

A dangerous game, honesty. "You know, Anna, I don't think talking about things always makes them clearer."

It wasn't so much what he said as the matter-of-fact way he said it, as if at the center of him there was some neat little vacuum of emotion. To her surprise, rather than making her mad it made her feel almost tender toward him. She lifted her hand off him, but he reached out and pulled it back, lacing her fingers tightly into his. "Look, I'm not saying any of this to hurt you."

"I'm not hurt," she said firmly. "But you don't start something and then stop."

He sighed. "Okay. What was the question?"

"Does she know that you fuck around?"

He didn't speak for a moment. "She knows that I have, in the past." In her mind she saw the luggage carousel again, the Busby Berkeley dance of a dozen identical well-dressed cases, each with its own set of initials lovingly engraved. Samuel's girls. She had been right. He paused. "But she doesn't know about this."

The carousel stopped her case under the spotlight, a Ruby Keeler smile for the camera. "And what if she did?"

He held her gaze. "I think she'd be scared."

Something in her stomach tightened and released. "Why?" He frowned. She tugged at his hand. "No, why?"

"Oh, come on, Anna. You're not a fool. You know as well as I do what's happening here. We're taking a risk. And the longer we play around the more dangerous it gets."

"But I thought you told me that didn't happen to you."

"I told you it hadn't happened. In the past."

"But yesterday—"

"Yesterday I said what I thought it would take to make you change your mind. Because we were a long way from home and because I wanted you to stay." He paused. "And since we're being honest here, maybe you should admit that I said what you wanted to hear as well.

"Face it, Anna. You're as messed up as I am on this one. Would you have stayed yesterday if I told you I might consider leaving my wife? If I'd started talking joint mortgages and trips with Lily to the cinema to get to know her better? I think not. I think if that had been the case you'd have been on the first plane home. Because you don't want a partner any more than I want another wife. Or at least that's what you thought. That was what we both thought. That's why you were into this as much as I was, guilt or no guilt. That's what made it so equal and so sweet."

"So why are we using the past tense?" she said, the air grown still between them.

He didn't answer her immediately, simply laced his fingers more firmly through hers and pulled her toward him. She resisted, waiting. "Because the real risk is that I don't know what I want anymore," he said quietly. "And I'm not entirely sure you do either."

Home—Saturday P.M.

EIGHT O'CLOCK ON SATURDAY EVENING AND IT WAS SO WARM that we decided to eat in the garden. Paul had found some chicken in the deep freeze and was doing something *nouvelle* with it on the barbecue while I had made a selection of salads. I'm good at salads; something about the quiet ritual of chopping.

Michael arrived at the last minute, bringing a bottle of champagne with him. It wasn't clear whether he'd expected to find Anna back or thought we needed cheering up. Either way, it was the right gesture. I watched him come up to Paul as he stood cooking at the fire and slip a hand around his waist, dropping a quick kiss onto the back of his neck. Paul pretended to ignore it, but I spotted the sigh of his hips as he moved himself back into his lover's body.

From Paul, he came to me, and in place of the usual smile delivered a clumsy spontaneous hug. I was surprised by how much it warmed me. Anna had told me that Paul was only his second big romance, but for all his youth and energy there was a definite homely quality to him, as if his gayness were somehow incidental to his search for something domestic and nurturing. What other kind of man would have taken on not just Paul but his strange other family with such ease? It made me think—not for the first time—how there are some gay men who feel like a genuine loss to womanhood: men who in the nasty illiberal past would have been forced to settle for marriage, kids, and hidden affairs and yet might have got, perhaps, some kind of alternative pleasure out of the pretense. Was everybody happier now? The question was academic. It seems you can't argue with sex. It always wins out in the end.

"Lily asleep?" Mike asked as he poured the booze.

"Just," I said.

"How is she?"

Paul and I exchanged looks. "She knows something's wrong, but she's going along with the idea that it isn't," he said sagely. "On the other hand, she swam and played so hard today that she couldn't help but conk out."

It was true. It had been an exhausting afternoon. Torn between wanting to keep life as normal as possible and trying to give her everything we could as compensation, we had stayed longer than planned at the fair, going on every ride and trying every game, some of them twice. Paul had won her an abnormally large panda by throwing a neat hand of darts (not a talent I associated with him), and she had got herself a punchball balloon for finding the right number on a duck's bottom. By the time we had left, the afternoon family–cotton candy crowd was shifting into knots of noisy Saturday-night teenagers in search of nonexistent action. Lily was so wiped out we had to stop her falling asleep in the car. We bought fish and chips on the way back; then she and I watched a video about a young girl helping a flock of geese find their way home. She was too tired for a bath but kept awake long enough to insist on a story from each of us. She didn't say a word about Anna, simply curled over onto her stomach and went out like a light. The last time I had checked she was sound asleep. I couldn't decide whether to be relieved or worried.

From the champagne we moved on to wine, and I went upstairs to get the photos and the personal ads. I watched their faces as I laid them out on the table.

"You really think this might have something to do with her not coming home?" It was clear Paul was not convinced.

"In the absence of anything else, yes, I suppose I do. Why? What do you think?"

He shook his head. "I can't see her going off for some dirty weekend without saying something."

I shrugged. "Maybe she felt weird about telling us."

"Why should she feel weird?" Mike was leaning backward, balancing on the back legs of his chair, the photo of her in his hand.

"Well, getting your lovers through the want ads isn't exactly something to boast about."

Paul smiled. "You've always been a snob when it comes to sex, Estella."

I laughed. "That's a generous way of describing decades of failure. Anyway, what if I am? I still don't think it's the sort of thing Anna would shout about."

"Why not?" Mike cut in quietly. "Paul's right. This stuff is kosher nowadays—you know, ads and dating agencies. They're all over the place. The world is full of busy single people who've got money but not enough time. Advertising is a way of spreading the net. Nothing to be ashamed of—loads of people do it."

Spreading the net. It sounded vaguely biblical, like something you did before spending your seed. "Do they?"

"Sure. It's a laugh. Especially this kind. You just pick out a few interesting-sounding ads, you give them a ring, and if they deliver, you leave a message."

"Have you done it?"

" 'Course—when I first came to London and I didn't know anybody. I had to start somewhere. I thought the *Guardian* would do a good line in cultured gays."

"And?"

He shook his head. "Not as rich a harvest as I expected."

"But did you see any of them?"

"Oh, sure. I met a couple. An adult-education lecturer from Surrey—he was okay. And this guy from Wandsworth, a computer analyst. He had a great collection of jazz records. Except I wasn't into jazz."

By his side Paul was looking at him affectionately. "Did you fuck him?"

"No. He was too earnest. Don't look at me like that. I can't believe you haven't at least followed up a few messages in your more colorful past." Paul gave a studied noncommittal shrug. Mike dug him in the ribs. "See. And I bet you *did* fuck them."

Lovers' talk. It was rather sweet to be eavesdropping on it.

"Certainly not. I never even met any of them. I just . . . well, they didn't sound . . ."

"They didn't sound dirty enough for you, I bet." Mike laughed, filling Paul's glass and then leaning over to do the same to mine. A bit of me was entranced, sitting there watching their relationship unfold. Anna would love this, I thought: the booze, the company, the teasing, and the chatter. It reminded me of evenings we used to have a long time ago when we all had more time and energy. But Anna wasn't here, which is why we were. I shook my head. "I think it's different for women. For gay men it's probably another kind of cruising."

Paul smiled at me benevolently. "This, darling Stella, is not cruising—far too round about the houses. Cruising denotes action. This is more head-entertainment."

"Yes, well, at some point she stopped talking and started doing as well. Or at least that's what her phone bills say."

I had found it in a folder after I'd put Lily to bed. The telephone quarter to the end of June showed the Soulmates number clocking up pound signs in clusters of three and four sessions a week through the end of May into June. Then, midway through the month, it stopped. It was now the middle of July. We all sat looking at them.

"Boy, this stuff is expensive." Mike whistled softly. "No wonder I never had any money those first few months. Does this bill mean a lot of calls or just a lot of windbags?"

"The latter, if my experience this afternoon is anything to go by.

But see when the phoning stops? Either Anna got tired of listening or she found someone."

Paul shrugged. "And you say you called some of these guys that she rang?"

I nodded.

"They were still available?"

"Not all of them. But a few were."

"What were they like?"

"Pretty hopeless."

"Not the kind of men Anna would go for?"

"Not at all. Not unless . . ." I hesitated over the words. "Not unless she was in some way desperate." There was silence. "I wondered whether maybe you two getting together has made her feel . . . I don't know, more alone, excluded."

"We've been very careful around her." Paul, immediately on the defensive. "She knows it won't change anything."

"I know that—I'm not attacking you. I just—"

"I think you've both got it wrong." Mike, cutting in, sounding quite sure of himself.

"Got what wrong?" I said.

"This whole thing. Anna. I don't think she's desperate at all. I think she's just been thinking about this stuff."

"What stuff?"

"Men. Sex."

Paul looked at him for a moment. "What makes you think that?"

Mike pulled his chair back from the tilt and laid the photo down on the table. "Well, for one thing, she's been getting more into how she looks these last few months. She's been experimenting with her hair color, using something to lift up the black."

"Has she?" Paul again.

"Yeah, she and I talked about it. Which shades would go best. It's my speciality, color and light. She went for a mahogany shine. It was perfect under the right light. And she's started to wear different clothes, more of the body and less of the drape. She's definitely become a bit foxier."

"Foxier?" I repeated, thinking what a wonderful word it was, all earth smells and sharp teeth.

"Yeah, foxier."

"So what else has she said to you, apart from discussing hair color?" said Paul, and you could see that he was really interested, not just in what he was finding out about Anna but in what he was learning about his lover.

"Nothing really. But it's obvious, isn't it? I mean Lily's not a baby anymore. And however much Anna loves her, she has to recognize that fact. I think she needed to spread her wings. Or try to. Just to see how it felt again."

And as he said it, it struck me that maybe knowing Anna as long as we had done didn't help us here. That while we saw a woman somehow fashioned by the past, by old wounds and the all-encompassing love of Lily, Mike had met someone who had come through that, someone who perhaps had more sense of the future.

Paul frowned. "So if she didn't tell you, how do you know all this?"

Mike smiled. "You know, your trouble is that you think being younger than you means knowing less."

"I do not!" Paul guffawed. "What a fucking cheek."

Mike grinned, enjoying the joshing. "Listen, it's simple. I watched Megan go through this same thing last year. Megan's my elder sister," he said to me as an explanatory aside. "Her husband walked out on her, what, three years ago, leaving her with two small kids. She's been a really good mum, got on with the job and not played around, but she also gets tired of it. Sometimes she needs to blow out a bit, to have something for herself as well as for them, see if she can still do it. I think something like that is what's been happening to Anna."

We both sat and thought about it. I hadn't seen her since that visit at the end of April when she had been busy and working and had bought new clothes and seemed intermittently so high. Then there had been the missed phone calls, and the ones where we didn't talk much because of work, hers and mine. Maybe she'd sensed I wouldn't approve. Or maybe with my settled life I hadn't been the right person to tell. Something similar could be said of Paul, with his expanding business and his new sexy love affair. He'd appreciate his lover more after tonight, though. The vein of compassion and intuition revealed would make Mike even more of a match for him, adding further spice to their relationship. It seemed strange to admit that Anna's absence might actually have achieved something positive.

"So what do we think?" said Paul. "Do we tell all this to the police? Stella?"

"I don't know. What is there to tell? You're right. We have no proof that her not coming home has anything to do with these ads. And even if it had, how would we ever know which one it was? She circled ten or fifteen. She could have called a hundred. She might have answered ads elsewhere, or even put one in herself. We could be chasing them for weeks."

"Yeah, I suppose. If you're getting up, Mike, can you bring out another bottle of wine from the rack? And stick your head into Lily's room. Check she's asleep?"

"Sure." He gathered up the plates and walked to the kitchen door, then turned back as he got there. "Hey—have you guys got the answering machine on?"

Paul and I exchanged glances. "No," I said. "I turned it off when I checked the messages. Why?"

"Because I think there's someone talking in the hall."

Away—Saturday P.M.

As HE STOOD ASIDE FROM THE DOOR SHE HAD TO STEEL HERSELF not to run.

This time she noticed everything. The four other closed doors on the landing, the bars on the window halfway down the stairs, the main door at the bottom, dark, heavy wood apparently impenetrable. She had a sudden vision of a woman in a vermilion dress pulling frantically at the lock, yanking it open, and flying down a path, the bottom of the dress catching on the undergrowth, the sound of someone in pursuit after her. But she couldn't tell if the woman was herself or someone taller. She brushed it aside.

Downstairs they passed further closed doors on their way to the single open one. Even if he lived like a hermit, he would need a kitchen and a bedroom at the very least. In one of them would be her passport and ticket, and a window that opened onto the world outside. Don't rush it, Anna. First Lily and food. After, she would put her mind to ways of leaving.

The place was transformed for evening: fat church candles on the mantelpiece and windowsills, and music, devotional, young voices recorded in old spaces, echoing through the room. On a blue damask tablecloth laid on the floor in front of the fireplace was the food: a dozen dishes on bright ceramic plates, generous helpings of cheeses, meats, bread, salads, cooked fishes, and roasted peppers. And next to the food, a bottle of red wine. The whole thing was almost sinister in its perfection. Nevertheless the very sight of the food made her salivate. She turned away from the fire and looked around for the phone. It was already in his hand. She thought of his obvious lie when he had tried to call the taxi. He wouldn't dare try that again, would he?

"I'll dial for you," he said quietly. "To be sure you get through to the right place."

He punched in some digits. She hesitated. Did he really know her home phone number? He'd claimed to have called it the night she had arrived to tell them she would be delayed, but that had to have been a lie, hadn't it? Lie or not, he seemed to know what he was doing. She watched his finger hitting the numbers. She had an image of her kitchen in the summer evening twilight. Lily would almost certainly be asleep by now (Paul was more scrupulous about bedtimes than she was), and he and Estella would be stalking the phone, waiting for her to call. If he got through to either of them, would he put the phone down? Certainly a foreign man asking to speak to Lily would make them immediately suspicious. Even if he hung up immediately it would be enough to alert them. Or that, at least, was what she hoped. It was the most and the least she could do. Could you trace an incoming number from a foreign destination? He would no doubt know that, too. She felt her stomach knot again. She took some deep breaths to get her voice ready.

He looked up at her. "The number is ringing."

It wouldn't take long. If it was the answering machine it would pick up after a couple of rings. He listened for a few seconds, then thrust the receiver abruptly toward her.

"Remember," he said, as she took it from him, his fingers rested above the disconnect button. "Only what we agreed."

Away—Saturday P.M.

His words lay between them, a teasing invitation to honesty.

Sometimes it is hard to know what is more painful, telling the truth or lying. Now would have been the perfect moment for her to confess. It wouldn't take that much. "Remember that first night at the restaurant, Samuel? Well, I didn't tell you the whole story, either. I'm not exactly the woman you think I am. . . ."

In the right circumstances such an act of confession could be its own erotic activity. Penance comes with in-built absolution. The sexuality of submission. She formed the words in her head. But it turned out not to be the right moment after all.

The cry burst in through the shutters like breaking glass, and it was clear from the first note that this was the voice of a child in pain. The jagged howl was followed by an equally sudden out-of-control sobbing, full of panic and fear, as if he or she had been struck viciously or had sustained an instant terrible injury. On the bed Anna lifted her head to the noise like an animal reading a scent in the wind. She recognized the cry as that of a child around Lily's age, and its distress turned her stomach over. She disengaged herself from his arms and sat up.

The sobbing continued for what felt like the longest time. Surely someone must have got there by now? Eventually, a woman's voice could be heard rising up, intervening between the yells, and gradually the hysteria subsided, softening into a gulping tearful sound; more familiar, more confined, a sign of comfort given and received. Anna could almost feel the weight of the child's body on her own lap, touch the sticky heat of the tears on flushed cheeks. In her experience no adult could be both so monstrously hurt and so utterly comforted. It spoke of a different passion from the one unfolding in the room, and its intrusion served to break the spell between them.

"What time is it, Samuel?" she asked suddenly.

He smiled, acknowledging the loss of her gently, as if it were a bet that he had always been willing to lose. He stretched across the sheets and down to the floor where his watch was lying by the edge of the bed.

"See. No need to panic," he said, scooping it up and presenting it to her face upward. "She'll still be awake. It's always an hour earlier in London."

He pulled himself off the bed and moved across to the shutters to let in the pastel shades of a gathering twilight. "Give me a couple of minutes to get dressed and get out of here. I'll order the first course while you phone."

Home—Saturday P.M.

THERE WERE A NUMBER OF WAYS WE COULD HAVE MADE EXCUSES for ourselves: the night was hot, the outside patio inviting, there had been music coming from a nearby garden muddying the silence, and the kitchen door had blown half closed. We had been talking intently, voices overlapping with the odd rise of laughter in between, and we had all had a sufficient amount to drink. It wasn't enough. If the phone had been ringing in the house we should have heard it. The fact was we didn't.

Paul made a grab for the receiver on the wall at the back of the kitchen. I heard him shouting "Hello!" as Mike and I sprinted up the stairs into the hall where the machine was located. We nearly made it in time.

In her full-length nightgown and tumbling hair she looked like a small pale ghost that had lost its way. She was standing by the hall table, the receiver still in her hand. Through the earpiece we could hear Paul's voice, insistent, almost angry: "Hello? Hello? Anna, is that you?"

He had obviously startled her. Him or someone else. As I approached her she shoved the phone straight out to me, partly to protect herself, partly as if it was suddenly something she didn't want to touch anymore.

I bent down until I was level with her and took it carefully from her hands. Paul's voice had gone. The line was dead. I heard his footsteps bounding up the stairs. I opened my arms to her, but she did not come inside.

"Did the ringing wake you, Lily?" I said softly as I heard Paul arrive behind me in the hall.

She gave a little shrug, half yes, half no.

"I'm sorry. We were in the garden. We didn't hear it." I motioned to the other two behind me to stay back. As I did so I caught Paul's eye. He looked strange. I thought about what it must feel like for her, the three of us bearing down on her.

"How clever of you to get to it first," I said, smiling. "Who was it, darling? Did they leave a message?"

She gave her little frown. No wonder she seemed lost. She was probably still half-asleep. "It was Mummy. She said she'd be back soon."

Part
Two

Home—Saturday P.M.

MAYBE SHE ONLY CAME TO ME BECAUSE MY BODY WAS THE RIGHT shape, its softness and angles in the same places as her mother, and because at times of stress everyone needs familiar comforts. I think Paul was hurt that she chose me over him, but his voice had been so insistent and anxious through the telephone receiver; he was sensitive enough not to argue with her decision.

We were sitting in the garden, her on my lap, a glass of fizzy water in front of her on the table, a piece of leftover chicken in her hands. She was telling us a story. It was not the first time we had heard it, but since it changed fractionally with every telling we needed to be sure. Although she was, I have no doubt, disturbed by the event, there was also a sense of occasion about it, and she was not unaware of her place at the center of it.

We had got to the bit where we were asking her questions: same facts, different angles.

"She must have been surprised it was you who picked up the phone," I said brightly.

"Yes. She asked me if I was in bed."

"I hope you told her that you were," said Paul with mock severity.

"Yes, but I said I wasn't asleep yet."

I gave her a small squeeze. "You were when I looked in."

"I had my eyes closed," she said solemnly. "I'm very good at that."

"And she definitely said that she'd called earlier?"

She nodded. She had already grown tired of this one, but Paul kept returning to it.

"Did you tell her we hadn't got the message?"

She shrugged, then nodded again, but it was hard to know whether that was because she had told Anna or because it was what Lily thought we wanted to hear.

"But she said she'd be back soon." Me, this time, trying to shift the subject.

"Yes."

"On Monday?" Paul again.

Lily frowned. "I think so. She said she was going to pick me up from school."

"Because the planes were full until then?"

She nodded impatiently, though it was clear she really didn't have a clue. I noticed her jaw tighten, as if she was clenching her teeth, a warning flare that she was feeling cornered.

"Paul," I said lightly. "How about we leave it for a bit and have a cup of cocoa? And maybe a biscuit. What d'you say, Lily?"

Mike walked back in while the kettle was boiling. He shook his head. "You can't do it if it comes from abroad. They don't have the technology."

"But if we'd dialed *out* they'd have an automatic record of the international number," said Paul. "It's itemized on the bill."

"Yeah, well, that's how it works. But not the other way around."

"You sure?"

"Listen, I rang the operator and he rang the supervisor."

"Maybe the police could do it," I said quietly, when Lily had her attention focused on the biscuit tin.

"Nope," said Mike. "Apparently not. I asked them that, too."

"Jesus, and this is supposed to be state-of-the-art technology."

Paul slammed the fridge door shut. "You should have asked to talk to the manager."

"I did, Paul. It's ten o'clock on a Saturday night. He or she is out having a life. Hey, don't shoot the messenger, okay?"

Paul sighed. "Sorry." He went over to where Lily was sitting and squatted down in front of her. She kept her attention stubbornly on the biscuit. Careful, Paul, I thought. "Listen, little lumpalink. I know you're tired, but I just want you to tell me one more time. Mummy didn't say where she was calling from, no?"

She shook her head, her mouth full of chocolate chip.

"And you said that we were all here waiting for her, right? Stella too?"

"Yes." And a bit of biscuit got spat out with the words. "I told you that already."

"I know, love. I know. But can you remember exactly what you said about us?"

She shook her head, her jaw clamped together. I wouldn't want to be in Paul's shoes now. Silence.

"Lily," he prompted. Then, more firmly. "It's important, darling."

She snapped her head up at him and her voice exploded out. "I said you were in the garden, all right?" she yelled. "Didn't you hear me the first time?" Then she flounced her body away from him, shoulders hunched right over, head down, enclosing herself in her own storm, blocking out any further incoming signals.

At full throttle (which, luckily, isn't often) Lily's temper can strip wallpaper. There is an internal incandescence to her fury. While other children shout and scream she goes into closedown, total absence, deafness like a form of civil disobedience. Paul put a hand on her knee. She jerked her leg away. As a strategy it had got the British out of India, and it would defeat us here tonight if we didn't think fast. Once they locked horns we'd be here for hours. I glanced at Mike over the top of his head. He made a small face, then laughed out loud.

"Hey listen. Anna didn't want to talk to us because she phoned to talk to Lily," he said merrily, coming up and putting a hand on his lover's shoulders. "If it had been me, I would have done the same thing. Sounds like you're jealous, Paul."

Paul scowled. Lily spotted the look. She shot Mike a fast glance to check whether she was being humored, thought about it for a while, and decided to let him do it anyway. She relaxed her shoulders. I swear I saw them fall. The air around us began to move freely again.

I let it circulate for a while. "And I'm sure she'll call us later," I said when I thought the coast was clear. "After you're in bed." I paused. "Speaking of which, do you know what the time is?"

She sighed, but the weather was clement now and it was more a breeze than a harbinger of a gale. "Oh, Stella . . . it's Sunday tomorrow," she wheedled, the old Lily back again.

"That's as may be, but Stella's right, it's still time for bed," Paul chipped in, looser this time. "Come on. Who do you want to take you up? Me or her?"

She paused and looked at us both. "Can I have another biscuit?"

"No," we said together, laughing.

She gave a shrug and pointed to Mike.

He grinned. "Good choice. It would be my pleasure. Just so long as we don't have to read the story about the giant-eating man again."

She took his hand and let him lead her out. I watched them go. Harmony restored. How can anyone believe that children are powerless? They know more about fighting than the average German Panzer division. Yet their real strength is how to make peace.

Although some would no doubt find it precocious, I love the way Lily knows how to handle adults. It speaks of a certain confidence about the world—something that had always eluded me as a child, though it has to be said that circumstances were not on my side.

At the door she turned. "If Mummy calls again, will you wake me up? There was something I forgot to tell her."

Paul nodded. "Yes, of course. Up you go now, pumpkin. I'll come and say good night in a minute."

They went off together, as if it were something they did every night. I thought again of how substantial Mike had proved himself to be this evening and how this crisis could only serve to deepen their relationship. It was interesting, seeing Paul with a younger man. In contrast to Mike's casual style, Paul's now seemed more focused, more regimented. Maybe Mike had just allowed Paul to grow older at last (it has always seemed to me that good-looking gay men carry the burden of others' sexual expectations upon them), to become more himself.

It had also been illuminating to watch him with Lily; the up-front questioning, the domesticity, the edge of discipline along with the love. It made me realize how in the past I had only ever seen him as the supplementary parent, more likely to be playing Mr. Nice Guy to Anna's primary mum. How much of his tougher stand was about chronic worry and how much it reflected his own style of parenting was hard to tell.

It is, I think, time to say something more about this strange un-nuclear family of which Lily is the center and in some ways the key.

I know academically speaking the jury is still out on nature versus nurture, but I have to say that fifteen minutes in the company of Lily as a baby would have sorted most people out on that one. Because Lily didn't simply arrive, she came equipped with her own game plan. The only child of a single mother. What was needed here? An essentially sunny disposition, an ability to sleep through the night at an early age, attachments to other adults if and when they proved trustworthy, and a kind of innate belief that the world will do unto you as you do unto it, and thus you will be charmed and loved forever. Lily. Outgoing and self-contained at the same time. If you could have used her as a political weapon the debate about nuclear versus dysfunctional families would have taken a whole new turn.

Of course, we have helped. Right from the beginning the three of us have provided a structure and a security in which this unusual plant can flourish. My side consists of regular visits, me to them and them to me, large phone bills (I talk to Lily on her own almost as often as I do to Anna), and a growing proportion of my more than adequate income spent on games and books and the more extravagant bits of a child's yearly wardrobe.

Perhaps more unexpectedly, given his other life as a gay man, Paul has shown a similar level of commitment. Maybe he always harbored a secret desire for a child and knew that this would be his only chance to have one. I don't know him well enough to ask, but I do know that he's always been there for them both, financially as well as emotionally. From the acorn of that computer graphics course at which he first met Anna thirteen years ago has grown a sturdy software business, and as his income has risen so has his level of financial commitment. It took Anna a while to accept it, but in the end it seemed churlish to refuse. His support has made their life easier. Just as their life has made his richer.

For years now there has been a routine to his care. He stays on Friday, and occasionally Saturday, nights, takes Lily out for part of the weekend, and looks after her if Anna is away. During this time he has also had a succession of lovers—his gayness has always been openly acknowledged and talked about—but none of them have ever been particularly serious or, to put it another way, none of them have been allowed to affect his commitment to Lily. And with Michael's acceptance into the family it looked as if that wouldn't change now. It was that security of care which gave Paul the right to say what he did about her on that Saturday night. He had evidently been worrying at it for a while.

"I don't get it," he said almost angrily. "How could Anna possibly not ask to talk to one of us? She must have known we'd be out of our minds with worry."

"Not necessarily. Not if she believed she had already left a message for us."

"But she hadn't, had she."

"The trouble is we don't know that for sure, Paul. What if it was on your mobile?"

He shook his head. "In that case we'll never find out, because my bloody secretary canceled the whole thing before checking. But there wasn't, anyway. I mean, I checked the messages first thing on Friday morning, before I went into the meeting. There was nothing there, and she was already twelve hours late by then. If she was going to call she would have done it before."

"Maybe she got held up. Why would she say to Lily that there'd been a message if there hadn't?"

He sat silently for a second, picking bread crumbs off the table with his fingertips, then flicking them into the grass. "You don't think Lily was just telling us what she thought we wanted to hear?"

"What do you mean?"

"Well, you saw how angry she got when we questioned her."

"Oh, come on, Paul, she just lost it. I thought we were lucky she went so long. We were pushing her."

"You mean I was pushing her?"

I shrugged.

He sighed. "Do you think I'm being unreasonable? Don't you think Anna should have talked to us?"

"I don't know. Maybe she wanted to and Lily hung up before she got the chance."

He shook his head. "She hasn't called again."

"The line's been engaged, remember. Mike was checking with the operator."

"Yeah, well, the line's not engaged anymore."

We sat in silence for a while. Upstairs in Lily's bedroom I heard the murmur of voices. They'd be well into the second book by now, and Mike probably wouldn't even have noticed the join. I poured myself another glass of wine. The sky was thickening from gray to black; one month on from the summer solstice and the light was already on the turn. It is the mark of a committed pessimist, looking for winter in the middle of summer. Despite my recent successes, the older I get the more I find myself in need of the light. Maybe that was why I was holding out against Paul now. I could feel it building up in him. Still I didn't say anything. Which meant that in the end he had to.

"She's not going to call," he murmured when the wine was halfway down in my glass.

"What are you trying to say, Paul?"

He sighed. "Listen, nobody heard the phone ring, right? We were all out here with the door open; the music wasn't that loud, yet we didn't hear it and she did. If she had been asleep—and you and I both saw her—it would have had to ring a number of times to wake her, yet we still didn't hear it. And when I picked the receiver up in the kitchen the line was completely dead. There was definitely no one on the other end. It was like the sound you get when someone has had the phone off the hook for too long. Was Lily actually talking when you found her in the hall?"

"No. But that's because you were shouting down the receiver at her. Wait a minute. Are you saying you think that Lily made all this up? That it wasn't Anna on the phone?"

"Look, Stella, I don't know what I'm saying. All I know is that if Anna had called, she should have talked to us. Or at the very least to you, when she heard that you were here, too. It doesn't make sense that she didn't. And, well—well, it *is* possible. I mean you know what Lily's like. Always wanting to make things better for everyone. I think she might have just decided to say all that because she knew we were worried. Or maybe she did it because *she* was worried—pretended to talk to Anna to make herself feel better. She's always been a great chatterer when it comes to fake phone calls."

"Yeah, but that was when she was younger and we all knew it was fake. She hasn't done anything like this before."

"There hasn't been anything like *this* before, has there?" He sighed. "You and I both know that Lily's got a pretty powerful imagination. She can hold on to a story when she wants to, even when it's made up. Anna told me how she came back the other week with some number about how all the kids in her class had got chicken pox. Kept it up for ages. It was because she didn't want to do gym next day in school. Anna had to call one of the other mothers to check."

Maybe she's just better at fibs than you are, I thought, though clearly it wasn't the time to say it. "But this isn't the same. I mean, this evening she retold the same consistent story under questioning."

"It wasn't exactly a complicated one, though, was it? Mummy called, said she'd been delayed, they talked about what she'd done at the fair, then Mummy said good night and that she loved her and that she'd be back soon. Nothing about where she was or why she hadn't called sooner. I'm sorry. It just doesn't sound convincing to me. And you saw how mad she got about it."

I sighed. "I don't know. I think in her shoes I would have got mad, too. She's a smart kid, Paul. Somewhere underneath all this happy-weekend stuff she knows it's falling apart. I'm surprised she hasn't lost it sooner, really."

We stopped talking. It occurred to me that Paul would almost certainly think that he knew Lily better than I did. And that in some ways that might indeed be true. I also knew that he was right; Lily's version of the phone call didn't completely make sense, but I really didn't want to think about what that might mean. Because, of course, it affected the next question we had to discuss.

"I still think we have to tell the police," I said tentatively.

He sighed. "If we didn't speak to Anna directly I don't think we can vouch for the conversation."

"Paul! They've got people working on this, out there looking for her. It really could be that she just missed a plane and you didn't get her message. In which case we're giving them false information if we don't tell them."

"Well, you've changed your position since this morning, haven't you? I got the impression you didn't think they were doing enough then."

I sighed. "Yes—well, that's when you suggested she was disturbed."

"And we're still sure that she isn't?"

I stared at him. "Jesus, Paul. What is this? What do you think is going on?"

"That's the point, Stella. I don't have a clue. One minute she's missing and we're all freaking out about it, the next minute she's with some guy because she's changed her hair color and needs to get laid, the next minute it's none of those things and she's on the phone chatting to Lily about coming home but not to us. Meanwhile we don't know where, who, how, or why." He shook his head. "I'm just wound up about it, that's all. And I can't bear to see Lily in trouble."

He glanced up at her bedroom window; the night-light was on now, flickering in time to the dancing silhouettes. Mike would be on his way down. What if Paul was right and Lily had made up the call to make us feel better? What if something really had happened to Anna? If it wasn't her on the phone there could be no other explanation for this length of silence.

The space across the table between us was filling up with the night. I put out a hand and laid it on his. "What do you say we compromise? I'll carry on thinking she called, you keep thinking she didn't, but we won't decide whether or not to tell the police till tomorrow."

He sighed. "Okay," he said, giving my hand a brief squeeze back. "I'm sorry, Estella. But this is fucking me about."

"Yes, I know. I feel the same. Listen, why don't you get Mike to stay here with you tonight? Lily won't care and we both know it would be okay with Anna."

He nodded. Then he said, "You know, I've remembered where I saw Chris Menzies."

"Where?"

"It was reporting on some Mafia scandal in southern Italy. Two, maybe three months ago."

I frowned. "You don't think . . ."

"What do I know? But I sure as hell don't have any other explanation. I mean, I don't think there's been anyone else. But I can't swear to it. These last couple of months have been so busy. And like I told you, I think she *has* been strange recently. If Mike was right . . ." He trailed off.

I shook my head. "You wait. We'll tease her about all this when she gets back. Just you see."

Soon after that we closed up the garden and went to bed. Nobody had called the police.

Away—Saturday P.M.

YOU EAT NOW. WE HAVE AN AGREEMENT, REMEMBER?"

The mention of food churned up sour juices in the pit of her stomach, but the sound of Lily was still singing in her head and she was scared of letting him see how shaken she was.

If Anna hadn't expected her daughter to answer the phone, she'd been even less prepared for the impact of her voice, plucked from a warm bed and bursting with tales of family dinners and a Saturday spent coddled and spoiled. Terrified that if she said too much she might break down and then he would cut them off, she had kept to her word, saying as little as possible, and when the questions came—as she knew they would—making light of missed planes and dwelling instead on her return with promises of pickup from school gates and pizza in front of the TV. It was only at the end, as they said their good-byes and Lily got suddenly needy and tearful, that her own voice grew sticky with pain and he, realizing her distress, brought his finger down on the bar and severed the connection too early.

She gulped back the tears, fury colliding with pain. No, we don't have any agreement, she thought. It was all she could do not to throw the telephone receiver at his head. Except it wouldn't do enough damage. She searched the room for something that might. When she found it she could barely keep her eyes off it. A full wine bottle could open a man's head up if you brought it down with enough force. I don't care about your sorrow or your grief, if that's what this is about. You're a weird, fucked-up man and I'm going to get out of here the second you make the mistake of turning your back on me. Which you will do, as soon as you start to feel more comfortable with me. As soon as . . .

I'm coming, Lily, she thought. I'm coming.

"You're right." She took a deep breath. "I need some food."

He took a plate from the table and knelt down at the tablecloth, careful to keep her well within his sights. He was close enough now for her to catch the scent of him again, the chemical smell mixed with a cloying aftershave, as if too much of one had been applied to disguise the other. She remembered the pine tree in the car, and the carefully ironed creases in his jeans. Mr. Clean, Mr. Tidy. He had given her the shivers from the first moment she had stepped into the car. Why, oh why, hadn't she stepped out of it again? She stared at the top of his head and tried to imagine glass in the bone, wine and blood matted into the hair. A nasty experience for a man who didn't like mess. And for a woman who didn't like violence. Whether or not she could actually do it—hit him with enough vicious power to knock him senseless—she had no idea. For now the fantasy would have to be comfort enough.

He was scooping a little from each of the dishes onto her plate: anchovies, cheeses, peppers, pickles, salamis. Her hunger was getting the better of her. She felt a flood tide of saliva rising in her mouth. He made a move toward the wine. "No," she said loudly, having to swallow to avoid spitting. "No, I don't want any alcohol."

He turned and looked at her. "There is nothing bad in it," he said quietly. "You agreed to stay. I don't need to drug you now."

"I know," she said hurriedly. "It's not that. I'm too hungry to drink. It'll make me sick."

He put the bottle back on the floor and handed her the plate. "Here," he said. "Eat slowly."

He sat back on the sofa and watched her.

She couldn't wait any longer. The taste of the anchovies exploded onto her tongue, their saltiness so intense that she had to shove in a chunk of bread to mop up her own juices. It was so long since she had eaten it felt like an alien activity. She thought of Lily, shoving in too much food and then grinning across the table at her with her mouth open. She made herself chew slowly until her jaw hurt from the scrape of her teeth. The real flavor started to seep through, sour, sweet, exquisite, overwhelming, flooding her brain as well as her mouth. She closed her eyes to hold it in. Nothing will ever taste this good again, she thought. Every time I sit down to a meal, every time I open a fridge, I will be here, reliving this moment. If, that is, I ever get home to do such things.

She glanced sideways at him. He was sitting absolutely still in his chair, watching. The penetration of his stare was like trying to look into a torch beam. She shifted her gaze away from him, letting her eyes drift to the wall of pictures above the fireplace. Her alter ego was everywhere, smiling and laughing in half a dozen expensive outfits: animated, busy, the hands—nails colored to match the clothes—in conversation along with the mouth. Each of the photos on this wall was carefully cropped so all you could see was her, never the person she was with. Since it seemed logical that he was the photographer, this meant that he must have framed each one with considerable, almost obsessive, care.

Then across the room there were the other, different studies: more intimate, close-ups where she was looking straight into the camera, smiling or simply staring openly, with no sense of self-consciousness. I could never be that at ease with a camera, she thought. Even in repose the woman's face had tremendous energy and power to it. You could feel how her presence would light up a room. It was hard to imagine them together. Her so vital, him so dead. It seemed wrong that in reality it was now the other way around.

Do I really remind him of her? she thought. Is it as simple and as stupid as that? What if he actually meant it: three days of talk and companionship and then a lift to the airport, a desperate way to get through a desperate anniversary. He was disturbed enough for that. No doubt about that. Sitting there in the warm evening air, she felt suddenly tired of being scared, tired of the way her body was all knotted and hollow with it. She took another mouthful of food and felt the warmth thaw further into her rigidity.

"You're right," she said after a while. "I was hungry."

"The taste is big, yes? I do this sometimes. Stop eating, then have a slow meal."

"Do you drug your drink and lock yourself up in a room for days as well?"

"I am happy you picked that dress," he said, failing or choosing not to notice the sarcasm. "I always like it. Red is your color."

If I didn't know better, I might think you were a polite, rather boring man, she thought. But I do know better. And so do you.

"There is polish as well, you know, for the nails. In the drawer by the bed."

So then she'd be just like the photograph. Perfect in every detail. Is that what he wanted? Oh no, she thought. Not that crazy, please. She took a breath. "You know, we don't know each other's names."

"No," he said, not taking his eyes off her. "I am Andreas." He didn't offer a surname.

"Good. I'm Anna, Anna Franklin. But then you know that already, of course, from my passport. And my daughter is Lily. She's six years old, almost seven." She paused. Do you know about children? she wanted to add. About how much they need love and security? How much damage you can do by depriving them of the people they love? But she didn't. Tread softly, Anna, she said to herself. The more relaxed he becomes the more chances you will have. "What was your wife's name?"

He didn't answer immediately, as if he didn't want to have to admit to the two of them having separate identities. "Paola," he said at last. "Her name was Paola."

Paola. Had he used that name two mornings ago? She could no longer remember. "Paola? She was Italian? I thought perhaps she was English."

He grunted. "Her father was English, her mother was Italian."

"Ah. So she spoke both languages."

"Yes."

"And it was she who taught you?"

He nodded.

"She did a good job."

He didn't answer.

"Is that how you met?"

Still nothing.

"Was that here or in England?"

In the next gap between the words, the choral evensong that had been whispering its way through the room drew to an echoing close. With God gone the space was suddenly colder. She registered a tension building up inside him, that smooth fat layer of politeness being eaten away by something. Maybe it was because she was doing the talking now, taking control. Was this how they had been together—he with a ramrod stuck up his soul, she unable to thaw him? It was not inconceivable that she had died to get away from him. Six years in an isolated house in the wilderness. It must have been like being buried alive.

She glanced toward the bottle on the hearth. It was a long way away. Take your time, Anna, she thought. You may only get one chance.

"You know, Andreas, I'll tell you the truth. I'm scared of you. And when I'm not scared, I'm angry. I want more than anything else in the world to be home with my daughter. But you say that you won't hurt me, and that if I keep you company for a few days you'll let me go home. In which case we are going to spend time together. But I can't pretend to be her. I can only be myself, you understand? And for this to work we are going to have to talk to each other. Otherwise there is no point. Otherwise I might as well go back to the room and stay there." She paused. "So why don't you tell me something about her?"

He gave a little grunt, then bent down and picked up the wine bottle from the edge of the grate. She watched it go. Don't panic, she thought. There will be others. He pulled the cork out and poured two glasses full. He offered her one. She took it this time and scooped a tiny mouthful. Like the food and the clothes it tasted rich. How convenient, she thought, to have enough money to finance one's madness. It would be interesting to know which side of the family it came from.

"When I saw you in the shop I knew you will be like this."

"Like what?"

He was still looking down at his glass, as if this conversation made him shy. "Like her. I met her in that shop, the one with the horse." He shrugged. "It was different then, a serious place, for books, for study. She was just arrived in Florence. She had grown up in London, but her father died and she came home to be near to her mother. We started talking. She spoke so perfectly in English. I knew it from school and from my business. But I wanted to learn more. She offered to teach me. Conversation lessons. I was not a good student." He paused. "It took me a long time to get better. Long enough time so she will fall in love with me too."

It was the first time he had said anything that could even remotely be interpreted as humorous. She found herself almost shocked by it. She watched his face carefully. When she didn't respond he looked up at her and there was a ghost of a smile. Had this been the charm? The shy boy in the big man? It didn't seem enough. She tried to imagine them together, heads over a book, she correcting his stray words. The secret of a language is in the shape of the lips. Could the repetition of all those precise little English vowels really have driven them into each other's arms? Why not? His personality was more pursed than extravagant, more English than an Englishman's. Maybe some people were simply born into the wrong culture, got lost early on trying to form the wrong set of sounds. "So then you married and came here?"

"Yes."

"It's a long way from Florence?" He gave a shrug. If he saw the question as probing he didn't register it. "Very isolated. She didn't mind that?"

"Not at all. She wanted it. She chose it. She said that the house was full of the silence of women, so it would make a good home. We worked on it together."

I bet she didn't design my room, she thought. I bet that came later.

"The silence of women." If the photos were anything to go by she hardly conformed to the pattern herself. It wasn't the only image that jarred: a woman with that kind of wardrobe shoving plaster onto walls and laying floors? Something not quite right about the thought of all that chipped nail varnish.

"What about children?" she said, already knowing with utter certainty that this man had never been a father.

"Children? No, there was no children." He paused. "She couldn't have children."

"I'm sorry."

He shrugged. "It was not a problem. It always felt as if we were enough."

She wondered if Harlequin had an Italian imprint. The picture had so much soft focus in it she was beginning to lose any sense of depth. She saw them going up that elegant staircase together at the end of a long day of do-it-yourself in haute couture, his hand teasing the zip down the back of her dress as she walked: the red sea parting to reveal a vision of white land ready for the taking. But the image choked on its own triteness, and anyway, he seemed more like the kind of man who needed to fold up his clothes before getting into bed. When she tried to push it further her imagination lost the signal, static coursing across the screen. That was the other alarming thing in all of this; there seemed to be no sex in him, or certainly none that she could relate to. Grief can do that, of course, using up all the juice on tears, but that wasn't the problem here. All she could feel here was sticky sentiment, like the leftovers of a man masturbating into his own hand. And from what she could see, the woman in those pictures would have had no truck with that.

"And you took all these photos of her?" she said to clear her head of the image.

He nodded.

"Is that your job?"

He shrugged. "Sometime. More it is my pleasure."

"Do you still work?"

"Oh, yes," he said. "I have a lot to do."

She took in the misunderstanding but let it go. The woman sat between them in the room. "She was very photogenic. How old was she when she died?"

"Thirty-six years. These were taken not long before she died."

"But you have others?"

"Yes."

"How many?"

He gave a shrug, as if the question were too hard to answer.

"Do you keep them—I mean, like this, hanging in other rooms?"

He nodded. Was that what was behind all those closed doors? A house as a museum. No wonder he would be having such trouble forgetting her. "You're a good photographer." She paused. "But it must be painful for you, seeing her all around you like this."

It took a while for him to find the answer. "I think it is worse if she is not here."

There was nothing to say to that. "Can I see some of the others?"

The question hung in the air. For all his neediness he was not a man to be rushed. "Another time perhaps."

Tomorrow and the next day, she thought. That's all you've got, remember? Was this what they would do with their time then? Revisit the past through English conversation and admire photos of the dead?

They sat silently for a while, the atmosphere unexpectedly calm between them. In the candlelight his face looked better, almost relaxed. She took another sip of wine. Even on half a glass she could feel it playing games with her head as well as her stomach. One of the candles on the other side of the room flickered in response to a draft through a slice of open window. Was it like the one in her room, doctored to open only a fraction? It didn't matter. If she got out there she would find herself in the wilderness without money or passport. Not tonight, she thought. Tonight I'm too tired. Tonight let him feel safe with me, and let me sleep alone.

She saw the room above and the lock on the door, and how the chair would be no protection at all if he decided to come in. Except he hadn't yet and there had been ample opportunity. She thought back to the image of him folding up his clothes. Maybe not all screwed-up men are screwed up about sex, or not in the same ways. Maybe he did it all with his camera. She thought about how many times he must have snapped the shutter on this dead woman called Paola, how many hours he would have spent caressing her face or sliding her body to and fro between his fingers in the developing tray.

Of course—the smell. She knew now what the smell meant. It was the aroma of a darkroom, the sticky-sweet stench of developing and fixing chemicals. He was still at it, filling up the time turning negatives into positives. But if he had the ability to endlessly re-create his own wife, then why did he need the company of an inferior look-alike? Once again there were too many things in this that didn't make sense. Once again she could feel herself getting scared. She put her glass on the floor.

"I want to go back to the room now, please. I'm feeling a little ill. I think the wine has made me sick again." He didn't answer immediately, as if he was weighing it up: her needs against the terms of their deal. Was it her imagination or could she feel a tension starting to flood back in, like someone turning a stopcock key? "I think it's the remains of the drug. Tomorrow I'll be better," she added carefully.

"Of course." He got up. "I understand. I will take you up. Oh, but I forget. First I have something to give you." He bent down and slipped his hand under one of the large cushions on the sofa, pulling out a small parcel wrapped in silver paper.

She took it gingerly.

"Open it. It will help you sleep."

She had a sudden panic that it was something compromising, some intimate object of their life together for her to share. She thought of the nail varnish and the wardrobe full of newly cleaned clothes. Please, God, don't let it be underwear, she thought.

"Open it. Please."

She split the seam of tape carefully and folded back the paper. Through the tissue underneath, her fingers encountered a long thin ridge. The feel triggered a memory, and suddenly she knew what it was. She ripped away at the remaining covering. Lily's wooden horse fell onto its side in her lap, its front leg prancing into empty air.

"See," he said. "Now you can believe what I say. In a few days you will be home and then you can give this to your daughter. Like it was you who bought it for her."

She couldn't speak. As she ran her hands over the cool flanks, she saw herself back in the shop, a woman in love with her child, yet in need of some excitement to prove she was still herself. Is that what had attracted him to her; the smell of her restlessness? The world was full of other women with dark hair and pale skin. He could have picked a dozen others.

What was it Estella and she always used to say when they were younger and life slapped them around a bit? It's not the cards that you're dealt, it's the way that you play them. For many years she had assumed it had been Chris and then Lily who had made up the hand of her life, the one that would decide the fundamental balance between happiness and sorrow. Now she knew with awful clarity that that had only been a practice run and that the real hand, the one that would decide everything, was the one she was playing now.

"Thank you," she said, half under her breath, and she smiled, not because she necessarily believed what he had said, but because for that instant she did indeed feel grateful.

"See," he said quietly. "I was right about you. Look. You even smile like her. You should do it more often."

Away—Saturday P.M.

SHE WAS SITTING CROSS-LEGGED ON THE BED, THE SHEET DRAPED around her shoulders. The room had cooled down with the dark. Or maybe she no longer had the heat of his body to rub up against. She looked at her watch: 9:20 P.M. In the restaurant he would have finished his drink and be thinking of food. For once she felt like making him wait. She dialed the number again, but this time when it connected all she got was the engaged tone. Maybe Lily hadn't put the receiver back on the hook properly. It wouldn't be the first time.

The conversation between the two of them had been easy, peppered with tales of swimming lessons and fun fairs, until, that was, the last few moments when Lily had somehow picked up a shadow in her mother's voice and responded to it by suddenly wanting her home again. Anna had tried to jolly her out of it, but had been undermined by the catch in her own throat, and the call had ended a little abruptly. Now she wanted to check that everything was all right. She redialed. Still the sharp persistent engaged signal. Oh, Lily, she said under her breath, it's not a toy, sweetheart. You have to remember to put it back properly. . . .

She thought of home and everyone gathered together for Saturday night. How fitting that Stella should have chosen this weekend for a visit. They hadn't talked to each other in two or three weeks. Was that why she'd come? To check up on her?

Maybe she should have told them what was going on. Stella or Paul. An affair with a married man would hardly have offended Paul's morality. In the past the two of them had had a history of such confessions, embroidering tales of sexual fiasco to make each other laugh over late-night glasses of brandy. But since the arrival of Mike, their previous easy camaraderie—their intimacy without intimacy—had faded a little. And so she had said nothing to him about Samuel, and he in turn hadn't been aware enough to ask.

With Estella the reasons were more complex. Like many best friends they were very different; Anna's spontaneous, often irresponsible style complementing Estella's deliberately defensive one. But at root, for all her unpredictability, she, Anna, had always been the stable one, able to earth the painful detachment of a friend who had lost her mother at the age of ten and coped by closing down on all other offers of intimacy. Over the years the intensity of their friendship had been a surprise and a delight to them both. It had only been shaken once, during Anna's affair with Chris and the fallout that followed it. Then Anna had no longer been the buoyant one, and her despair had proved dangerously contagious, so much so that when she had taken the train north without telling anyone it had partly been Estella's overwhelming, almost panicky concern that she had needed to get away from. Of course she had never told Stella. It would have hurt her too much. But even when she had healed herself their relationship had taken time to recover, and the remaining scar tissue left Anna wary of telling her best friend absolutely everything, particularly when that everything included a married man whom she already knew she wasn't going to resist.

• • •

This thing between her and Samuel had all happened so fast anyway. What had started out as a joke—a drunken Saturday evening spent exploring the lonely hearts column—had, by the next week, turned into an article sold to a features editor fretting about her paper's reach into the thirty-something market, not to mention the barrenness of her own love life.

"What if I decide I want to go to bed with one of them?" Anna had asked her, with a gentle cruelty.

"All the better, so long as you change the names and it doesn't turn into a date-rape piece. Nobody cares about those kinds of stories anymore."

But Anna had already known she wouldn't sleep with them. Their voices had told her that the first night, something about the mix of supplication and arrogance in the tone. Still, she had entered into the spirit of things and left a few lively, encouraging messages. The take-up had been such that she had to get Patricia to baby-sit twice that first week.

She'd met them both in one of the less flashy restaurants of Soho over the course of two evenings. Both of them were nice guys, but boring copy: one a divorced civil servant who, it emerged, very much wanted kids but didn't seem that interested in the woman he'd have to live with to get them; the second a self-employed heritage consultant who had dropped out of the rat race but had recently grown tired of staring at the computer screen in his South London semi and was looking for a way to get out and meet people again.

She in turn had arrived with a bag full of alternative lives to play out, but to her credit she had quickly realized there was no point in lying about all of it, that to write the article at all she had to feel something, and to feel something she had, at least in part, to expose herself. So she used what she could—which was Lily, her house, and her friends—and she turned the journalism into part-time English teaching at a local sixth form college. A full life, but not without its fault lines, she had thought as she unfolded it carefully before them.

The evenings had played out with remarkable similarity. In both cases they had set out their stalls and admired each other's fruit, but it became clear early on that no one really wanted to buy, not wanting or willing enough to take the risk of what felt in some way like soiled goods. In both cases the conversation had started to flag toward the end of dessert and they skipped coffee, splitting the bills and saying their good-byes respectfully while still at the table, thus allowing them to leave separately. She had written them up in her head as she drove away.

Later she found herself quietly depressed, as if the world were shot through with thin veins of sadness—not the dramatic stuff of tragedy, but the small everyday pain, enough to cause slow poisoning in the most balanced of people over the course of a lifetime. Thank God for Lily, she had thought fiercely, she burns brighter than any of them. But that night as they lay tangled together in bed she had a sudden image of her daughter all grown up and striding out of the house, independent, complete, a profound silence growing up in the wake of the door slam. Sentimental shit, she thought, as she went downstairs to get herself a glass of wine. But next morning she rang the Soulmates line and left a message of her own; funky, almost angry, rewriting Marvell's "Coy Mistress" sentiments to throw down a gauntlet to the opposite sex. When she listened to it she realized with a slight shock that although it was fake it was at the same time real. At least it would make for a better article. Only men wanting to buy need apply for this one. Welcome back to the Anna who took risks, and wasn't bothered with consequences.

She rang it herself next weekend to check it was in. Amid breakfast chaos and the scramble to make the swimming lesson on time it sounded outrageous, almost drunk. By Monday night she had had six calls: life stories, sad chat, a flash of bravura here and there. His had been number four. It was not like any of the others:

"Hi. I'll tell you what I think, all right? I think this whole exercise has got more to do with the voice than the content. Okay, so I know not everybody is their voice. You old enough to remember Terence Stamp? Or maybe you're more the Julie Burchill generation. But they're the exceptions who prove the rule. So while you may or may not be what you say you are, your voice has got something about it. No doubt you'll have already formed your own impression of mine.

"Either way I suggest we give each other a get-out clause. There's a restaurant at the top of the Oxo tower on the South Bank where the food isn't worth the money but the view is good. I'll be eating there on Tuesday of this week at nine P.M. Table 110. I've already booked it. You could come and have a look, and if you like what you see you could sit down. If not, don't bother. There's nothing lost. You could have a drink and appreciate the skyline. Who knows, you might meet someone else. I won't ever know if you came or not. No one can miss what they've never had, eh? Though sometimes I think I already do. Good hunting."

He would, she thought as she listened, make a great article.

She dressed down and was deliberately late. She parked the car on Waterloo Bridge and walked along the river beside the concrete sprawl of the National Theatre's new extension. It was one of the first really hot days of summer, and there were people out everywhere walking and drinking, pretending that they were living in Paris, the Thames doing its sluggish best to fit in with the illusion. The walk had reminded Anna of how much she liked the city: its chutzpah, the way the eighties had reinvented it, teaching it how to pose. It had been a while since she had felt so benign toward it, so willing to play.

At the top of the tower the bar had thinned out from the after-work crowd, but the restaurant was buzzing. The diners got the prime view—St. Paul's and the City—the drinkers had to make do with new business developments and the occasional run of lights. *Blade Runner* it was not.

Table 110 was next to the window. The waiter was keen to take her there himself, but she insisted she go alone. She wove her way through until 110 and its inhabitant were clearly in view. Because she had not allowed herself to feel anticipation it seemed unfair that she now experience disappointment.

He was tall and well-dressed and at a generous estimate he might soon be celebrating his twenty-sixth birthday. It was less that he was bad-looking than that he was unformed, the smooth bits and the creases more like the ones from the original packing case than the results of any real living. His neck, she noticed, had a prominent Adam's apple. It was hard to believe that that voice could emerge through such a narrow tunnel. He looked up and it was clear that he was waiting for someone. She turned quickly and managed not to catch his eye.

She retreated to the bar. The wine came in a tall glass with a cool little Oxo logo imprinted on it. She glanced back at him. Was it his age or his face that made him creepy? Since when did good looks guarantee good sex, except in the movies? And who said she had to sleep with him anyway? This was about getting copy, not getting laid. She had a commission to deliver three thousand words on the dangers of the lonely-hearts culture. What the hell was she doing deciding not to meet him, now that she'd come this far? She felt as if she had caught herself out in some kind of lie, though she wasn't exactly sure what it was.

She started to construct a different kind of piece, refashioning her disappointment into something witty and clever, laughing at herself, then willing herself to be surprised. She slid off the stool and turned back toward him. He was on his feet, too. But not, it appeared, for her. Between the tables a small young woman with a mass of curly red hair was striding toward him. His smile grew wider to meet her and the narrowness of his neck seemed less of a problem. They kissed in a way that made it clear they had been there before, and she sank into the seat opposite.

At the bar Anna stood holding her drink, for a second completely nonplussed.

"All I can think is that he must earn more than I do."

It was the voice. She looked down and registered a guy sitting along from her at the bar with a book in his hands. She caught what might have been the word "Redemption" on the cover, but she was too busy trying to read the man to bother with the full title. "Table 110, right?"

He made a grimace. "Meant to be, yes."

He was not as tall as his voice, but there was a chunky, solid feel to him. He had cropped dark hair flecked with gray and a big face that had done a lot of laughing and some of the other. Nothing to set the world alight, but there was something about the eyes that made it clear he didn't give a toss about that. Not another rewrite, she thought, not yet. Without realizing it she wrapped the cloak of work around her a little tighter. Disguise. The great trick of it is that in the right circumstances it can allow one to be even more oneself.

"I thought you said you booked it."

"I did, but obviously his influence is greater than mine. I gather it was an anniversary."

"Of what?"

"What do you reckon? The first time he wore long trousers, or the first time he took them off?"

She glanced over at the two of them. They were smiling at each other. "Oh, I think he's already taken them off," she said. "Don't you?"

He frowned. "I'm surprised she's interested. If you were her, would you be?"

She shrugged. "Well, I was and I wasn't. Or were you too caught up in your book to notice? But, that's not the point," she said quietly. "You're not looking properly. It's not about sex. It's about love."

"Oh—love." And the way he undressed the word made it clear he didn't have a lot of time for it. "No wonder I didn't get the table." He paused, holding her eyes. "I did get another one, though. Unless, that is, you'd prefer to stay drinking?"

She looked out at the two views. On one side St. Paul's, luminous, almost airborne on its floodlights, on the other scaffolding and eighties office blocks. "You lied about the view from the bar, you know."

He sighed. "I think 'lied' is a bit strong. Let's say I exaggerated a little. The food will make up for it, I promise."

Once at the table he seemed to lose interest in her, more focused on the menu and the art of getting the meal right. Anna, being largely bored by cuisine and its elevated place in modern culture, chalked up his first black mark. Great opening, no follow-through, she thought, knowing that she would remember some but not all of the running commentary when she came to put it down later that night. She looked at him looking at the menu. They were, at least, on first-name terms now. Samuel (long for Sam, no doubt). No second names yet. But at least this way she hadn't had to lie. She already wondered about him.

He glanced up. "Sorry. This won't take long."

She shrugged. He went back to work, evidently a man who was used to being indulged. Monstrous confidence.

The waiter came and they chatted together about the finer points of the braised lamb. She sat sliding her fingers up and down the wine stem. Maybe this impresses some women, she thought.

"So," he said, business finally complete. "Here we are. Voice to voice. How shall we start? We could do work, past relationships, present ones, or top ten favorite movies. Do you have a preferred itinerary?"

Yes, monstrous confidence. But at least it wasn't boring. Yet. She gave a short laugh. "How many times have you done this before?"

"Well, more often than you, obviously," he said, smiling. "Which is why I've changed my tactics."

"What? Voice over content?"

"No. Substance over small talk."

"The cooking time of the lamb notwithstanding."

He shrugged. "It costs an arm and a leg here. And not everything on the menu is worth it. I wanted to make sure we got the best we could. Anyway, it's done now. So. Was it a flirt or serious?"

"What?"

"Your message."

"I thought you could tell from the voice."

"So did I. On the tape you said you had a life, but that you could do with another one, though not all the time."

"Yes," she said evenly. "Well, that's more or less how it is."

"Does that mean you're married?"

"No."

"Kids?"

"Yes."

"How many?"

"One."

"You want to tell me any more?"

"A girl. Six and a half. Lily."

"Lily? Nice. Does her father help support her?"

"No," she said, her irritation showing for the first time. "I do."

"So he's not in the picture?"

"Tell me, Samuel, what do you do for a living?"

"Unh-unh. Boring. We decided against that."

"Excuse me. *You* decided."

He paused. "I sell art. To companies."

"How interesting."

"No, it's not," he said abruptly. He sat back in his chair. "Would you like to start this again?"

The remark took her aback. "I don't know. How far back could we go?"

He shrugged. "Well, we've ordered. We wouldn't want to do that again, since it was almost certainly when the problem started. I am right, yes? That is when you got pissed off, isn't it?"

She gave an exasperated laugh. "Let's just say it was a little dull after the opening."

"I know." He sighed. "Food. My great failing. I have to say I like it almost as much as sex."

"You eat regularly, do you?" she said dryly.

"Yep. But there's always room for more," he said, and this time he grinned, showing off those laugh lines at their best. I bet this has them eating out of your hand, she thought. Or maybe using their mouth elsewhere. Nevertheless, she was not having a bad time herself, although if she had thought about it she wouldn't have been completely sure whether that was professional or personal.

"So how about you, Samuel? Are you married?"

He nodded. "Yes, I am."

"Children?"

"No, no children."

"How long have you been together?"

"Eight years."

"That's a long time. Is it successful?"

"More or less."

"So is this the 'less' bit?"

"Not really." He frowned. "Listen, in your message you made it clear you weren't looking for a husband."

"I'm not."

"Good."

She laughed. "Why, what are you looking for?"

"Same as you, I hope," he said quietly. He broke off to fill her glass and then his own. "I'll tell you how it is. I live abroad—in France—but I have to spend a couple of days in London every month on business, and during that time I feel . . . well, far away from home. Almost as if I was another person. I like that feeling. It makes me—I don't know—more whole." He paused, in case she wanted to add something, but she didn't speak. "Last year I had an affair with a woman I met on the plane coming over. It lasted two months. I enjoyed her company and I was sorry when it ended. I've been rather hoping that I might do it again."

"And you thought the dating ads were a good way to find someone?"

"As good as any, yes."

She gave a little shrug. "Well, at least that's honest."

"I am," he said, looking straight at her. "Honest, that is. Honestly. For some people it makes up for a lack of morality. Not for all, though." Gauntlet down. He gave a wry smile. "Listen, as far as I'm concerned there are no rules, okay? So if this isn't what you wanted, if it's too much or too little, then you can call it quits any time you feel like it."

She stared at him for a moment. Though his words were cynical they hadn't come over that way. On the contrary his voice had considerable warmth to it. It could be argued that she was the cynical one;

writing it all down in her head for further use later. "Thanks. I'll re-member that. Who'd be expected to pay for the meal, by the way? I mean, if I walked?"

He grinned. "Since I plan to try some of yours, I think it's fair if it's on me."

She nodded. "And what happens if you're the one who wants to leave?"

"I'd eat first." He looked up at her. "But I don't. Want to leave, that is. And if it doesn't sound too bigheaded, I don't think you do ei-ther. Not yet, anyway."

She stared at him and the tiniest stab of desire registered inside her, somewhere around where the top of the cervix meets the womb. Biol-ogy, she thought, survival of the species. That's all it is. Easily ignored.

She took a breath. "I love my daughter," she said, absolutely not intending to.

"I know how you feel. I love my wife."

She made a little clicking noise with her tongue, but it wasn't ex-actly anger. "I don't fuck my daughter."

He missed a beat, but only one. "I don't fuck my wife." He smiled. "Well, not much. Not anymore."

She didn't smile back.

"But I have to tell you, Anna, I would really like to fuck you."

Since he was too good to have made such an elementary error at this stage, he must have known that she'd be up for this. Or at the least not put off by it. You could easily stop now, she thought. You've got a great article here, you don't need anything more. Unless there is something else here that you need—or want?

"You don't think this could be reflex action on your part, do you?" she said. "You know, like hunger and then food?"

He laughed. "I grant you it may look pathological, but I assure you it isn't. I would have no trouble leaving here alone. I've done it in the past." He paused. "I warned you I was honest."

"What? Same table?" she said, professing indignation.

He gave an apologetic shrug. "Last time I got number 110."

She glanced in their direction. They were eating and talking, merry busy chat, so much to say; easy, domestic, rather than vibrant. A couple, whatever that meant.

"And what if it's no good?" she said, turning back to him.

"The sex, you mean? Then we'd have had a decent meal and seen the view. But it won't be no good. With the right person I'm better at it than eating. Trust me. Trust yourself."

She sat back in her chair and stretched her legs out under the table. Her foot met his. For a moment he did nothing, then he slid his hand down and took hold of her bare ankle, slipping his forefinger under her foot and flipping off the shoe. He ran a slow, slick finger over her sole. Flesh on flesh. He knew what he was doing. She couldn't claim it wasn't nice. If maybe a little corny. "I've got a better idea," she said. "Why don't we just miss the meal?"

He stared at her, and for the first time she saw him confused, watched the contest playing out behind his eyes. Even his touch grew halfhearted. Once upon a time she had been good at combining mischief and passion; something about the confidence of not being hurt. I want it back, she thought. I'm ready for it. She laughed so loudly that the neighboring table stopped to check them out.

As she spoke, somewhere, somehow, something had been decided. "Well, at least you didn't lie about *that*," she said, pulling back her foot gently, then taking pity on him. "I wouldn't want us to peak too early here."

He too laughed out loud at that one. He lifted his hand from under the table and held it out across the napkin and the knives and forks, as if greeting a business associate.

"So, Anna—what's your second name?"

"Revell," she said, with barely a missed beat. "Anna Revell."

"So, Anna Revell," he said. "I'm Samuel Taylor. I'm very pleased to meet you."

The room had grown dark around the memory. On the bed the phone exploded under her fingers. Home, she thought, grabbing for it. They've managed to trace the call.

The restaurant was noisy, Italians doing what they do best. "Hey, I'm about to go hypoglycemic here. Should I call an ambulance or the waiter?"

You could always call your wife, she thought, surprised by the exposed edge of irritation in herself. "Start eating," she said instead. "I'm almost out of here."

She pulled herself up from the bed and went looking for something to wear. She dug down into the new bag and pulled out a clean top, realizing too late that it was the one she had wrapped Lily's present in. The wooden horse tumbled onto the floor, its prancing front leg hitting the tiles at an angle. She heard the crack. Damn. She picked it up gently to survey the damage. The wood around the knee joint had split open on a seam. The horse still stood, but would need veterinary superglue to make it whole again. Her carelessness made her angry, as if it were a symptom of maternal neglect. She rewrapped the animal with exaggerated care and returned it to the bottom of the case.

In the bathroom as she turned on the light a cockroach skittered across the floor and disappeared under the wash unit. Dirt in the cleanest of places.

"What's your problem?" she said out loud. "Don't you like it with the lights on?

"And how about you?" she murmured under her breath, staring at her reflection in the mirror. "What do you see?"

The face that looked back at her was pale, the skin almost spongy with faint purple bruising under the eyes from sleeplessness: a woman under the influence of sexual intimacy. She thought again of home: Paul, Stella, and Mike dining in a summer's garden without her while Lily scampered downstairs to answer the phone. Was that the real risk in all of this? That opening up to a lover would mean somehow closing down on them? She had a job, a daughter, and a home. A life. She didn't need another one. Or if she did, what did that say about the one she'd already got? She looked at herself again. Was the difference she saw behind or only in front of her eyes? It's just sex. If I chose, I could walk out of here and never see him again, she thought. True or false?

Stupid question. Why should she have to? Was it really so impossible to have both him and them? After all, men did it all the time. The trick was to learn to keep them separate, learn how to compartmentalize.

She had dug into her makeup bag and started dressing her face when the phone rang again.

Home—Sunday A.M.

I WOKE TO THE SOUND OF NO SOUND IN THE MIDDLE OF THE NIGHT. No sound, but something wrong. My first thought was that someone was in the house, my second that it was Anna. I got up and pulled on her dressing gown quickly as I moved to the door.

In the gloom of the landing I could just make out her silhouette sitting on the top stair like a goblin, body bent over itself, arms wrapped tight around her knees. If it hadn't been such a warm night I would have thought it was a gesture against the cold. But I knew that really she was hugging herself.

Scared that I might make her jump, I called her name very softly. I could feel her attention, though she didn't reply, just shifted her head a little until it lay on her arms. I took it as an invitation and sat myself down next to her.

"Hi," I said quietly.

"Hi."

"Couldn't you sleep?"

A small shake of the head.

"Too much fun during the day, eh?"

"You're wearing Mummy's dressing gown," she said, her head still at an angle but her face obscured by a tangle of fallen hair.

"Yes, I forgot to pack my own. I don't think she'd mind, do you? Do you want to share it? There's loads of room."

Another little shake. We sat for a while. I wanted to put my arm around her, to make her safe inside my warmth, but I didn't know if it was the right thing to do. If I were Anna, I would know automatically. That's what being a mother is all about.

"You didn't hear the phone again, did you?"

She shook her head once again, this time abruptly. I felt a little wave of hostility coming out of her, but whether it was directed against the world in general or just toward me I couldn't tell. How will we ever cope if Anna doesn't come back? I thought. How will we ever make it through the night?

"Would you like a drink?"

She shrugged. I waited.

"Do you think you might sleep better in Mum's bed?"

Still nothing.

Once, the summer before last when they'd been staying with me, and Anna had gone to a midsummer night's concert in the park, leaving me to baby-sit, Lily had woken with a nightmare, something she had never done with me before, and when I'd tried to comfort her she had grown dreadfully agitated, overflowing with what felt like boundless rage. I had found myself almost frightened of her. She had cried for what seemed like hours (though I know it was only thirty-five minutes because I kept checking my watch). Then, all at once, she had stopped and come and curled herself on my lap and fallen asleep. I was so nervous about moving her that she was still there when Anna got home.

Anna had been sanguine about it. She'd said it happened maybe once or twice a year, and that it was only so upsetting because of Lily's usually sunny disposition. Looking into the pit, she called it. The drop went so far down you felt giddy and all you could do was stand by and be there for her until eventually, when she was ready, she would come back, knowing you were waiting. We had talked about it for hours afterward: how almost everyone has a darkness somewhere in them, one that is born rather than made, and why should we somehow expect less depth of personality just because there have been fewer years? It had made me think again what a good mother Anna had turned out to be because she wasn't afraid of that. What a good mother, and what a good friend.

Apparently after my own mother died it became a habit of mine to go into her bedroom in the middle of the night—a kind of sleep-walking grief, I suppose. My father would wake to find me sitting on her side of the bed: no tears, no nothing, just sitting there wide-eyed and blinking, not saying anything or responding to any of his questions. Like Anna he had some aptitude for other people's pain. If it was a cold night he'd put a blanket around me; otherwise he'd just sit with his arm around me and wait till I was ready. He would ask if I wanted to go back to bed and eventually I would say yes. In the morning I couldn't remember anything about it. Just like I can't remember anything now.

It could be that I was trying to work it out for myself, the problem of where she had gone: same house, same room, same bed, one morning she had been there and the next night she hadn't. Maybe I needed to test the absence for myself. In retrospect I can't see that I was so damaged by it all. The wisdom of the time, of course, decreed that talking about it should help. I know my father took me to see somebody. I used to think I could remember the face of the woman I talked to—or rather who talked to me—and the pattern of the wallpaper in her room, but now I think I was just embellishing details given to me later. I have no idea if the therapy did any good. As it happened I did my own healing later in ways he wouldn't really have understood. But at least he tried.

Ever since he'd told me about it—what, it must be ten years ago now—I've had this image of children as potted plants: pushy little seedlings that need basic but regular monitoring. Forget to stake them up at the right time, give them too little or too much Baby Bio, and you can affect their emotional growth for years. The tyranny of Freud. I think it's one of the reasons I never wanted children of my own. Anna, luckily, has always been more phlegmatic. Her line is that potted plants survive the most appalling abuse and that children are more resilient than any of the advice books would have us believe. She would know. Maybe my mother would have known that too. If she'd stayed around longer, perhaps I would have learned it from her.

If only I could remember what her loss had actually felt like, rather than just the flat dull memories of the day-to-day living without her. Presumably it was a way of blanking out the pain. No doubt that's what I was scared of now. That somehow the loss of Anna would tap into something even bigger in me, something that had hitherto been submerged. Was that why I chose to believe that it had been her on the phone? Because it was just too awful to contemplate anything else?

"You know, when I was little I used to go and sit on my mum and dad's bed in the middle of the night sometimes," I said, looking down onto the hall beneath with the phone silent on the hall table.

She liked that one. I sort of knew she would. "Why?"

I shrugged. "I don't know. To make sure they were still there, I suppose."

"Your mum's dead, isn't she?"

"Yes. But she wasn't then," I said, working some swift revisionist magic to protect us both.

She didn't say anything for a while. Maybe I'd scared her. "Was she nice?"

"My mum? Oh yes, I think she was."

"Do you miss her?"

No point in lying too much. Lily would spot it, anyway. "Well, to be honest I don't remember her very well anymore."

"Why not?"

"Because it was a long time ago that she died."

"How old were you?"

"Oh, old—I mean much older than you—nearly ten."

"Ten. And you don't remember her? You must have a bad memory, Estella."

I laughed. "I suppose I have."

She had shifted herself a little in my direction, so that now I could feel the warmth of her right leg against my own. I slipped an arm around her. She leaned into me. I felt myself go soft inside. We sat staring down into the swirling darkness of the stairwell. I thought about death, and I wanted to guide us both away from it.

"Don't you find it spooky sitting here on your own in the dark?"

She shook her head. "Mummy says that the dark is only frightening because we're not cats. She says the world is full of animals that love the dark. And they have to have some time for themselves when they can catch food and play."

Sensible idea. "Well, she's absolutely right, don't you think?"

"Mmm. We saw a hedgehog once, you know. On the road. When we were coming back from the cinema. It went under the car. We gave it some cat food."

"Did it like it?"

She shrugged. "I dunno. It wouldn't come out. We pushed the bowl underneath the car. It was empty in the morning."

"But it might have been the cat?"

"Yeah."

The darkness had softened around us, images of Beatrix Potter overlaying those of Stephen King. I glanced at her. There would be no better time than this. "It must have been nice, talking to Mum this evening."

She said nothing, but gave the smallest of nods.

"You haven't been worried about her, have you?"

She was silent for a while. "No. But everybody else has."

I laughed. "Oh, we haven't been that bad, have we?"

She gave a little shrug.

"You know, I think Paul just wanted to talk to her. Which is why he was upset with you."

"She said to give him her love. She hadn't forgotten him."

"No. What did she say about me?"

"She said—that's nice."

"What?"

"I told her that you were here, and she said, 'That's nice.'"

"Is that all?" I said, and I must have let my indignation show because she squeezed my arm. "She said it in a big voice. Like she meant it."

I smiled and squeezed her back. Paul was wrong. Lily had talked to her mother. This was no elaborate child make-believe. We sat for a moment, held in the heart of the night. I imagined a campfire and a legion of little furry animals poking their noses out of the gloom. Maybe we tell children bedtime stories to keep at bay adult fear of the dark.

"She sounded funny," she said at last.

"Funny? How, funny?"

"I dunno." She gave a little shrug. "When she said good-bye to me, she sounded sort of . . . sad, like she didn't want to go. It made me cry. I tried to say something, but she wasn't there anymore. And then Paul shouted in my ear and you all came running out and I got scared."

I felt a terrible sick lunge in my gut, as if a black hole had opened up and I was being sucked inside myself. Why is it that when the heart hurts most it always tears at the stomach?

"Oh, Lily." I gave her a hard hug. "Darling. She was probably just upset about missing the plane."

In the gloom I saw her squeeze her eyes together tight to stop herself from crying. It was a gesture she had perfected when she was first beginning to walk and would fall over a lot. "I don't think Paul should have shouted at me like that."

"Oh, he didn't mean to. You know Paul." I paused. "Did she hear him shout? Were you still talking to her when he came on the line?"

"I don't know. I don't think so."

"But she knew you were all right? Yes? I mean she asked you how you were?"

"Yes."

"And what did you tell her?"

"I said I was fine."

Fine. It was Lily's word for everything: the day, her life, school, everything. *Fine.* In our time she and I have had complete telephone conversations with her finely monosyllabic. I was so impressed by the technique that I once tried it on a business colleague. It worked quite well. Fine, in fact. But not now.

"I told her you'd won me a duck," she added because she obviously thought it would make me feel better.

"*I* didn't win it. You did that."

"Yes, but you helped me hold the net."

"Did you tell her about the panda?"

She nodded.

"Well, I expect that's why she was sad. She heard about all that and she wanted to be here having a good time with us."

"Yes." She thought about it. "I think that's what she wanted. So why doesn't she come home?"

"Oh, she will, darling, she will."

We sat for a while. She extracted herself from my grasp. I couldn't tell what she was feeling, and I felt suddenly nervous about making a mistake.

"After your mum died—I mean, when you were little," she said at last, not looking at me directly, but keeping her eyes fixed on the stairs in front, "did you miss her then?"

Did I? I stood in my parents' room again, staring at my mother's side of the bed, the cover so smooth and shiny like still water, and for a second I felt the pit open inside me. "Yes," I said. "I missed her a lot. But, Lily, your mum's not going to die. She's just going to be late home."

We sat for a while. Everything else I could think to say sounded fake and unworthy. I could feel her fingers fluttering in mine. Help her, Stella. Think of a way.

"Do you want to sleep with me for the rest of the night?" I said, giving her a little squeeze. "Do you think that might help?"

I didn't really expect her to say yes, but she did. I put my arms around her and carried her upstairs.

Away—Sunday A.M.

IN THE MIDDLE OF THE NIGHT HE UNLOCKED THE DOOR TO HER room.

She was lying in the bed, her hand curled around the body of the wooden horse. She was not asleep.

After he had left her she had sat replaying the encounter between them like some eager lover trying to decode deeper messages out of a first date. It didn't work. The more time she spent in his company, the more the ground moved under her feet. The less he said the more she suspected, and the more he confided the less she believed. The woman was real enough. The photos confirmed that. He had had some kind of relationship with her, that much was clear, but surely not the one he was claiming. The old-fashioned courtship, the happy marriage, the sad demise—not even fiction came so sugarcoated these days. So why go to such lengths to convince her that it did? That was the strangest part. All of this—the kidnap, the captivity, the hospitality—all of it spoke of obsession, but with whom? Her or a dead woman? Was she meant as a replacement or merely as a witness? It was almost as if he needed her to believe it before he could believe in it himself. In some way he didn't even seem that interested in her; he looked through her rather than at her. Did that mean he might keep his word and let her go? Would she keep hers and stay compliantly until he did? The answer to both of those questions seemed obvious.

Either way there would be little sleep tonight. The food had done its work, replacing the lost, spacey feeling of the day with a restless energy. She moved through the room again, searching for anything she might have missed. When she had exhausted the bedroom and bathroom, she had turned out the light and lay under the covers staring up at the ceiling, moving around the rest of the house in her head, testing doors and windows, picking her way through locks and out into freedom, while in her imagination he slept the sleep of the disturbed, curled around bottles of developing fluid in a blacked-out basement.

In her mind she kept coming back to that darkroom. If he spent so much time in it, would he have gone back there now? The depth of his infatuation and the smell of his clothing suggested it might be a habitual haunt. Yet at some point even he would have to sleep—if not there, then somewhere close enough to be able to hear if she became troublesome in the night. The fact that he hadn't responded that first night when she tried to break down the door didn't mean that he couldn't hear, simply that he had chosen not to listen. For some reason it seemed important for her to know where he was, to be able to place him in her mind as he could place her.

So when the key entered the lock in the blackest deepest part of the night her panic was made all the greater from the fact that yet again she hadn't heard him coming. Did this man really know how to walk on eggshells, or could it be that he had been there all the time, waiting outside the door, his mind keeping pace with hers as it prowled its way toward freedom? The lock clicked free. Her body lit up with fear, a pulse exploding inside her head and her stomach going into spasm. Under the covers her fingers clasped themselves around the neck of the horse. She had tried it both ways; grasping the body with the legs as sharp jabbing spikes, or using the head as handle and the body as the cosh. This hold she had decided could do more damage. Somehow she managed to stop herself shaking.

There was silence. Then another small scrape, as if the key was now being withdrawn. She lay rigid, waiting for the door handle to turn. What came next? If this was going to be about sex, he was going to have his work cut out for him. He could have made it easier on himself. A man who could spike coffee must have a dozen tasteful things he could do with red wine or anchovies. Yet she was wide awake now. So was he ready to fight? Was that what he wanted? With all his talk of love among the English verbs, he seemed almost too sentimental for rape. But then what did she know? This was her first weekend away with a psychopath.

She lay and waited.

Nothing happened.

The door remained closed.

Her fingers shivered over the wood. This time she could hear the muffled thud as his feet hit the floor. He was moving away from the door, along the corridor and down the stairs. What the hell was happening here? First he bolts her in, then waits until the middle of the night, unlocks the door, and—what?—just walks away again?

Had he lost his nerve at the last moment? Pulled upstairs by the elevation of his cock only to find that the fantasy couldn't sustain itself through the time it took to unlock the door? She knew that couldn't be it. It had to be something else. She toyed with the idea of repentance: their romantic evening opening up a well of empathy in him which in turn freed her and sent him running to the local priest for confession and absolution. It didn't wash. For all his talk of love and sorrow, this didn't feel like a pathology that encompassed repentance.

There was only one other answer. It had to be a trick of some kind. Did he want her to wake up and find the door open, so she would come and look for him? Maybe it was a test to prove her compliance, to see if she would betray their agreement and try to escape. So then he could use her broken word to break his own.

In which case she wouldn't oblige him. Black silence descended again. She lay completely still, her eyes closed, her breathing even. Outside, through the wedged-open window, there was a rush of wind in the pine forest; a shimmering rippling noise, like a wave on a beach, every particle of the sound alive with movement. In the emotional maelstrom of the last two days she had found herself growing almost fond of the sound. Then she heard something else: the distinctive growl of a car engine igniting and catching once, twice in the night, revving a few times before its wheels pulled harshly across gravel then out onto firmer earth and away, the noise eventually dissolving into the night.

Her heart started thumping uncontrollably. There was absolutely no mistaking the story of sound that had unfolded in her ears: first someone had unlocked her door, then someone had driven off into the night. It had to be him. If she had been asleep, probably neither of the sounds would have been loud enough to wake her. But she had not been asleep. She was awake and now the door was open and the car was gone.

She thought back to the confessional booth and a man in tears for a love that had driven him mad. Whatever the answer, she couldn't simply lie there and wait for him to come back. It spoke too much of being the victim.

She got out of bed and slipped on her shoes. She had slept in her clothes, and the silk dress was scrunched and clinging to her body, its creases scoring uneven latticework on her skin. No time to change now. If she got out of the house she would still have no passport, no ticket, and no money. It didn't matter. She could walk or hitch her way to freedom. All the rest could come after. She grabbed a jacket from the wardrobe and with the wooden horse still clamped tight in her hand she quietly opened the door.

Nothing happened. No alarm screamed, no lights flashed, no arm shot out of the darkness to stop her. She moved to the top of the staircase. The large hall window let in slivers of light from a young crescent moon above. It broke up the dense dark, but with it came shadow and what felt like movement.

She steadied herself. She could deal with this. Living alone with a child makes one an expert in night paranoia; while burglar alarms can persuade insurance companies, the imagination demands subtler protection. If Lily were here now, she would be too busy containing her daughter's fears to indulge her own. She formed her empty palm into a fist, imagining the fluttering of a smaller hand in hers. Besides, she said to herself as she walked downstairs, what was there to be frightened of? She already knew that there was no one there.

At the bottom she made straight for the front door. She slipped off the upper and lower bolts and turned the main handle. It stayed locked. She hadn't really thought it would be open, had she? That would have been too easy. Nevertheless, she turned swiftly back on herself, half expecting to find him standing behind her mocking her naïveté. After forty-eight hours of captivity she was already behaving like a prisoner, nervous of freedom, guilty about moving without chains. She walked swiftly along the corridor, trying each of the doors in turn. She was tired of finding them all locked. As she turned the handle of one of them she threw herself against the wood, using her shoulder as a battering ram. The only thing that gave was her flesh. She accepted defeat and moved toward the living room.

Inside, the air was ink-black. There must be shutters on the windows to create such an intense dark. Should she risk the light? What if he was standing outside watching, waiting for some kind of sign to come back in? With her free hand she felt her way carefully across the room to the table near the fireplace where the telephone had been. Of course it was no longer there. He wasn't that careless. She moved quickly in the direction of the open window she had remembered from dinner, but as she turned her hip caught the edge of the table and sent it crashing to the floor. The noise was deafening and she heard herself yell out, losing her grip on the horse and feeling it spin away into the darkness. It was okay. It was okay. If the house was empty then no one could be listening.

Still, it increased her sense of urgency. She left the horse where it had fallen and went for the window. When she found it, not only was it locked but there was no handle anywhere, no way to get a purchase on its wooden surrounds. She thought about picking up a piece of furniture and smashing it against the glass, but it wouldn't make any impact on the shutters outside. The place was impregnable. There was no way out.

She felt shaky, as if the air had grown suddenly cold. Fear rose in goose pimples on her skin. None of this made sense. She was wandering around a darkened empty house in which everything was locked and bolted. Why had he bothered to let her out if there was nowhere to go? Or maybe that was precisely why he had let her out. Because he wanted her to understand how total her imprisonment was. How without his consent she could never get out, even if he wasn't there to stop her. If she went back up to her room now, would he know? Would there be broken threads across doorways or footprints in flour, so he would have proof that she had roamed and tried to escape?

She realized that even with him gone she was still afraid. How was it that she had become so scared of everything? That must have been why he had singled her out. People like him made a decision in these things. There must have been dozens of English-speaking tourists with dark hair and fair skin in Florence. Yet he had picked her, had detected her vulnerability across a crowded shop, as strongly as if it had been crude animal scent.

She hadn't always been like this. There had been a time when she used to be able to walk on water, or at least not be frightened of drowning. But somehow since Lily's birth the world had become an infinitely more threatening place. She had spent so much energy protecting her daughter from life's fault lines that she had stopped appreciating the beauty of their drop, and so, gradually, had lost her own head for heights. Emotional as well as physical vertigo. Well, she would never walk another cliff edge like the one she was walking now, and if she wasn't going to fall she had better find her balance soon. She could start by believing she already had.

If he expected her to escape she would do just the opposite and stop trying. If he wanted her to become frantic she would stay calm. If he was out to play games in the dark, she would put on the lights. She made her way back to the door and located the switch. The room burst into life, tidy, clean, the dinner things cleared away from the fireplace and the dining table, now pushed against the far wall, already laid for breakfast with a thermos of coffee and a basket of bread rolls under a cloth that was still damp. She picked up the bread and squashed it between her fingers. It was stale. So he was running out of fresh supplies. Was that where he had gone, shopping in some distant twenty-four-hour supermarket? It hardly seemed likely. It rammed home the fact that she still didn't have a clue where he might be.

She started setting the room to rights, recovering the horse from where it had fallen. One of its legs had splintered at the knee joint on impact. Lily would have to bind it up. She was very good at Animal Hospital. Anna pushed the thought aside and moved on to the table. Nearby, on the floor, lay an arc of books that had obviously fallen with it. No wonder the crash had been so loud. She gathered them up. They were English paperbacks, their spines creased with use, their covers giving away their content. Well-groomed women with good-looking open faces set against exotic backdrops, romantic figures: stories to suit the upstairs wardrobe. She checked the inside covers. The last imprint on each of them was dated late nineties. So had this been Paola's library—now, presumably, meant to be hers? What did he think? That she would spend her days lounging about on the grass reading romance while he lovingly prepared the next meal? Married bliss with a captive.

As she moved away she caught a glimpse of herself in a mirror hanging to the right of the fireplace. She hadn't seen herself properly for three days and the sight shocked her. She looked extraordinary, her face pale and drawn, bits of hair standing up all over the place from the bed, the red dress a creased chaos of silk.

Without thinking, she brought up a hand to smooth her hair, tightening her face muscles out of their frown into an automatic half-smile. Woman's stuff: the involuntary communication between self and mirror-self. Even in a crisis it worked. She looked better. And felt better, too, more in control.

Immediately to the right was a portrait of Paola staring directly into the camera, also smiling. They must have been lovers by now for her to allow such an intimate exchange with the lens, both inviting and ignoring at the same time. Maybe she had liked it. She was clearly a woman who had an understanding of her own power. The mystery was why she should want to give it to him.

Anna glanced back from the photo to the mirror again. Was it just obsession warping his vision, or were they really alike in some ways, the two of them? No. Not when you thought about it. To start with, the woman in the photograph was prettier than she was, a broader forehead and a wider mouth, which made the smile more entrancing.

Anna returned to her own image, fine-tuning the smile, trying to get it to mimic the photo, to see if she could understand what it was he might have seen in them both. Lily had once caught Anna at this mirror game, demanding to know why it was she always changed her face when she looked at her own reflection. At the time she had been mortified, as if she had been caught in some trick of gender, guilty of inadvertently passing on the sin of female vanity to the next genera-tion. Since then she had spotted Lily at it herself; that shy, sly collu-sion with the glass, practice for the years to come. Ah well, she had thought. Maybe it is bigger than both of us. All of us . . .

She looked back at the photo. And suddenly she understood it. Of course. Why hadn't she seen it before? The familiarity was not about their looks but their pose. The woman in the photograph was coming from the same place she was: the way she held her head on a slight tilt, the ghost of a smile, half coquettish, half confident. A woman playing with her own image. A woman oblivious of the cam-era lens. A woman looking into a mirror. Alone.

She dropped her eyes, so they wouldn't give away what her brain was thinking. She feigned interest in the room again, glancing casually around the walls, reading the gallery of photos differently now. In the first section a young woman was caught going about her everyday business in public places, laughing and chatting with companions who were no longer there. As they were excluded, so she was enlarged; the devious art of the telephoto lens.

In the second gallery she was on her own: the public face now en-gaged in private business, charming itself, checking its own attractive-ness in a mirror. Subject and object at the same time. And meanwhile, the journey from the one to the other had taken place without any bride in between. No wedding shots or formal portraits, not a single photograph that showed the two of them together, no proof at all that in fact they had ever been intimate in each other's company.

Paola. His dead wife? Or just some interesting-looking woman plucked from the crowded streets of Florence into a house, a room, and a mirror?

Like her.

Now.

Away—Saturday P.M.

BACK IN THE BEDROOM THE SOUND OF THE TELEPHONE WASN'T coming from by the bed. Its tone was different too, more singsong, more like the warble of a mobile, only muffled. As it rang for the third time she traced it to the wardrobe.

There was nothing hanging in there but his linen jacket: too hot to wear, too smart to be left crumpled in a suitcase. In the inside pocket she found the handset. She pulled it out and it lay in her palm, so tiny and precise that you could almost imagine it as a medical accessory in some state-of-the-art heart surgery. The ringing had stopped now. The caller, unable to connect, was no doubt leaving a message.

She frowned. He hadn't said anything to her about having a mobile. If he had, she would certainly have asked to use it to call home while they were traveling, rather than having to wait until they reached the hotel. Maybe its reach didn't extend that far, though given the international map of his working life that seemed unlikely. Or maybe his wife checked the numbers on the bills. "She knew about the others. She doesn't know about you. . . ."

She studied the dialing bar. Sure enough, a small icon had already lit up, alerting him to the missed call. Nine-thirty on a Saturday night. You don't want to know who this is, Anna, she thought. It's nobody's business but his. But the intensity of their mutual confession had done its work, acting as a slow burn into her conscience, making the need to know as powerful as any niceties of privacy. She accessed the answering service from the menu and an electronic voice in her ear instructed her as to what to press to hear the missed call. Her fingers darted over the numbers. Maybe she just needed to feel guilty about a second family.

Sure enough it was a woman. *"My wife is French."* But this accent was American:

"Hi. Just to let you know, I spoke to our client this afternoon and while he's real excited, he's also impatient. Me, too, eh? Can't wait. I just want to check everything's okay on your end and that you made all the connections and can still get her back here as planned. I told him by the end of next week. I'm assuming we'll be home and dry by then, yeah? I can't tell who I want to see most, you or her.

"Oh, and speaking of people missing you, a Sophie Wagner phoned the office while you were gone. St. Petersburg, I seem to remember, right? Luckily she didn't have the right name and I took the call. You don't know how she got this number, do you? I wouldn't like to think you were getting careless.

"Anyway, let me know when you're getting back in. And don't wear yourself out too much on the job, all right? Remember, lover, you've got commitments elsewhere." And the voice splintered into laughter.

The message ended and the automated voice asked if she'd like to delete it, save it, or hear it again. She switched the phone off, then on again, checking to see that the message remained. He would never know she had heard it. She stood staring down at the receiver in her hand.

It's work, she thought. The woman is his partner, someone who knows him well enough to be rude, ruder even than his wife. But when she tried to swallow she found she didn't have enough saliva to complete the action. Whom was she kidding? "Me, too, eh? Can't wait. . . . speaking of people missing you . . . Remember, lover, you've got commitments elsewhere. . . ." Even without the words, the voice was a giveaway. The way it wiped its feet on the name "Sophie," the teasing insolence that comes with the confidence of sex. If this woman worked with him, she also slept with him. And it didn't sound like a one-sided arrangement.

She glanced across the room and saw herself lying on the bed, her limbs tangled together with his, his fingers in her crotch, his face studying hers as he watched her orgasm build. You come differently with somebody you trust. The air in the room was thick with his protestations of honesty and intoxication, with images of French wives no longer fucked and the confession of a sweetly painful mutual sense of risk. "You know as well as I do what's happening here, Anna. The longer we play around the more dangerous it gets." She felt suddenly sick, as if a dredger were at work at the bottom of her stomach, scraping deep into a flesh floor of memory and humiliation. Except why would he do such a thing? Why bother himself with exhausting lies when all the time he had some other woman—not even his wife—billing and cooing into his inside jacket pocket?

She reran the call in her head. And where did she, Anna, fit into all of this? Was she the "her" they were referring to, the "her" who should be back next week? Surely not. In which case she had to be the job that he shouldn't wear himself out on. And what about Sophie Wagner and St. Petersburg? Did that mean another hotel room somewhere, with the imprint of tangled bodies on the bed?

She remembered him standing with her in the corridor that first night in the London hotel, waiting for the lift to come, repeating her phone number back to himself. "I'll call you tomorrow," he had said as he kissed her good-bye, not offering his own number in reply. And he *had* called, the very next morning, warm and eager for more. "What if I need to get in touch with you in an emergency?" she had asked him later. "I've got an answering service," he had said. "I'll let you have the number." But somehow they had never got around to it. He had always called her, though he had never left a message, only ever spoken to her direct. Was there a reason for all that? "Luckily she didn't get the right name," the woman's voice had said. His name, presumably. Maybe if you don't know someone's number, you don't know who they really are.

The dredger was at work again, slicing into nerve ends concealed in the mud. She tried to steady herself. So this lover of hers had other lovers, other agendas. So what? In a way, so did she. She was the one who had gone through the want ads in search of a story. This wasn't like her and Chris. She had some agency here, some power. But first she needed to know what she was dealing with. She needed to talk to Sophie Wagner, whoever she was.

She looked at the phone in her hand. A traveling man would take his own directory of numbers with him. She looked at her watch. Almost 9:40. He was already impatient with her absence. She didn't have a lot of time.

She locked the door from inside. Sitting on the loo, she started work on the phone. The menu offered her up a directory of most-used numbers. She started punching buttons to check each of them. As they came up she realized she had nothing to write them down with. Lifting the hygiene wrapper off the tooth mug, she used it as her paper, grabbing a lipstick pencil from her makeup case as a pen. The first few numbers had no names attached. Presumably these were the ones he used all the time, and he didn't need to be told who they were. She wrote them down anyway. Two of them had a European prefix (not France) and one was in Italy.

Then came two with names attached. One sounded Russian but she couldn't be sure because she didn't know any East European prefixes, the other was American. Both men. She was writing so fast the tip of the pencil snapped off on the paper. She was moving to the door to get a better implement when she heard a knock on the outside door.

"Anna?"

On the little phone screen the name "Sophie" had flipped up followed by an initial "W."

"Anna?"

Then a number that she recognized as American. Area code 212. Manhattan. She frantically scrawled it down, what was left of the pencil crumbling completely under the pressure, so the last two digits were barely legible. 87. 87.

The knocking got louder. She heard him rattling the door. "Anna. Anna, are you in here?"

"Yep. Hold on a minute, I'm on the loo." She stuffed the piece of paper deep into her wash bag on the basin, zipping it closed. Then she flushed the toilet. "Just coming," she shouted over the noise of the cistern. She slipped the phone back in his jacket pocket on her way to the door.

"Sorry," she said as he stepped inside.

"What's with the lock? You all right?"

"Yes, fine. I was wandering around naked and they came in to turn down the bed."

"What have you been doing? I've been waiting for over an hour."

"Oh ... I ... I kept trying to get through to London, but it was engaged."

"But I thought you said you'd spoken to her?"

"I wanted to add something. Anyway, it's done now. You must be starving."

"I gave up, it was getting so late. We'll have to find somewhere else."

"I'm sorry. We can go straightaway. I'm ready now."

"Really." He gave a slight frown, taking hold of her hands and turning them over until her palms were facing upward. "What have you been doing to yourself?" he said, shaking his head in mock astonishment. "You look like a bride at a Hindu wedding."

She stared down and saw a crisscross of rust-colored streaks like henna stains running through her fingers and onto the palms. "Oh, it's lipstick pencil. It broke."

"Before it got to your lips, I see," he said. He put out a finger to her mouth, running it along her bottom lip, then prodded it inside. She caught at it with her tongue and pulled it further in. He smiled.

"You're almost enough to put a man off his dinner. Compliment. Eh? Come on. Let's go eat."

On his way out he plucked his jacket off the hanger. Was it her imagination, or did he slip his hand inside to check the phone was still there?

It took a while to find a restaurant that was willing to serve them so late, and once they found one it seemed easier to eat than to talk. And drink. The wine was his second bottle, her first. He went to the loo halfway through. Whether he picked up the call, it was impossible to tell. When he came back she decided to poke a little, just to see where it might go.

"Can I ask you something?" she said casually as she reached for the wine. "What will your wife be doing tonight? Do you know?"

"My wife? I don't have a clue. She's probably out with friends."

"What's she like? Does she look at all like me?"

"No. No, she doesn't look anything like you. Anna?"

"I was wondering what language you spoke when you were together. Is her English as good as your French?"

He frowned and put his fork down on his plate. "What happened here, Anna? Did you get mad with me because you felt homesick?"

I wish you were more stupid, she thought. I could find it easier not to want to fuck you. "Why does it make you nervous, Samuel? It's just curiosity."

"No, it's not curiosity. It's picking at the scab. I don't want to talk about her anymore. I don't want her at the table. I want to be with you. We don't exactly have a long time left."

"One day, two nights. It's enough."

Enough for what? But he didn't pick up the gauntlet.

"Okay. So tell me what you'll be doing in Geneva next week."

He shrugged. "Same as usual."

"Which is . . . ?"

"Going to see a man about some paintings."

"When will you be in London next?"

"Er . . . I'm not sure. Maybe week after next."

"Week after next? And will that be about work or pleasure?"

He held her gaze. "I suppose that depends on whether you forgive me for whatever it is I seem to have done." She shrugged, as if she didn't understand the comment. He put out his hand across the table and covered hers. His touch was very warm. You could see how one could mistake it for feeling. "I shouldn't have left you," he said quietly.

"When?"

"In the room, making the call. You've been traveling without me. And I can't get to where you've gone."

She stared at him.

His attention was like a search beam, throwing light into the darkest of corners. She dropped her eyes. "I'm sorry. I think I'm just tired."

He released her hand and topped up her wine. "Yeah, well that makes two of us. Why don't we just relax, eh? We're both slightly out of tune. Too much sex and too little sleep. It's a recipe for madness."

She smiled. Whatever it was that was going on here, it wouldn't do to have him too suspicious. "You're right." She sat back and sipped at her wine. "Sorry."

He finished his own glass and refilled it immediately. "You know, I keep remembering that old man today," he said after a while, staring into the red of the grape. "I keep seeing his face light up when he was delivering that Dante. It was great."

"Better than the tabernacle painting?"

He didn't answer immediately, as if he was conjuring up the image again, checking it over. He shrugged. "In my line of work, you've seen one Madonna, you've seen them all." He took another long slug of the wine, drinking it more like water than alcohol, as if he were now the one who was too tired to care.

"You don't believe that."

He grinned. "No, you're right, I don't. But you can get oppressed by old paint at times. The flesh is a long time dead."

"Is that why you like the live stuff so much?"

The remark seemed neither to offend nor to surprise him. He

gave a deep smile, even a mildly drunk one. "Yeah, I suppose. Something like that."

And as he said it, she knew that she wanted him to make love to her again, and that whatever the possible deceit and the double-crossing, right at that moment it didn't matter.

Back at the hotel again she undressed while he used the bathroom.

When he emerged, she was sitting on the bed flicking through late-night Italian TV with the remote. He threw himself on the other side next to her with a long groan. "God, I'm bushed," he said, the words broken by a long yawn as he put out a hand and casually ran it down her back.

She turned to look at him: his body was splayed out on top of the covers, his cock curled and cozy, already settled in for the night, evidently uninterested in her presence. From the depths of the wardrobe a snaky American voice insinuated itself into her ear. "And don't wear yourself out too much on the job. Remember, lover, you've got commitments elsewhere." What else could it refer to but her? What other job was there?

He caught her watching him and smiled lazily. She lay back on the bed next to him. Suddenly their very closeness seemed strange. She felt aware of her own nakedness, like Eve after the apple. She wanted to get up and go somewhere else, curl up in her aloneness and fall asleep. But she also wanted him to make the first move, to prove that whatever it was that was happening between them, it was about desire as well as work.

She flicked off the TV. They lay for a moment in silence. She ran a teasing finger down his chest. "Hmm. Nice." He opened an eye. "You're gorgeous," he said absentmindedly, and pulled her toward him, cupping her inside the crook of his arm as if he were cradling a baby, removing her hand from its exploration as he did so. They lay there glued together, unmoving. It was clear he would soon be asleep.

"Do you want to make love?" she said, trying to sound casual, but the words stuck in the air, harsh and exposing.

He laughed lazily, seemingly oblivious to both her anger and her fear. "Oh, Anna. Though thou art as lovely as the dawn, I'm afraid I'm finished for the night. You should have got me before the second bottle of wine. It's all that driving. I have to sleep." And he pulled her closer to him, as if the smother of the embrace would be its own fulfillment. She lay there, her head on his chest, his heart beating a staccato bass track in her soul. He must have registered her tension because he gave her a little squeeze. "Tomorrow we'll have breakfast in bed. Eh?"

His head fell to one side and almost immediately his breathing evened out, his arm around her body turning dead and weighted in sleep.

"Don't wear yourself out, lover. . . ." The words were like barbed wire; whichever way you tried to pull them out, they tore their way further into the skin.

She lay inside the grip for a while, poking at her ego to assess the level of damage. A memory like a smell wafted into her mind: a moment from the end of her affair with Chris.

The worst had already happened, the Dear John bit delivered through a stunted phone call and a brush-off from his secretary. She had been nursing the wound for ten days, by which time it was clear it had gone septic. It was then that she had decided to call him at home. He hadn't been there. Instead she had listened to his voice on an answering machine inviting messages for him and his family. She had sat in shimmering silence failing to do as he asked and speak after the beep. It had been the longest forty seconds of her life. She had felt like a child whose sense of self hadn't been sufficiently nurtured by its parents, from whom something vital had been withheld, something that at this moment would have sustained her, instead of ripping open her stomach and pouring her insides onto the floor.

That phone call had proved the beginning of a violent downward spiral that had ended six weeks later on an achingly cold lakeside beach outside Windermere: her crouched against the wind holding both hands deep into freezing water and watching the skin bruise with the cold till it was the color of the blue-black pebbles beneath them.

In that instant she had realized that she was either going to get over this or she wasn't. That it was as simple and as apocalyptic as that. Her choice. And suddenly what had felt impossible became almost easy. She had removed her hands from the water, sucked her fingers back into life in her mouth, and walked back up to the hotel, where a message from Estella had been waiting at the front desk and from where the world started again, with Anna as a stronger pulse-beat within it.

Then and now. The left side of her body was gradually going numb under his armlock of sleep. But she wasn't going with it. She shifted herself in his grasp, and when he didn't wake she pulled up his hand and slid herself out from under him. He grunted heavily, like a prodded animal, then flopped over to one side and sank further into the deep. By the time she had dressed and rescued the torn piece of paper from the wash bag in the bathroom, it was clear that he was underground, sleeping as still and deep as rock strata. It was time to find out who this lover of hers really was.

Home—Sunday A.M.

I LAY WITH HER UNTIL HER BREATHING GREW EVEN AND I WAS SURE she was asleep. I studied her face in the gloom: the exquisite way her cheeks curved and plumped right up to her eyes, how the lashes lay like black little fans upon them. If you looked carefully you could see her eyelids twitch occasionally, as if she were a cat dreaming of flight-less birds. She was utterly calm, utterly quiet. There didn't seem to be anything wrong even in her dreams.

If my father had let me sleep in his bed after my mother's death, might it somehow have helped us both? He must have thought about it. I suspect he was too shaken by his own sense of devastation and the fear that having me next to him at night would only have rubbed salt into the wound. In my twenties I went through a period of thinking that it meant he didn't love me enough, but I've felt more benign toward him in recent years. At times of stress you do what you can. It is not your fault if that isn't the same as what you should. With Lily there beside me now, I think I understood how he must have felt. Her very calm made me more agitated. Her sleep made me more awake. My body felt as if there were a fire inside it, small flames of panic flaring up and scorching me awake, however many times I tried to throw a blanket over them. The infinite beauty of a sleeping child. As an adult, I found it almost unbearable.

I tucked the sheet around her and went downstairs to check that the phone was still on the hook. The dial tone was noisy in my ear. I rang my own number to see if there were any messages. René had called from Stockholm to say he'd be back on Monday; could we make a date for next week? Would I leave a message on his answering machine? His voice took me by surprise. I hadn't thought about him since last night, as if what was happening here was my real life and he only an occasional sideshow. I realized that I wasn't sure if he and I would survive this crisis, even though it had nothing to do with him. I couldn't even feel disturbed by the thought.

Above me I heard the attic door open and the heavy tread of footsteps on the stairs. "Anna?" Paul's voice, whispered, tense, from the middle landing.

I walked into the pool of light at the bottom of the hall so he could work out his mistake himself. "No. Sorry, Paul. It's me. Stella."

"Stella," he repeated flatly.

"I didn't mean to wake you."

"It's okay. I thought . . . What time is it?"

"Three, three-thirty? I couldn't sleep."

Behind him Lily's door was open. I saw him turn to check on her.

"She's not there. She's in with me. She woke up about an hour ago."

"What happened? Did she have a nightmare?"

"No. I don't think so. She was just awake. She needed a bit of reassurance, that's all."

"You should have called me."

"I don't think it would have helped. We had a chat and I put her into Anna's bed."

"What about? What did she say?"

"Nothing, really," I said, aware that I should be giving him more, but unwilling to recount a conversation that contained so much of my own pain. "We just chatted."

"Did you talk about the phone call?" And it was clear from the edge in his voice that he was worried that it hadn't been him on the stairs in the darkness holding her hand.

"A bit."

"And?"

"She still insists that she talked to her. I must say I believe her."

"Yeah, well . . . I would like to have heard it too." He stood for a second, not willing to leave it, but not willing to push it either.

I thought about telling him not to worry, that we were in this together and there was no way anything would come between us. But to say that would have been to acknowledge the fact that something already had, and once out in the open, it would be neither easily forgotten nor quickly resolved.

"You can talk to her about it in the morning," I said mildly. "She's bound to be up before me. Listen, I'm sorry I woke you. I hope you sleep all right."

"Yeah." He gave a small grunt. "You, too. You've left the answering machine on, right?"

I checked the little light under the hall telephone. "Yep. No problem."

I stood and watched as he climbed back up the stairs. He left their bedroom door open this time.

The encounter had done nothing to help me sleep. Even the house seemed alive with anxiety. I made my way quietly upstairs into her study and over to the filing cabinet by the wall. I pulled out the top drawer and stuck my hand down the back of it, feeling my way until I found what I needed: a small plastic bag strip-sealed along the top. Inside there was a clump of grass and a packet of papers. Enough dope for a couple of emergency spliffs.

Even with Anna gone, her hospitality remained. Though she herself no longer really smoked—not since Lily (she had been afraid that being stoned she wouldn't know how to cope in a crisis), it was a long-standing tradition that she always kept a stash for the nights when I needed to feel at home. I could only hope it would do the trick for me now. I cleared a space on her desk and started on the ritual: separating out the seeds from the leaves and crumbling them carefully like a dynamite trail along the middle of three gummed papers. And as I did so I thought about Paul's suppressed aggression on the stairs and how he and I had coped so well over the years, all things considering. Surely it wouldn't fall apart now. There was too much past to support it.

Anna and I had already been best friends for years when she first met Paul in the mid-eighties. They'd even slept together once, I seem to remember, before discovering that they did much better out of bed than in. A year or so later, when Paul had his road to Damascus about such matters, it was Anna he talked to first and the result was that while he became exclusively, triumphantly gay, they became even firmer friends. It's hard now to imagine that they had ever been lovers, though the occasional echo of intimacy filters through their irritation with each other as well as their affection.

He had really proved his worth during the cataclysmic times of Chris and their aftermath. I think in some ways he may have been more help to her than I, his energetic promiscuity better able to empathize with her sexual meltdown than my ignorant anxiety was. Then, after Lily was born, he was also there. He had the knack of ringing just at the moment when the going got tough, as if he could hear those vibrating angry-bee cries clear across the West London night. He was the first to discover how much Lily liked the car, how she would instantly fall asleep on the second turn around the Hogarth roundabout, even if she had an equal tendency to wake up again on the straight stretch of Chiswick High Road home. And she in turn got used to seeing his broad good-looking face as he strapped her in and out of her car seat late at night.

For a while we provided between us something of a triangle of care. I was the first to fade away. International law firms have little enough truck with the legitimate kind of parental leave, let alone the nonparental type. I kept up a weekend schedule for a while, but in the end we all got tired of the disruption—it is, I discovered, not possible to live in two places at once—and I reverted to a monthly and then three-monthly cycle.

As I rolled the spliff between my fingers I tried to remember how excluded I had felt by that discovery. But the truthful answer is, as far as I can recall, not at all. I had always been the least adept at the baby stuff, more frightened of the right way to pick her up, less able to cope with the tears or the demands. Maybe biological time clocks also bring with them an ability to tell the time. And anyway, as was already becoming clear, we had got better and better as she grew older.

Words proved our breakthrough. We seem to share a verbal gene, Lily and I, and have always found it easy to chatter, even about the most mundane and meaningless of things. While her first word—"Mummy"—was directed at Anna ("Paul" was harder to say than "Daddy" and took much longer to perfect), her first phrase—"Cup of tea, cup of tea, cup of tea"—was kept for me when I walked in for one of my quarterly visits one afternoon and put on the kettle. And from then on the more we talked the more we discovered we liked each other.

As for Paul—well, he, too, has achieved something unique, and because of that over the years I have grown to respect him very much. But I cannot say that were the two of us to find ourselves together on a desert island one of us wouldn't choose to swim. Nothing personal, you understand, just something about not being soulmates. Given the pressure we were under at this moment it was not, therefore, surprising if we were feeling the strain. But we would come through it. Of course we would.

I had a sudden flash of the three of us, Paul, Anna, and me, all sitting in a church pew together years from now watching proudly as Lily stood at the altar, all grown up and gorgeous in some fancy frock with a hunky man at her side. Father and mothers of the bride. Outrageous. Camp.

The image shifted. Paul and I were still together, but this time the service was different. On the altar there was a flower-laden coffin next to a discreet oven door, and the third figure in the pew was Lily, sitting between us, each of her hands held tight in one of ours. Except that when you moved the camera into close-up you could see how we were trying to pull her in different directions.

The image did not bear thinking about.

I took the coward's way out and lit the spliff.

The sound of the grass crackling against the paper created a familiar static in the night silence. The very act of pulling the smoke inside relaxed me, triggering a Pavlovian memory of release, like the pleasure of taking off a pair of shoes that are too tight. From my lungs the smoke song started filtering up into my head. Brain-talk. It wouldn't be long before we were singing in there, too.

I like being stoned. It has always been a mystery to me why some people are so scared of it. When I first discovered it in my teenage years I was still shadowboxing with my mother's absence. Dope achieved more than therapy ever could. To begin with, it made me laugh. It made the world absurd, rather than just plodding and flat, and, wonder of wonders, it made my own mind more interesting as it got looser. And as it got looser, so my mother started to find her own way in. I don't know quite how or when it happened, but I discovered that I was thinking about her. And that rather than being a black hole of memory, she began to take on substance, to have a form and a personality. I found myself studying photographs of her, imagining her face in movement and wondering what her voice would have sounded like, what she might have thought about the Bay City Rollers, or Watergate, the maxi skirt or the end of the Vietnam War. I practiced these topics on her, along with my own responses, and then sometimes, when I felt more confident, I tried them again on my father. Of course I never told him where I had got it all from. That would have been cruel, since his pleasure in my newfound voice had so much to do with his worry about my previous silence.

I daresay it had its dangers. No doubt it could have all gone horribly wrong, grown into obsession and psychosis; a child on drugs resurrecting her dead parent for company. But it never felt like that to me. After a while she sort of faded away (I suppose my own life took over and I found other people to talk to, other ways to spend my time), but afterward I felt as if I had known her a little better, even if she had been constructed of smoke rings. Since then, dope has always been somewhere where I go to be at home, where I can feel looked after, or maybe where I have just learned to look after myself.

Now even the smell of it reminds me of solitude, of time then and time now, years of Friday nights spent in my Amsterdam apartment sitting on the floor by the open windows on a summer's evening after my phone call to Anna, some concert or opera on the airwaves, BBC Radio 3 sneaking its way onto my foreign dial like a subtle cultural imperialism. I turn up the stereo and let it take over the space inside my head as well as the one in the room. I love the fact that I know nothing at all about classical music. I like the way it rolls back away from us in time, like a country whose history I have never learned. It is one of the things that make me feel really good about the idea of growing old: that there will be so much time and space to discover it in.

Perhaps not surprisingly, when I paint this fantasy I am always alone in it, a teenager grown old, with no need of anyone else to share it with. Not lovers. Not even best friends.

But what about Lily? What would happen to my life if Lily had to be included in it? If Anna really didn't come home and we—me or Paul—were left holding the baby?

"She sounded funny. . . . When she said good-bye to me, she sounded sort of . . . sad, like she didn't want to go."

Her words on the stairs came back like a sudden howl round in my head.

Just occasionally dope can let you down, can curdle contentment into paranoia, pleasure into palpitations.

I stubbed out the joint and made my way back to the bedroom, to check she was all right. Somewhere in the middle of an Italian night Lily's mother was in some kind of trouble, and there was nothing, nothing I could do to help her.

Away—Sunday P.M.

AT FIRST SHE JUST WANTED TO SMASH IT. TO PICK UP THE table and hurl it at the mirror, watch it plunge in glorious slow motion through the glass wall into the room behind, watch him and the camera reel to the ground, showered with glass, shards of it everywhere, in the lens, in his eyes.

The need was so great that she had to dig her fingernails hard into her palms to stop herself from doing it. Where would it get you, Anna? she thought fiercely. Nowhere. What would you do next? Climb through the hole to finish him off? Even if you incapacitated him enough to get away there would still be no way out. Don't waste the chance. For once you know more about him than he does about you. Keep it that way. Use it, make it play.

She made herself walk over to the table and pour a cup of coffee from the flask. The very domesticity of the act, the mixing of the milk and the stirring of the sugar, earthed her a little. She went back to the books, selecting one with a glamorous blond woman on the cover, red dress, red hat, her face bathed in a rosy light. The title was *Memory and Desire.* It was heavy, a weighty story inside here. She opened it and read the first few lines.

From the vantage point of the mirror he would have her perfectly in shot now, the light a halo behind her head. It would make a good photo, warm, relaxed, convincing. She let him have his fill of it. Then, after a while, she put down the book and yawned. It wasn't fake. Her body was greedy for the oxygen it gulped in. She got up and moved casually past the mirror, then stopped, as if her own reflection had caught her attention again.

She turned into it, as if she was surprised to find herself there, as if there was something worth seeing. She indulged her vanity more fully now, lifting up her hair in one hand and holding it on her head, studying the change it made in her face. She sucked in her cheeks, then checked what might be a blemish on her chin, careful not to get too close in case she should find herself able to spot the joins. She sighed. What was it Stella had said to her? That she had had an impressive ability to spin a good lie. The truth, but nothing like the truth, so help her God.

She kept on looking.

Then she tried a shy smile at herself. "That's better," she murmured aloud to her own reflection. "See. You don't have to be so scared all the time. It's not as bad as you think. He's not a monster. He unlocked the door and let you out, didn't he? That has to mean something."

She paused. The woman staring back at her remained unconvinced.

She frowned. "What if he's telling the truth? If all he wants is your company. It's only two days. You talk, get to know each other, see him through a bad time, and then you go home. He lets you go. He keeps his word and you keep yours. No one has to know. It's your secret. Between the two of you. You can do that, can't you? For Lily's sake you can do that."

She gave herself—and him—a bright smile as if in answer to her question. And then, at last, she heard it: the small but unmistakable noise—half click, half scrape—that placed him at that moment on the other side of the wall. It ran a scalpel into her gut, cold and clean. Go on, keep on snapping, take as many as you want, she thought. Because I'm going to get out of here. And when I do I'm going to be taking your films with me.

She dropped her eyes and moved back toward the chair. And as she did she thought she heard another move, more muffled this time. Another roll of film, or had he had enough? Somewhere close by, the darkroom would be waiting. Was it the same room or somewhere else? Wherever it was, he wouldn't want to risk her hearing him go there. Not now. Better to wait until she had left before he made his move.

She glanced around the room. The horse was still on the table, wobbly but still standing. They needed to be reunited before she could leave. She gave another yawn, bigger this time, equally genuine once it took hold, then, placing herself between the mirror and the table, she gathered up the wooden animal along with the book. From there she walked slowly and noisily out of the room, snapping the light off behind her.

She kept up the obvious soundtrack as she mounted the stairs to her room and opened and closed her door loudly. Then, slipping off her shoes, she retraced her footsteps silently, downstairs, along the corridor, and back into the living room, to a vantage point just inside where she couldn't be seen, but from where she could hear everything.

Sure enough, now he thought she was gone he was noisier. She could hear him quite distinctly now, footsteps on stone, then the sound of an object dragging or being pushed. Except somehow she had got the geography wrong. Because the sounds weren't coming from the other room, they were happening right underneath her, below the very floorboards on which she was standing.

She processed the information fast. Somewhere down below . . . To have got himself back into the house again from where he left the car would have taken time, however quickly he moved. He couldn't or wouldn't have risked coming in on the ground floor, because he must have known that she might be up and about by then. Of course, that was why the front door didn't open. It was never meant to. The real entrance to the house was not there, but underneath. In the cellar. The perfect place to hide all manner of darkness. And the only way in and the only way out, which was why he could afford to have her roaming around elsewhere, while he darted between the floors creating his glorious works of art.

That would be what he was doing now. Believing she had gone to bed, he probably wouldn't bother to check, just deliver his precious film into the darkroom and start to play with her in his developing tray.

She had to find a way down to him.

She shifted her weight slightly and the noise beneath her suddenly stopped. She froze—he couldn't have heard her, could he? There was nothing to hear. She imagined him standing underneath, staring upward, puzzled. If he even suspected she was still there, he would need to know what she was doing, just to check. Her silence would make him too nervous.

She was right. About twenty seconds later she heard him moving again, underneath the hall this time, then making his way upward, not, as she had first assumed, into the room next door, but from another set of steps. She heard a door open somewhere in the darkness under the stairwell. Got you, she thought. Got you. . . . She slipped herself behind the living room door. He wouldn't search here first, not until he had checked the rest of the house.

As soon as she heard him move upstairs she slid out of the living room, across the hall, and into the recess under the stairs. She pushed herself to the back, sliding her hands frantically across the wall in search of the door which she knew had to be there. Above, she could hear him in the bedroom now, lights snapping on and off, doors opening, furniture being pulled this way and that, his movements as urgent as her own. He would be getting agitated now. In a house with so many locked doors there were only so many places where a person could hide.

Her fingers located an edge and she followed around it until she found the handle. She yanked it down but the door stayed shut. She had to bite her lip not to let out the moan of disappointment. He had locked it. He had locked it. How could he have done that so quickly? She had found the way out but she couldn't get to it.

Above her she heard his footsteps coming down the stairs.

Away—Sunday early A.M.

At THE BOTTOM OF THE STAIRS, THE RECEPTION AREA WAS empty. Anna rang the bell. After a while a man came out, mid-thirties, comfortably unfashionable in a cardigan and slippers. According to Samuel's guidebook it was a family hotel, not exactly five stars but charming in its way.

"Sorry to disturb you," she said in Italian. "I'm from room fourteen."

"Yes. I know," he said, and his gaze hovered nervously over the ugly bruise that was coming into flower above her right eye. "Can I help you, Signora Taylor?"

Mrs. Taylor. Appendage to Mr. Taylor. Of course. He would have registered her on his passport. The Italians didn't give a toss anyway. It was more to do with employment for bureaucrats than with morals. "Er . . . my husband is asleep and I need to make a phone call. I don't want to wake him."

"Of course. There is a phone in the lobby. You speak Italian very well."

"I used to. A long time ago. It's long distance."

"Fine. Shall I put it on your room bill?"

"Er, no. I mean—I wonder if I could pay you in cash. It's just, er—well, I mean it's a private call. I don't want my husband to know."

He made a small face, midway between a shrug and a smirk. His wife was a pretty woman, plump and pouty with deep brown eyes and spreading breasts. It seemed doubtful that he had ever wanted to call anyone else while she was in the house, but presumably, like all men, he reserved the right to imagine. "Of course. No problem. Why don't you call from the office? It's more private in there. I'm in the back if you need me."

She sat herself down at the desk and picked up the receiver. She found that her fingers were shaking. Two in the morning. It would be five—no, six—hours earlier in New York. Anyone with a life would be preparing to go out and enjoy it. She dug out the crunched-up piece of paper. 87 87. The last two digits.

The number connected and an answering machine came on, an Ella Fitzgerald track offering a few sassy well-chosen lyrics before the music faded and the woman's big voice cracked in:

"Hi, Sophie Wagner here. But not in person," it said with that neon optimism which nestles so close to depression in many Americans. "Why don't you—" Then the machine cut out and another voice cut in. Same timbre, not quite the same irrepressible bounce. "Hi, it's me."

"Sophie Wagner?"

"Yeah. Who's that?"

"Er, you don't know me, but I got your number from a friend. I'm calling you from Italy, actually."

"Italy. Great. Who's the friend?"

She took a breath. "Samuel Taylor."

There was a pause. Then: "I'm sorry. I don't know anybody by that name." But the voice was still up, perplexed rather than hurt.

"Oh . . . Oh dear. He said . . . I mean . . . Well, it's possible that when you met him he used another name. He's an Englishman? Tall, maybe six one, six two. Late thirties, early forties. Firm build, slightly graying hair. Full face. Attractive. Smiling eyes. Good sense of humor." There was a short pause. How else could she put it? "Good in bed."

"Hey. I don't need this," Sophie Wagner said, and the line went dead.

Anna held the receiver in her hand while her heart returned to its normal tempo. Then she dialed again. This time it was engaged. She counted to twenty and repeated the operation. The answering machine kicked in. It ran the whole message this time. As the beep came she imagined Sophie sitting at the table, curling her fingers nervously around a wineglass, trying not to give a damn.

"Listen, Sophie, I'm really sorry to bother you. My name is Anna Franklin. And I need to talk to you about this guy. Because . . . Well, because I'm sure you know him or knew him and I need some advice. I'm a professional woman, sorted, not a hysteric, but I think I'm in trouble and I need your help. So please, if you're there, will you pick up the phone?"

She waited. She saw the apartment: small, cleverly designed to make the best out of no space. If Sophie was really lucky she was high enough to get a glimpse of the city: an abstract of rooftops, or a bird's-eye swoop down a grid street, a wind tunnel of light and glass. But however much it thrilled the eye it still wouldn't give her a life. Maybe she was one of those women who needed a man to do that. The phone line clicked and the machine disconnected.

"Okay. I know this guy," said Sophie Wagner, the voice tough as old Californian skin now. "Talks a good line, knows how to schmooze and when to pick up the check. In bed he likes the woman to do most of the work during the warmup, then he comes on like a hurricane at the end. Gives good head if he's got enough energy left."

Anna thought of the hurricane, all blown out and puffless upstairs. Despite herself it made her smile. "Yes. I believe we're talking about the same man."

"Only his name wasn't Taylor. It was Irving. Marcus Irving. And the only advice I've got to give is, if you're still hanging out with him, take a pair of garden shears and slice it off. Only make sure you dump it someplace where no one can find it, so he can't get it sewn on again."

So what if life hadn't treated Sophie Wagner that well? At least she had kept a sense of humor about it. We could all wish for so much, thought Anna. "Can I ask what happened between you?"

"How far have you gotten?"

She considered how to put it. "I'm beginning to doubt his sincerity."

On the other end of the line she heard a whoop of delight. "Whooh. You guys have got such a way with understatement. So? What? He's wined and dined and fucked you, right?"

"Right."

"Has he started talking serious shit?"

"Yes . . . Sort of . . ."

"Okay. Then you're almost at the finish line."

Something turned quietly in her stomach. "What do you mean?"

"I mean he's going to dump you."

"But why—I mean . . . I'm sorry, but can you tell me what happened to you?"

"Where did you say you were calling from?"

"Italy."

"Is he with you now?"

And from all the way across an ocean and half a continent Anna heard something go tight in the woman's voice. "No, no," she said quickly. "But I'm due to be meeting him. Tomorrow morning."

"Invited you on a trip, right?"

"Er . . . Yes, yes, he did."

"So how did you get my number?"

"I found it. In his address book."

"Jeez. You must have sharp eyes. Was I one of many?"

"Er . . . I didn't see. You were on the front page."

"Oh, really," Sophie said, her voice like sour milk.

"Listen, please—I mean I know this must be difficult, but . . . will you tell me what happened?"

She gave a snort. "It's your phone bill." She paused. At the other end of the line Anna thought she heard the sound of a match being struck and the intake of breath. A New Yorker who still smoked. He would have liked that. Enjoyed the lack of PC about it. "I . . . I put an ad in a magazine. A serious magazine, literary, respectable, with an international academic readership. *The New York Review of Books.* He answered it and we met for dinner."

"This was in Manhattan?" Anna said quickly, phone in one hand and pen in the other, scribbling down notes in a fast loopy hand.

"Yeah. He told me he came here a lot. For work. We met once, twice, then we got into the sack, and after about a month of fairly mind-blowing encounters he invited me on this trip to St. Petersburg."

St. Petersburg, of course. The woman had mentioned that on the phone. "St. Petersburg?"

"Yeah—neat, huh? He went on and on about snow on pre-Revolutionary boulevards, Hermitage art, pepper vodka like frozen spice, that kind of thing. It was a hell of an in-flight movie. I was up for it."

"Who paid?" Anna asked quietly.

"Good question. I mean, since we were both consenting adults"—Sophie's tongue hit the syllables with exaggerated care—"I bought my ticket and he took care of the rest, hotels and stuff like that. Sound at all familiar?"

"Yes," Anna said in a small voice that was not entirely fake. "A little. What happened then?"

"Nothing. We had the greatest time. Just like a movie." And for a moment the memory of the pleasure blotted out the pain. "He was the perfect lover—bought me presents, told me how important I was to him and how we were going to make it work for each other, then sent me off on my plane to New York glowing like some radioactive romantic." She paused. Maybe she was watching herself walk back into her apartment from the airport, her stomach a tumble-dryer of emotions. She had probably got through the jet lag by making room in her closet for another set of clothes.

"And then?"

"And then—boom, it stopped. Just like that. Nothing. Zero. Not a word. Not a phone call, a letter, a postcard. I never heard from him again. He dumped me."

At the hotel desk Anna's pen had frozen in midair. "But, why? I mean, why bother to tell you it was serious if he wasn't going to follow through?"

"You think I haven't asked myself the same question? I have no idea. All I know is that one minute he's got his face in my crotch and he's talking marriage, the next he's disappeared from the surface of the planet."

"Marriage?"

"Yeah. Joke, huh? Marriage? I have a pretty reliable bullshit detector when it comes to stuff like this, and still I fell for it."

"So he didn't tell you about his wife?"

She gave a snort. "No, no. I got the one about his divorce. How he'd been on his own for two years and was ready for something real now. He put it very well. Very emotionally articulate for an Englishman. So, he's married, huh?"

"I don't know. I mean, that's what he told me."

"And you didn't mind that?"

"Er, no, well, not really . . . it, well, it suited me."

"Well, isn't that a coincidence. Tell me, how did you meet him?"

"Through the want ads." Anna paused. "A quality paper."

"Hot dog," Sophie Wagner said in triumph. "There you go. And does it still suit you that he's married?"

"Well . . . yes and no. Anyway, I mean recently he, er . . ."

"Don't tell me—he's thinking of leaving her, right?"

"Oh God," she said softly into the phone, but more in solidarity with Sophie Wagner's pain than in expression of her own. Because right at that moment Anna didn't feel any pain. Whatever there had been was gone, wrapped up tight and swallowed down with a wad of saliva until it was deep in her stomach, a drip-feed of gastric juices working it over, dissolving and eating away at it. With it gone, she could see for miles, a dazzlingly clear vision over a landscape of revenge. She felt so little pain it almost scared her. Upstairs he slept on soundly.

"Hey," said her American cousin kindly. "Don't let it do you in. You should be grateful you found out in time."

"Yes. Thank you. Tell me, how long ago did all this happen?"

"Let's see. St. Petersburg in February. 'The most beautiful time of the year,' " she said, mimicking an English accent badly. "What does that make? Five months."

Five months. Five months of waiting for the phone to ring. Even the toughest of souls would find it hard to prevent scarring.

There was a silence, the first between them. Sitting in her New York apartment stubbing out another cigarette, Sophie Wagner would be starting to feel a little exposed now, would be looking for some exposure in return. Otherwise it wouldn't be a fair transaction. "I suppose this trip to Italy is my St. Petersburg," said Anna quietly. "Maybe I should go home now before he arrives. But . . . well, listen: I mean if I do stay—if I do see him, would you—do you—want me to say anything to him from you?"

Sophie gave out a gale of laughter, a veritable Bette Midler of sound. "Yeah, sure. Just before he sticks it in why don't you give him my regards. I'd love to see the look on his face. Maybe he'll have a heart attack." And down the phone line, if you listened carefully, you could pick up the howl of pain that followed the words. "No. I don't want him to know anything about me, d'you understand? Nothing. I don't want you to mention my name, or say you've spoken to me. And if you get hold of that little black book again, I want you to tear out the page with my number on it."

"No problem. I'll try my best."

"Oh, and one more thing," Sophie said, the voice still big in disguise. "When you get home, make sure to change your locks, or you're going to be paying for your orgasms out of your insurance money."

"What do you mean?"

"Look—I have no proof of this, right? But two days after I got home from Russia, I went to work and came back to find my apartment cleaned out. VCR, computer, stereo, two antique rugs from my grandmother, all her heirloom jewelry, my CD collection, everything—all gone."

"And you think it had something to do with him?"

"All I know is I don't broadcast my address around town, and if you were coming in to rip me off you'd have to know where the alarm system was to deactivate it or else everybody in my building would know you were here."

"And he did?"

"You bet your ass he did. He fucked me standing right next to it one time. Keeping his eye on the job."

"But why . . . why rob you? From what I see he has loads of money."

"Yeah, and where do you think he gets it from? All that bullshit art-dealer talk over the last few months. I've checked out every gallery in the whole goddamn country of Switzerland. No sign. Oh, I bet he sells stuff, all right. He just doesn't buy it first. Can you imagine how many of us 'independent women' are out there looking for a good lover and a little respect?" She twirled the memory of Aretha Franklin around the last few words. "Enough to dress him in Armani as long as he can keep it coming, that's for sure."

Sitting in the drab décor of the hotel office Anna flashed on her own house: ten years of Habitat and Ikea mixed with some items of superior junk and a bit of Conran when she had the money. If he was looking for golden eggs he had most certainly picked the wrong goose. On the other side of the world, Sophie Wagner was waiting. "Have you told anyone else about all this? I mean, did you go to the police?"

"Oh, please . . . You guys watch too many TV shows. New York cops don't catch criminals, they just verify insurance forms. You think anybody's going to be interested in some flake Englishman who fucks his way through alarm systems? Anyway, what name would I give them? Marcus Irving or—who did you say he was?"

"Taylor. Samuel Taylor. He's got a passport."

"Sorry. So did Marcus Irving. I saw it."

"God. I don't know what to say. I can't tell you how grateful I am—"

She laughed. "No, you're not. You wish you hadn't heard any of it. So would I in your shoes. If it's any consolation, I've been around this racetrack a while and I've seen a lot of the horses in action. But I never came across anything quite like this guy. The best you can do is take comfort from the fact you're getting worked over by a class act, then pick his wallet from the bedside table tomorrow night and get the hell out of there. If you did that you could write my name along with yours in lipstick on the mirror. Just make sure you get all the credit cards, too," she said, dabbling her fingers for a while in the healing waters of fantasy. "Good luck."

And the line went dead.

Anna put down the receiver and sat for a moment with her face in her hands trying to take it all in.

When she looked up, the hotel owner was hovering in the doorway watching her. She wondered how much cash she had upstairs. Maybe she would find herself having to pick his wallet anyway.

"All right, Signora Taylor?"

She got up from the desk. "Just wonderful, thank you. How much do I owe you?"

He had a pad in one hand. He looked at it almost mournfully. "I'm afraid it's one hundred and nine thousand lire," he said with a crooked smile.

Forty quid, she thought. God. At least it would make a good story. She reached for her bag. "Could you give me a receipt for that?"

Home—Saturday P.M.

I CRAWLED INTO THE BED AND CURLED MYSELF AROUND HER BODY. She was warm and calm, but it did nothing to soothe me. I lay and listened to the night, or the little of it that was left. Somewhere in the plane tree across the road an overeager bird was already up and celebrating the dawn. I closed my eyes, but I was too stoned to sleep. Too stoned to think straight, either. The dope had me spinning on a pinhead. All I could do was to replay Lily's remark on the stairs. "When she said good-bye to me, she sounded sort of . . . sad, like she didn't want to go. . . ."

What would happen if Anna didn't come home? I gave in to paranoia and let my mind run with it. We would have to think about it sometime. Better to have been prepared. Without Anna, what the hell would we do?

In the will that had been drafted soon after her birth, Paul and I were named as joint guardians. Of course we had never talked about what that would mean. The very act of signing our names seemed to protect against the possibility of anything like that ever happening.

But what if it did? What if it already had? A child can't live in two places at once. Paul loved Lily, and he was a good parent to her every Friday and Saturday. No one would deny that. But for the rest of the time he had his own life and his own business and now his own lover. Did a part-time father really want to be a full-time one? Would he even be given the chance? With no parents and no brothers or sisters it would be left for the court to decide. Would they give her to him or to me? There was no doubt that in some ways it should be him. She saw him more often, knew him more intimately. Even at my most mean-spirited I would accept that. But a gay man running a full-time business and involved in what might be deemed a casual relationship with a lighting designer thirteen years younger than himself? It would be the stuff of tabloid meltdown. If Paul had given it any thought over this last twenty-four hours (and surely he had) then he must have realized that.

Yet, when it came down to it, would my CV read much better? Single professional female married to her work and living in foreign city. I saw my apartment in Amsterdam with its open interiors full of desirable arty objects and its floor-length canal windows opening onto sky and water. For years, whenever Lily came to stay I had kept the windows locked, terrified by a horror story of a rock star's son who had danced his way across their skyscraper New York apartment and out to his death. If Lily came to live with me, would she, at seven years old, be old enough to cope, or would I have to put up bars? Or move? If Lily came to live with me . . .

The list of questions was long and loud. Home? School? Holidays? Friends? Care? Without a job I couldn't support her, yet with one, my life was so eaten away by work that it would need a full-time wife to include a child within it. Hey, René. Ever thought of turning a commitment to the casual into a ready-made family? Hardly. Our very success was based on absence, and after two days away I could barely remember who he was anymore. You can't make a family just to house a child. Anyway, how could you ever take her away from the house where she grew up? Even my father had known it was better to live through that pain than try to cut it out. So would I have to come here? Could I do it? Leave the flat cool spaces of my head and my house to become a surrogate single mother in a city I had long since disowned?

No. The truth was that we all loved Lily, but as Anna's child. Anna was the pivot of this fabulous piece of emotional geometry we had all created. Without her, it would disintegrate and fall apart, leaving the rest of us to pick up the debris.

I saw my father's face as he stood by the kitchen table that morning trying to find the right words. Welcome to the void.

Away—Sunday A.M.

IF SHE COULD HAVE HIT HIM THEN SHE MIGHT REALLY HAVE DONE some damage, but the angle was wrong and in the darkness she could barely see him, let alone tell a skull from a shoulder blade. And because there would be only one chance she couldn't risk mucking it up.

Still, there was no doubt that she caught him off his guard, looming like a specter into his path at the bottom of the stairs.

"Hello, Andreas," she said, the brightness in her tone surprising even herself. "Were you looking for me?"

After so much of her own fear it was a pleasure to watch him jump. As he whirled around she thought he might go for her, but instead he stopped abruptly, as if someone had frozen him in his tracks, plunging his hands deep into his pockets as if to avoid the temptation of violence.

"I scared you. Sorry." She laughed nervously in his face. "My door was open. You must have unlocked it after I went to bed, yes? I woke and found it like that, I couldn't sleep so I came downstairs. Had a cup of coffee. Hope that was all right?" She was gabbling, the words running away with her, deliberately careless, deliberately gullible, like the woman who talked herself into believing his goodwill in the living room mirror just now.

"What were you doing under there?" he said at last, his voice almost a whisper.

She shrugged. "I was looking for you, and then I found this door at the back. I thought it might be your darkroom." When are the truth and the lie the same thing? "But it was locked. Is that where you work?"

She drew in a breath.

She still couldn't see his face, just feel his tension. It was different from before. She kept on talking. So what if she sounded nervous— it would make her appear less of a threat. She repositioned her fingers around the horse's neck. "I found some books. In the living room. I suppose they belonged to Paola. I took one, in case I couldn't sleep. I hope that's all right?" she said, moving her right arm slightly as if to explain its place behind her back. "Where did you go? I thought I heard a car drive away. You must have come back in very quietly. I didn't hear the door open," she added. "I think we must have scared each other."

God, Anna, why don't you just hit him now? she thought as the words tumbled out. Just take a swing at the side of his head and get it over with. Why do women always have to try and earth things, make them better with words rather than letting them explode? Here and now is the best chance you're going to get. But her hand stayed behind her back. Either she couldn't or she wouldn't do it. She realized that she didn't know which one it was. She would find out soon enough. I'm not going back into that room, she thought. And you're not going to put me on your walls.

He was standing in the middle of the staircase, hands still lost in his pockets. She took another fast breath, as if there still was much more to say, and she just needed to get ready to say it, but this time nothing came out. It was as if the connection between her brain and her voice had been suddenly severed and there was nothing she could do about it. The breath skittered away in a noisy sigh.

The silence grew around them, then snaked its way up the stairs and along the corridor. What was happening here? He had barely listened to what she had said. It was as though he had blanked off from her, as if the conversation between them had been too much effort and now he had let it go. Maybe that was why she had kept on chatting, to get him to join in the game again, to inject the normality of his abnormal politeness into this fucked-up relationship.

But something had changed. What? She thought frantically. She hadn't even tried that hard to escape. Instead, she had given him exactly what he wanted, standing in front of his camera and letting him snap his mirror images of her, offering him smiles, intimacy, even tears. Everything he desired. Just like Paola. He had them both now eye to eye in his lens. What more could he possibly want?

What more?

What else could there be apart from sex? she thought, staring at him across the gulf of silence. And that's not what this is about. I know you already. She thought back to the meeting in the gift shop, then the conversation in the station and the car, in her room, over the bottle of wine. In all that time he had never come near her, never even so much as lifted a finger in her direction. In fact, the only moment he had touched her at all must have been when she was unconscious.

But if he didn't move soon, then *she* was going to have to touch *him*. He was standing right in her way and it was clear he had no intention of moving.

So be it. "I have to go back to my room now," she said softly, the manic energy faded. "I'm tired and I want to sleep."

She waited for him to move aside and let her pass. When he didn't budge she took a step closer. She felt his body go rigid and watched a muscle twitching in the side of his face. Fear or fury?

One more step. She was within striking range now. Whatever happened next there would be no more presents or promises of freedom or intimate meals in front of the fire. No more talk of lost love. Despite her confession into the mirror, despite all the games and the reassurance, he wasn't going to let her go. She knew that absolutely now. And so did he. She could smell him again, the leftover chemicals mixing with sweat, sour upon sour, like something rotting inside him.

Somewhere on his body there was a key to the room downstairs and somewhere in that room were her passport and ticket and the way out. Get it over with, she thought. One way or the other, get it over with.

"Listen," she said, lifting her face into a smile as if she were staring at him in a mirror. "I know how much you miss her, Andreas. And I'm truly sorry for you. But . . ." Her words hung there, deliberately soft, almost coaxing. And as they did so, her right arm roared out of the darkness, with Lily's horse heavy on the end of it.

She deserved better than she got. Stella was right. Anna was a good liar, and she had played it as well as it could be played: the mirror talk, the chatter, the calm, even the caress of her voice. It wasn't even that she was queasy about the violence anymore. No. Once she had decided, she struck him as hard as she could. Or at least she would have done. If he hadn't hit her first.

You wouldn't expect such a constipated man to have such elegant action in him. It was almost as if he had known what she was going to do before she did it. His hand rose out of his pocket like a bird in sudden flight. The one blow was all it took, fast, efficient, perfectly aimed, his fist connecting to her head on the right side just above the eye.

Away—Sunday A.M.

THE CENTRAL PIAZZA RESEMBLED SOMETHING OUT OF A SCI-FI movie: ghostly, emptied of life and cars. Under the glow of badly placed halogen lamps, the cobblestones undulated like pebbles beneath shallow water, the whole square apparently tilting to one side as if somehow defying gravity. Bibbiena after the aliens had landed. Not even any bodies left to snatch.

Except for hers. She was sitting on a bench under an old and stately chestnut tree, staring out over the scene. She was trying to think, but she wasn't getting very far. The illusion of water on the cobbles was distracting, reminding her of the ice-rink floor in the Fiesole apartment that first night. It seemed so long ago. Everywhere in this story there were hidden depths, surfaces that couldn't be trusted. It became hard to hold on to what you knew. She would have liked to be asleep now, but the phone call had wired her brain into an adrenaline feed, and although her eyes hurt from being open she knew that if she closed them sleep wouldn't come, particularly not if she was lying next to him.

At first the fresh air had helped, the night so clean, the temperature so balmy and perfect. It was always a delicious shock for English skin; to be warm in the darkness, to feel the sun in the night air. Expansive climates make for expansive temperaments. That's what makes Americans so flamboyant, she thought. They spend their lives expanding and contracting to the extremes of mercury. Would a Spanish or a Norwegian woman have had a different reaction to the seductive arts of a con man? If that was indeed what he was?

She strode through the streets pulling at the tangled ball of facts, looking for the end of the thread so that she could start to unravel it the right way. Where to start? With a man who set out to rob women? To woo and entrap them, then fuck them—in all senses of the word—and walk away with what? An enlarged ego, a tired cock, and whatever he could raise from the sale of their valuables?

It didn't make sense. Too much effort for too little reward. So Sophie Wagner's grandmother had left her some antique rugs and pricey jewelry? Hardly enough bait to spend the best part of a month wooing her in New York and then five days of nooky in St. Petersburg hotels. Maybe the burglary had nothing to do with it. It could be just the talk of an aggrieved woman desperately looking for an explanation for the emotional disemboweling that had been inflicted upon her. But then without it, the whole thing made even less sense. Even the most sadistic gigolo culture has to feed on something more than vanity and humiliation. It has to be about money, too.

There were other things that she hadn't got right. His job, for instance. Marcus Samuel Irving Taylor was almost certainly an art dealer. Or at the very least he worked in one of those Swiss galleries that Sophie had called. She needed to get hold of that number. He would know it himself, of course. And if he dialed it enough he might use the directory to save himself the use of his fingers. Technology makes us lazy. Thank God.

She had reached the main square now. She sat on the bench and dug out the crumpled paper from her jacket pocket. The first two numbers had European prefixes, but she didn't know which one applied to Switzerland, and anyway, there was not enough light to make out the writing properly.

She went back to Sophie Wagner and the love affair from hell. Whatever it was, the scam had been complete there, which must mean that from his point of view it had been a successful business operation. So how? She played through it again, slower this time.

First act: He had found her through the want ads, which meant that although she could be traced he could not. Second act: He had wooed her and won her, been taken to her place, but not returned the favor, nor offered a phone number or even his real name. Third act: He had taken her to St. Petersburg, where he had—what had been her words?—"been the perfect lover," unfolding the city like a carpet beneath her feet and sending her home warmed by promises of eternal love.

Stop there. Why St. Petersburg? It would have been cheaper and warmer in Florida. It would have been sexier in the Caribbean. But no. He had wooed her with a deliberately romantic vision of ice and culture. "Snow on pre-Revolutionary boulevards, Hermitage art, pepper vodka like frozen spice." Clever, really. As she had said, the right in-flight movie for the right woman, the kind who would advertise in *The New York Review of Books*.

St. Petersburg and *The New York Review of Books*. *The Guardian* and a weekend in Tuscany. As dating games went they were both clichés. What was the garden of delights that he had laid out before her that morning in the Fiesole restaurant, when she had been so caught between staying and leaving? The monastery of St. Francis and a great collection of Della Robbias . . . Hermitage art and pepper vodka . . .

Of course. That was the connection between the two. The art. But then it would be, wouldn't it? After all, art was his work. Buying and selling. So was this about some kind of art scam? Using a tourist–love affair trip as a front for dodgy dealing. But what and how? There'd been no time for him to do any business. They hadn't seen any art worth talking about (the churches hardly counted; the most exciting thing had been the altarpiece and that had been an "almost" rather than the real thing), and by the time they got back to Florence to catch an early Monday morning plane the weekend would be over. Unless he stayed on and did it then. In which case, why did he need her with him in the first place?

No, there was something she wasn't getting here. Her head hurt from trying to work it out.

Two ... three ... The bell in the clock tower echoed into the silence. From across the other side of the square she could make out a low buzzing noise, like a chainsaw starting up in the night. From a small side street opposite a scooter zipped into sight, moving more like a kid's remote-control toy than the real thing. The driver was a young guy with long hair, his pillion passenger, arms clinging around his waist, a girl in a very short skirt, her thighs bare to the night air. They drove fast right across the middle of the cobbled square, the engine buzzing angrily along the uneven surface, zooming past her and down the street to her left. The noise died slowly behind them. An Italian pair on their way home after a late night. One could only hope that the household wasn't up waiting for their return.

She thought of them saying good night on her doorstep, a quick snog before the lights snapped on in a room above. The image brought back her own date, sprawled across a bed in the best hotel room in town. She painted him more clearly in her mind's eye.

He liked to sleep on his stomach, that much she already knew: head turned to one side, face half-squashed into the pillow, his breathing heavy. In repose his shoulders and upper torso were chunky with muscle and what was—if you looked hard enough—the beginning of flab. But it still looked good, still offered an invitation to touch. She could feel the texture of his skin under her fingers, strong and supple at the same time, conjuring images of sweat, like beads of water, clinging to it. She ran her eye and her hands farther down his back toward the small of his buttocks, her voyeurism making her gaze cool, almost cruel in its assessment. There were traces of love handles above the hips, the leftovers of all those expensive meals. And she'd seen better asses. In her time. She imagined someone (herself?) slapping him on the buttock. "Come on, boy, wake up here. Start doing your job. There's a lady here who needs servicing." As he turned over, groping his way out of sleep, she noticed how his jawline had grown almost slack, and his eyes dull.

She froze the image and studied it, gorging herself on its grossness as if in some kind of *Clockwork Orange* aversion therapy. I don't like your body, she thought. It's too ripe with its own success. I don't know why I didn't notice it before. I don't ache for your hands on me anymore. I'm not even sure I could make love to you again.

She opened her eyes and the square exploded back into view, calm and silent, confident of the beauty in its age. She felt an almost palpable sense of relief. What is it with you and men, Anna? she thought to herself. Why is it you have such lousy taste?

She thought herself back to her kitchen table: saw Paul and Michael sitting on one side of it, a half-drunk bottle of wine between them and a game of Clue laid out in front. Opposite them sat Lily, kneeling up on her chair, clasping the dice in her fat little fingers, ready to throw, concentration in capital letters on her face. On the board Miss Scarlett was chasing Reverend Green around the house with a spanner, and the gay boys were having fun watching. There was laughter in the air, and a quiet kind of love. No, it wasn't true. She didn't have lousy taste in men. She just picked different ones for the fucking and the fathering.

Maybe in some bizarre way it suits me better, she thought: feeling both loved and left alone at the same time. In retrospect, she realized that she had been telling the truth about herself that first meeting in the Oxo tower. Not only did she not want a husband, she only sometimes wanted a lover. The worst sin she had committed here was waiting too long to get one, not recognizing the depth of hunger in herself, so that when she did eat she took in too much too fast, then felt sick afterward. It was a common enough female disorder, not knowing how to control your appetite. But given the chance, she could learn. Everyone can get what they want if they want it enough. If they want it enough . . .

So what was it he wanted? If it wasn't sex and it wasn't adoration, what was it about? She didn't know. But she would find out. As the clock chimed the half-hour she got up from the bench and walked slowly back to the hotel.

Home—Sunday A.M.

NEXT TO ME, AS IF SHE HAD HEARD MY THOUGHTS, LILY STIRRED and turned over, her left arm flopping over onto my chest. Her hand felt cold. I held it in mine for a while, then slipped it in underneath the sheets.

Above me I caught the creaking noise of bedsprings in the spare room upstairs. I lay and listened. Maybe I'd woken them with my wanderings. The sound stopped. I imagined Mike folding himself around Paul's body, like two spoons in a drawer. In the dark I looked at my watch. Almost 3:00 A.M. An hour later, European time.

I closed my eyes and let the dope take me where it wanted. It took me to Italy.

I imagined her in a hotel room, a man by her side, the phone neglected in the pursuit of orgasm. How good can sex be, Anna? Enough to rearrange your loyalties? Enough to make you forget your home? You tell me.

I tried again and found her at an airport, dozing uncomfortably in a bucket chair under strip lighting, the flight board silent in readiness for the next morning's rush. Everybody misses planes. It's part of life's rich pageant. But they still manage to talk to the right people, to reassure them back home.

Finally I caught sight of her in a field of resplendent high-summer sunflowers, her body lying between their fat stalks like a rag doll, the earth around her dark with spilled blood.

"She sounded sort of . . . sad, like she didn't want to go. . . ."

So many stories . . . So many possibilities . . . But then I'm good at make-believe. Always have been.

For the longest time after she didn't come home, I thought my mother had been run down by a bus. Well, how do you tell a ten-year-old girl that her mother's body has been found cut in two on a railway line in Hampshire, a one-way ticket away from home in her pocket? No note, no explanation, nothing, not even the faint imprint of a bruise in the middle of her back where someone might have helped her fall. It didn't make any sense. She sometimes took day trips when she was off work: checking out the gardens of stately homes for planting ideas, occasionally moving from one to another along a railway line, but with never a hint of *Brief Encounter* in the station bars. Except, of course, how would we ever know? It takes two to tell, and if one was dead the other might feel shy about speaking. I'm sure my dad must have thought about it; but then, only he would have known if the fault line of their marriage ran through sex or simply destiny.

In the years that have followed I have wondered if he would have preferred it if they'd never found the body. At least that way he wouldn't have had to cope with the horror. We could have pretended that she *had* really gone missing. Had had amnesia, got a better offer from Hollywood, run off with an exiled Hungarian seaman. The late sixties were wild times, after all. But bisected on a railway track? It was so macabre, so final. When did I first learn the truth? Playground gossip, no doubt. I wouldn't want the same thing to happen to any child I loved.

To redress the balance I wove a little white magic in the night, opening my eyes and bringing Anna into the bedroom, sitting her on the edge of the bed, her eyes bright with laughter.

"And remember that time you went missing?" I said, and because

I was still stoned, I think I might have said it out loud. "Christ, you wouldn't believe how worried we all were."

She laughed. "Yeah. I know. Sorry. Stupid misunderstanding, wasn't it?"

I nodded. "Certainly was. Well, just as long as you're back now."
Only she wasn't.

"For Christ's sake, where are you, Anna?" I said into the open air. "What are you doing now?"

Away—Sunday A.M.

SHE WAS LOOKING OUT THROUGH A WINDOW, THE LATE-AFTERNOON sun cutting a long shadow across the side of her face. She had a pair of sunglasses perched on the top of her head, pulling up a cloud of unruly hair from her scalp underneath. In half-profile there were little lines running from the edge of her nose toward the corners of her mouth, making her look tired, even sad. The cup of coffee in front of her was half-drunk. Her eyes were a long way away. She was thinking of something or someone else.

Then the mood changed and she was walking across a piazza after a shower of rain, the surface of the stones alive with light, the gleaming white façade of Santa Croce unmistakable in the background. She looked busy, intent, happy almost.

To the right came another series of close-ups: her with a glass of wine in her hand, talking to someone—a waiter, presumably—then eating in a restaurant. She recognized the blue check tablecloths; it was a place near the Boboli Gardens where she had drunk too much one lunchtime, then had to go back to the hotel for a sleep afterward. Later that same day she had walked through the city before dusk and sat for a while on the steps of the Baptistery. She looked lovely in this picture, fading sunlight the color of honey all around and her black hair fierce against the golden doors.

Laid out in a photograph album the pictures would be self-explanatory: Anna in Florence. Except you might perhaps add one more word—"Alone."

But then, she *had* been. That was the difference between her and the other woman. (Was Paola really her name?) If the pictures of Paola were more arresting it was not only because she was prettier, but because she had been plucked out of a life, busy, animated, while she, Anna, looked like a woman caught in transit, waiting for something to happen. It was hardly fair. He should have met her at home, where her world was full of friends, crowded places, chattering times. And Lily. How could you make a portrait of her life without Lily? Though you wouldn't want any such photos taken by him.

She closed her eyes and fell back on the mattress. The world spun in the darkness and the pervading stink of the chemicals made her feel sick. She pulled herself up onto one elbow and tried again.

The room was small, the ceiling low. There was no window, and only one door, closed. It was hot, despite the buzz of air-conditioning. A world underground. His world. So where was he? Her head hurt, but the pain seemed a long way away. He had put some kind of rough dressing on the wound. Underneath she could feel a spongy swelling and the burn of broken skin. How much blood had she lost? Did that explain the weakness and nausea, or was it something else? Had he given her another dose of syrup to keep her quiescent?

Get up, she thought. Get up and get out of here.

I can't. I can't.

She didn't want to cry, so instead she looked back at the photos. It was a strange feeling; being surrounded by images of oneself, yet a different self, a self seen through someone else's eyes. Like having your soul stolen away by the camera. Is this who Anna Franklin really was? So pensive, so sad?

He had been there all along, it seemed. Or at least since day two. Was that café on the first afternoon or the second? Before or after her visit to Santa Croce? She couldn't remember. Never mind. How weird that she hadn't noticed him. Too self-absorbed, no doubt. Not listening to the electricity in the air around her.

She shifted her gaze to the next wall.

Where she expected to find mirrors, instead she got beds. She recognized the green cover before she recognized herself lying curled under it. Each shot had been taken from the same place, a vantage point high above, in the ceiling—embedded in the light fixture, presumably. In sequence, they told the story of a night: an arm flung out here, a leg moved there, like one of those children's books where you flick the pages to make the animal at the corner turn somersaults, or a jump-cut television ad for a sleeping draft or a cold remedy. She looked peaceful, deeply asleep, no hint of the salacious or the erotic about her pose, just the creepy intimacy of surveillance, the blinking eye of a camera shutter. Had this been her sleeping off the drug, or the night after, when she had woken once to find the light on, puzzling as she was sure she had turned it off? Now she understood the composition of noises from last night. He had unlocked the door and driven away in the car because he had known all along that she was awake to hear him. Because all the time he had been looking at her.

Next came the mirror shots: a creative selection of them. Reading them now made them seem almost prophetic: a madwoman, disheveled and tense, pretending she wasn't. Even in the shots where the mirror had tempted her into vanity and the smile had arrived, sucking in the cheeks and opening the eyes, the effect seemed disturbing rather than seductive.

Where she had thought she had concealed doubt, the camera had found it immediately, in the flicker of the eyes, the parting of the lips to pull in a fast breath. Fear leaked out through the pores of her skin. To catch it so acutely would have taken sensitivity and skill. No doubt he would also have caught the next subtle shift of emotion, from fear into fury and sly determination. But there was no record of that shift on the wall. This gallery was selective, the story it told predetermined. She needn't have bothered with her monologue. He had never believed it anyway.

The remaining photos took up half of the last wall. He had been working hard, but the clock would have been against him. There had been no time to frame or even properly arrange here, just a run of quick blowups taped to the wall. Obviously he hadn't made up his mind about the selection yet. Some, the ones taken against the cellar wall, were simple and rushed, a body slumped, head down onto the chest, the wound hardly visible. Others, like those of her in the chair, were almost baroque in their elegance, the angry gash of blood echoing the deep red of her dress, her skin drained, white as an enamel sink.

From the still life of an ordinary woman in a café to the slow destruction of a special, chosen one. Half a wall left. Room for one more photo shoot.

She stared at the empty space. Her head was throbbing again, closer now, demanding her attention, willing her to close her eyes and lie down for a while. She lay back on the mattress. Her body gave a sigh of relief. She knew she ought to be doing something, spurred on by the terror that what she was looking at was a chronicle of her own death. But somehow she felt almost disconnected from it, as if whatever drug he had given her to relax her body had relaxed her mind as well. How extraordinary—to be looking at your own death and not to be alarmed by it.

She forced herself to keep thinking.

She thought of Lily, and with that a great sweetness flooded through her. She wished she could talk to her, one last time, a few last moments. She felt sure she would know what to say. The right words for the rest of Lily's life. Love without bitterness.

It had always been Anna's fear that Lily would die before she did. That she would open the door to the ultimate nightmare—the uniform on the doorstep and the words "I'm so sorry, Miss Franklin, I have bad news for you." At least now that wouldn't happen. On the contrary, her death would ensure Lily's longevity. Not even a godless universe is capricious enough to deliver the same horror over two generations. One murder would surely prevent another. She felt almost a sense of comfort in the thought. Stella would look after her. As an expert in such particular pain she would know what to do, how to comfort, when to leave alone. Lily would survive. That was all that mattered.

Was this how Paola had felt now? she thought. Did she keep fighting or did she give up as well? Had she been brought this low by the same means, a set of photos and tales of lost love? Or had she perhaps been the first?

It must have been so easy. She could see it all now. All you had to do was want it enough. The rest was planning and luck: the right stranger at the right time, someone with whom you had no connection, someone away from home who wouldn't be missed or pursued until you and they were a long time gone. She must have fallen into his hands; cheap hotel, obviously alone, no husband or boyfriend, just a guidebook and some rusty Italian. Travelers made such good targets. Any big city would supply the goods. Probably he didn't always pick Florence; more sensible to cast your net wide, that way it would take a while for the cases to match up. Maybe he let them all call home. Maybe that was one of the identifying features. Or maybe he had got cocky with her.

Of course, he wouldn't get away with it forever. They never did. Eventually he'd make a mistake and they'd find him. Find it all: the house, the bodies, the photographs.

The photographs . . . The ones on the walls were only his selection. There would be others: contact sheets, banks of negatives, film after film, step by step, shot by shot from the sunshine into the dark. Would they show them to the families? You wouldn't really want them to do that. Or even to have them hung up in a courtroom as evidence. These were not the pictures one would choose to be remembered by. Death was a private thing. Just between the two of you. Like sex or terror.

She felt a slow pain start to burn inside her stomach, vying for her attention with the lassitude and the throbbing in her head. She looked at the wall and saw her own fear staring back at her and she knew that the drug, whatever it was, was beginning to wear off.

No, better that they never saw this. She closed her eyes and went back to sleep.

Away—Sunday A.M.

SHE STEPPED OUT OF HER CLOTHES AND SLID UNDER THE SHEET next to him, careful to stay on the other side of the bed faced away from him. He didn't stir. She listened to his breathing: noisy, deep, a man at rest. Even with the distance between them she could feel the heat coming off him. She closed her eyes and tried to sleep. She was so tired she couldn't think straight, but neither could she stop thinking. The minutes ticked by. She was still trying when he gave a half-groan, flipped over from the side to the middle of the bed, and, finding her body in his path, threw a lazy arm around her waist. It lay there for a second, leaden, uninterested; then, as if realizing what it had found, the grip tightened and he pulled her toward him.

"Mmmn, you're cold," he said after a while, his voice muzzy, half-buried between her shoulder blades.

He had been asleep all this time, hadn't he?

She lay still, as if she hadn't heard, as if she were the one who'd been woken, not him. He ran his hand down over the surface of her left leg. "Freezing." And he sounded more alert now. "Where have you been?"

"Oh, just up for a while," she mumbled. "I couldn't sleep."

There was a pause. The hand kept on moving, methodical rubbing movements, slow warmth seeping into the chill. "Where's up?" And something in the way he said it made her decide not to lie.

"I went for a walk. I didn't want to disturb you."

"Silly girl." He nuzzled himself closer, like an animal burrowing deeper into earth. She felt the bristle of his stubble as he rolled his chin against the skin of her back; the finest of sandpaper, halfway between caress and irritant. Just a few hours ago she had lain next to this man desperate for him to touch her; now it was all she could do not to flinch away as he did so. The hand that had been working her left leg slipped itself deftly in between her thighs. "You should have woken me." She shifted her legs apart, but slightly, more out of politeness than invitation. "I could have helped you sleep," he said, the voice blurry but playful now, petulant almost, like a child's.

And as he said it she felt his prick stiffen against her left buttock. It sent a small shock wave through her, the line between old lust and new tension too close to call. He mistook one for the other and trailed his hand upward, his fingers meshing into her pubic hair, until he found the moistness underneath. "Mmm. Nice."

They lay like that for a while, neither of them moving, almost testing out the air. She thought about the portrait of him she had conjured up in the square, the flesh thick with ego and self-indulgence, then discarded it again. She could embellish it or let it go. Relax, she thought. Night fucks are the great freebies of sex, remember: bodies slipping out to play before the mind has had time to wake up. She moved her legs farther apart. Even bad men can do good things if you let them. "At last," he muttered, the words almost lost in her flesh. He played deeper, finding the entrance to her, opening it up with his middle finger, testing the temperature inside. She pushed herself down onto his hand, searching for the right pressure. They played for a while, then he slipped his finger out and, pulling her body back and up until the position was right, he slid his prick into her, each move so languid, so careless almost, that they might indeed have still been half-asleep.

The night sat thickly around them. He let out a long gasp as he pushed in and in the short silence before the next breath she heard the town clock hit the single chime of four-thirty. It would be dawn before long. She felt him moving to and fro, a calculated slowness, each thrust long and careful, savoring the moment. If you didn't know better you might think it was about art as much as pleasure. But then, like most men with a vocation, he obviously gained satisfaction from his own proficiency. "Come on, Anna," he said quietly into her ear. At the same time his fingers continued their plucking, searching for the right spot, the right rhythm with which to bring her inside the charmed circle. "You didn't think you could leave, eh? Time to come home."

He knows, she thought suddenly, the realization rushing through her like a shock wave. He's been awake all this time and he knows that I know. But how could he? It's not possible. She gave a little laugh out loud, and to her satisfaction heard a throaty darkness in it, the sound pulled from her body rather than her mind. You want me back, lover, you have to find me first, she said half to herself, half aloud. And with her defiance she ignited a flare of desire.

He felt it too. He pushed himself farther in, and at the same time his fingers found their mark and they both registered her sharp involuntary intake of breath. "There. That's better," he said, and the voice was firmer now. He turned his attention from himself to her, playing her more confidently now, connecting the catch in her flesh with that in her throat, perfecting the movement with each repetition, feeling the momentum build. She let him do it. How many times had they made love, he and she? Fifteen, twenty times? Enough for them both to know that she was on safe ground now. In a moment she wouldn't need him anymore; the dynamic of her own excitement would do it for her, the overwhelming tension of pleasure lifting her inside and out of her body until she was spinning and exploding in space, triumphant, alone, oblivious of him, his work, his vanity, even his pleasure.

He was waiting for the moment to join her, for her to give him a sign so they could do it like good lovers should, in the perfect gigolo illusion of togetherness, both of them in orbit at the same time. But she wasn't interested in him anymore, only in herself. As she wrenched her orgasm away from him into herself he realized too late and tried to catch up with a few deep plunges. But she was already gone; and when it was over, and love—or, at least, etiquette—required that she return to join him while he finished the job, she kept herself deliberately away, her mind and her body indifferent to his frantic rising thrusts. Now it was his turn to be too far gone to turn back. Men can fake everything but this, she thought. Even this man. Even when it contains nothing of himself. And the cruelty in her pleasure as she lay there, waiting while he battered himself inside her, both amazed and delighted her.

When he finally came—a fast, rather scrappy affair—and slid out of her, falling back onto the bed to get his breath back, she lay quietly next to him and thought of Chris and the moment all those years ago when Lily had been conceived. What was it that Samuel/Marcus/Taylor/Irving had said to her about that night as they had lain together on this same bed, swapping secrets in the amniotic fluid of mutual trust less than twelve hours before? "Sounds like you came out the victor in the end." And she wondered if the same could be said of her now, or if what had taken place was only a temporary victory in a much bigger battle.

They lay side by side not talking, until after a while he raised himself up onto one elbow and looked down at her. She opened her eyes and met his gaze. "What happened?" he said quietly.

She smiled. "Nothing."

"So where were you?" he asked lightly, and she was sure that they both understood the ambiguity.

"I . . . I didn't get back in time. Sorry."

"But you did get off?"

"Couldn't you tell?"

He shrugged. "I don't know. One minute you were there, the next you were gone. I got lonely."

She paused, despite herself impressed by the honesty. "I went to the town square."

If the change of direction disconcerted him he certainly didn't show it. He made a face. "The town square? That was a long way."

"Yeah."

"Why didn't you wake me?"

"You were tired. I wanted to be alone. I needed to do some thinking."

"I see. About going home?"

"Something like that."

He ran a finger down the line of her face. "So is that what you were doing? Getting used to having your orgasms alone again?"

She didn't break his gaze. "Don't flatter yourself," she said, but without particular malice.

He laughed. "I'm going to miss you, you know, Anna," he said quietly. Then: "You do realize that, don't you?"

"You'll manage," she said.

He looked hurt. It was almost convincing. "How would you feel if I told you that . . . that I was thinking of opening an office in London?" He paused. "And that if I did, I'd have to come over and live there for six months or so to get it going?"

She shrugged. "I suppose I'd wonder where you and your wife were going to live."

He smiled. "She's not an Anglophile, I'm afraid. She'd stay at home."

She nodded. She watched Sophie Wagner sitting by a phone in a Manhattan apartment, measuring out her life in the spaces between the wrong phone calls. "Why London?" she said. "Why not New York?"

He frowned. "New York? What made you think of New York?"

She shrugged. "I don't know. I thought the art market was bigger there."

He paused. "Not for me. So, what would you think? I mean, if it happened. Would that be excuse enough for me to meet your daughter?"

"I don't know, Samuel. I'd have to think about it."

"I see." He nodded slightly. "Well, anyway, it might not happen. It's only an idea at this stage."

Somewhere outside the window a couple of songbirds started up, rash creatures in a country where centuries of epicurean taste had decided that the smaller the bird the bigger the delicacy. Presumably they, too, could read a clock, would know it would be hours before all those brave Italian hunters would be up and about, eager to blow their brains out and roast their tiny bodies on supermarket spits.

It bestows an unusual and particular confidence, knowing when one is safe from the predator and when one is not.

"I have to sleep now," she said, lifting her head up to kiss him gently on the lips. "Just for a few hours."

He nodded, but didn't move, continuing to stare down at her. She closed her eyes. When she opened them again a few moments later he was still looking. She smiled. "You all right?"

"Yeah. Yeah, I'm fine. Just drawing something for memory. You go to sleep now. I'll wake you when it's time to leave."

"You're going to get up now?" It was hard to know whether she felt relieved or disturbed.

"I'm awake. I don't think I could sleep again. But you can. We've got all day. There's no hurry."

"What will you do?" she said, watching him get into his trousers and pull on a sweater, and finding something about the action suddenly unbearably painful, as if a shot of morphine had just worn off and she was plunged again into the raw ache of an open wound. What is this? she thought, frantically. Where did the numbness go?

"Oh, I'll go and sit in the lobby for a bit. See if I can catch an early breakfast. Maybe check out the church—the guidebook says it's a stunner—and find us somewhere to eat lunch."

It's because it's over, she thought. All of it: the pleasure, the pain, the sex, the seduction, the intimacy, all of it gone in the action of a man putting on his clothes. And because the only thing that isn't yet over, the betrayal, the double-cross—whatever and whenever it would be—wouldn't serve to wipe out the intensity of what had been before, however much she might wish it could. And for the split second when she registered that, it seemed almost preferable to make herself believe the lies again and so not let him go.

He slipped on his jacket as he came to the bed and leaned over her, kissing her lightly on the lips. "Sleep well. See you later."

Then, picking up his briefcase, he was up and out of the room.

She turned over onto her side and lay staring into the room, trying to deal with the pain, to breathe her way through it as she had once been taught to breathe through physical pain, as a way of absorbing and containing it. She focused on the window and the creeping new dawn. As she lay there the pace of change quickened, a gauzy, almost cotton-candy-tinted light seeping in, penetrating and dissolving away the gray, the color as tender and outrageous as a painter's brush. She had a sudden image of the restored tabernacle Madonna in the church holding the dead Christ on her lap, her robes a bright eager blue against the sallow shade of dead flesh. The painter had captured it so well you could almost feel the weight of his body pinning her down, before in turn he was lifted up and carried into the heavens. Men's bodies and the various ways in which women are called on to tend to them. It was not the end of the story.

Home—Sunday

I WOKE TO AN EMPTY BED AND THE SOUND OF LILY LAUGHING wildly, a jumble of high-pitched cartoon voices around her. I stood at the top of the stairs and listened. Why don't adults laugh like that? Is it something to do with the size of the larynx or the state of the soul? I felt as if I had been up all night, which, of course, I had.

In the sitting room Lily was curled under a duvet, a bowl of corn-flakes perched precariously on her lap, the Rugrats shining in her eyes. Angelica (my favorite and Lily's) was throwing another tantrum. I closed the door on her exhilaratingly bad temper.

In the kitchen Paul was standing alone at the open garden door smoking a cigarette. I couldn't remember how long ago he had given it up, and this wasn't the time to ask. He flicked the stub into the bushes as I came in. In happier days it would have been a gesture to drive the boys wild. But Paul was a married man now. And a worried one.

"Hi. How did you sleep?"

"Awful," I said, plugging in the kettle and warming my hands over it like a campfire, until it started to burn.

"Yeah. Me, too." He paused. "The police rang."

My head jerked up. "When?"

"This morning—around nine-thirty."

"And?"

"Nothing. They've checked all the flights for today and tomorrow coming out of Pisa and Florence. She's not booked on any of them."

I didn't say anything. There was nothing to say.

"But they found where she was staying. Tracked her down through the passport computer details. A Hotel Corri. In Via Fiesolana? Near the Duomo, apparently?"

"Never heard of it. What did they say about her?"

"That she checked out on Thursday afternoon, as planned."

"Did she say where she was going?"

"No. They assumed the airport. The girl on the desk said she asked her to call her a cab. She doesn't remember where to. She's not sure that she ever knew."

"But she did see her go?"

He nodded. I felt myself suddenly tremendously excited. As if somewhere in this one concrete piece of information lay the answer to all the questions. "So all they have to do is track down the cab."

He sighed. "It's not that easy. The cab company the girl rang said it would be a while, and Anna told her not to bother. That she'd get one in the street."

"Oh."

We sat for a while. Florence in high season. How many cabs? How many drivers? How many destinations in a day? Hold on to what you've got, Estella. It's better than nothing. "But whatever it was, we know that it happened between the hotel and the airport?"

"Yeah. We know that."

"Did you tell them about the phone call?" I said casually as I opened the fridge to get out the milk.

At least he had the decency to hesitate. "No." Then: "The milk's on the table if you're looking." I grunted thanks. But I didn't let him off the hook. "If they had found her name on one of the flights I would have done."

"How about the Soulmates column? Did you mention that?"

He shook his head. "It's not about a man."

"We don't know that, Paul," I said patiently.

"Yes, we do," he retorted, a flame of indignation rising within it. "I rang the paper this morning. Got the home number of the features editor she does stuff for. She told me that Anna handed in a story two weeks ago called 'Dating Games'—who you met, if they were kosher, that kind of thing. The *Guardian* Soulmates stuff was included in it. They haven't had time to run it yet. I told her to hold it till we knew more."

My God. So it was a story. The photos, the circled adverts, the phone bills, all of it. All of it?

I stirred the milk in and took a sip. The first hit of morning tea: like mainlining lifeblood. It's not the drug that counts, only the quality of your need for it. Last night's dope still hung around on the fringes of my mind, playing havoc with the notion of reassurance. "So you don't think it's possible that she might have met somebody more serious and decided not to write about him?"

"Why do you say that?"

I shrugged. "Only because it was you who thought she was distracted. And then there's Mike's comments about her appearance. I mean, something had changed in her. There has to be an explanation for that."

From the hall the sound of canned laughter grew suddenly louder, then came some zip-zappy music for the credits to dance along to. I put my finger to my lips to stop Paul replying. Ten seconds later Lily's head popped around the kitchen door.

"I'm still hungry," she said to anyone who was listening. "Can I have some toast?"

"Morning," I said. "Angelica got over her temper tantrum?"

She nodded. Nothing's so passé in a child's life as the last cartoon program.

"Brown or white?" Paul got up from the table.

"White, of course."

"Butter or margarine?"

"Margarine, of course."

"Marmalade or honey?"

There was a pause.

"Nutella, of course," they said together.

I was being treated to a floor show. For what purpose?

"Bring your cornflakes bowl in first," said Paul.

"Oooh, not now—it's *Spider-Man* next."

"Yes, now."

"Paaauuul."

"Hey—no bowl, no toast."

She gave a theatrical sigh and flounced out.

It struck me that if I hadn't been there he probably would have given in. Keeping things normal can be tough sometimes. The living room door slammed behind her.

He got up and started the toast anyway. "You want some?"

I shook my head. "Has Mike gone?"

"Yeah, he had an early call."

I paused. "Paul?" He looked up at me. "I really like him. I think he's substantial. A good man."

He grinned. "Yeah. Hard to find, eh?"

The invitation to the joke lay between us like a damp firework. It wasn't the morning for repartee.

"So, are you two going to move in together?"

He turned back to the toast. "We were."

" 'Were'?"

His back gave an angry sigh. "Well, it depends on what happens here, doesn't it?"

"Does it?" I finished my tea. "I don't see how."

"Oh, come on, Stella," he said, turning to me more aggressively this time. "You must have thought about it."

I took a breath. "No," I lied, putting down the mug and staring into the bottom of it. In the olden days (so old I don't remember them), women could study the leftover tea leaves to help them with the bits of life they didn't understand. With the advent of the tea bag we have lost our ability to see into the future. Sad. "No, I haven't."

He frowned at me for a moment, then came over and sat down opposite, leaving the toast unbuttered, or unmargarined.

He shook his head. "Sorry."

I gave him a "Hey, no need to apologize" gesture.

"I didn't sleep that well either."

"No." We sat for a moment in silence. "You're really good with her, Paul."

He shrugged, but didn't say anything.

"We'd cope," I said at last. "Between us we'd cope. And she'd be okay. But we won't have to, because it's not going to come to that. I know it's not."

He glanced up at me and smiled. I smiled back.

"No. You're right, it's not." He paused. "You can stay for a few days, right?"

"You know I can. I'll stay for as long as it takes."

He stopped. He was gearing up to something. You could feel it build. "I'm due to be in Scotland tomorrow for a meeting. First thing in the morning. It's about a deal with a Scottish distributor. Quite important. I've tried to get hold of him to cancel, but I don't have a home number."

I nodded. "Well, of course you have to go."

He still wasn't looking at me. "I could take the first plane at six A.M. Or the sleeper—they've probably got some berths left."

I paused. It was hard to know exactly what I was being told. "What were you planning to do—I mean, before this?"

He sighed. "I was going to go up this afternoon. Meet some colleagues this evening."

I shrugged. "Then why don't you do that?"

"What about you and Lily?"

What about me and Lily? What were we telling each other here? I realized I didn't know. "We'll be fine," I said. "No problem."

"You sure?" And this time he looked up at me, a man wanting to do the right thing, but needing a little space before he could work out exactly what that was. I, of all people, could hardly blame him for that.

I smiled. "Yes, I'm absolutely sure."

He smiled back. "Thanks, Stella."

Across the kitchen the bread popped out from the toaster. For a little while neither of us moved. Then I got up from the table.

"I'll get the toast, then."

Away—Sunday

No sight this time, only smells and sound. The chemicals were fresh now, sharp, pungent, acting like smelling salts kick-starting the brain back into consciousness. She could hear clattering, trays and bottles being moved around, water flowing, a tap like a fierce fountain hitting a metal sink underneath. The sound made her want to urinate. She remembered the time before when she had woken, desperate for the loo. How long had she been unconscious then? Seven, eight hours? Same drug, same sleep. Different kind of captivity. Her head was throbbing powerfully in time to her pulse now, no narcotic at work to soothe the ache. Nothing to smother the feelings. One thing was certain. She didn't want to die anymore.

She opened her eyes to see how it would happen.

She was propped in an armchair, a blanket over her tucking her in, her head held upright by a set of pillows carefully placed. Apart from the throb she felt comfortable—cared for, almost. In front of her the cellar unfolded like a painting: Joseph Wright of Derby, a man who knew a few things about darkness and light. Along the far wall was the photographic stuff: a bank of washing and developing trays, a light box, and an enlarger slung from the ceiling. And above it all a clothesline strung with damp new prints, a woman's body at the center of each, the borders glowing a mauvish white under the glare of the safe lamps. Outside of its reach the room was purple-black, alive with shadows and dark silhouettes. The only one moving was his.

He had his back to her, bent over the fixing tray, pulling a print to and fro between his fingers, lifting it out and holding it up to the light, then slipping it onto the line, droplets of chemical falling around him. She watched him carefully. There was something different to his movements, a certain grace and fluidity that she had never seen before, as if concentration had loosened up his joints, oiling away his tension and shyness. He was doing what he was good at. After all, everyone has a talent for something: his were photography and voyeurism. To which she could also add: violence and death.

She went back to the photos, bracing herself for more images of her own terror. Instead she got beauty: Paola in love with the camera if not the photographer, standing tall in a long white dress so sculpted onto her that it resembled snakeskin. The lighting played games with the glow of the material over her body, heavy breasts, the swell of her stomach against the silk, the outrageously rich curve of her ass. At a distance she was almost more landscape than body; erotic snow dunes, nature female down to the last wind-sculpted curve. On someone with less style the effect would be overblown. But this woman had the confidence to carry it off. She looked like the actress who played the actress in *La Dolce Vita*, a body ripe to the edge of rotting. Too much of a woman for any one man to hold. Especially this one.

She tried to swallow, but her throat felt coated with sand. She needed to drink. The cracks of her lips must have made a noise, because he had turned from the bench, hands cupped wet in the air, before she had time to close her eyes. She noticed an instant stiffness take hold of his limbs, a stand to attention almost, as if it was he who was scared of her. Ridiculous.

She glanced back at the woman. *La Dolce Vita*. Italian. A looser way with both the body and the tongue.

"*Ciao*, Andreas," she said softly, then took her time while the thought connected to the lips. "Head" was what? And the word for "hurt"? She tried it softly. "My head hurts."

He looked at her for a while, as if not sure what to do next. "What did you say?" And the language sounded better on him too, the words gentler, less manufactured.

This time it came out more clearly. "I said, my head hurts. I need some water."

"There is water on the table. But you have to take it slowly. The drug will still be in your system."

She reached over and took the glass, then sipped it slowly as he had instructed. It helped. It had been years since she had used her Italian for anything more than hotel bookings or chitchat on trains. But there had been one summer, when she was young and her fluency was still new and vibrant in her ear, when she had gorged on it, creating romance with a Tuscan boy she had thought she would love forever, but had in fact forgotten within a few years.

Coming back to Florence, she knew now, had been an attempt to rediscover that language in herself, to draw excitement from the present tense, to feel the pull of the future as well as the weight of the past. What a shame all it had led to was death.

"Who was she?" she said, gesturing to the woman on the clothesline.

He frowned. "I told you. She's Paola. She's my wife."

Now, in his own language, there was no excuse for getting the tense wrong. She said nothing.

"You don't believe me because you can't imagine how she would want to marry someone like me. I know that. But you are wrong. She's my wife."

She took a deep breath. "What about the others?"

"The others?"

"The others. Yes. Like me."

He stared at her for a moment, then shook his head. "I see you don't understand. There are no others. You are . . . you are . . ."

"The first?" she supplied softly, and because it couldn't have been the word that caused him the trouble, she knew it had to be the feeling behind it.

"Yes." And he said it so quietly that she almost didn't hear it. "The first."

"Oh. God." The first. He probably didn't even know what to do, how to do it. It would be messy and awful. "You're right. I don't understand. Why me? I don't even look like her."

"Not really, that's true. But you sound like her."

"Sound?"

"Your voice. I heard it that morning in the café on Via Guelfa. You were speaking in Italian to the waiter. 'Can I have a glass of water and an espresso please.' " And this time he fashioned the Italian differently, her accent roughening it up at the edges. "So perfect. English and Italian together. If I closed my eyes you were her. You were Paola."

Anna took another sip of the water. So he likes the sound of your voice in Italian. So keep on talking. "What happened between you?"

"You mean why did she marry me?"

Anna shrugged. "I didn't—"

"No, you are right, of course. Why should she? She could have had many men. They were flies all over her. But I had something they didn't have. I had money, you see. A lot of money. And I was very happy to give it to her. I didn't care what she did with it. Only that she used it to make herself happy. She liked that. It was a good marriage. Better than many."

"And the photos?"

"It was my hobby. She indulged me. It was not such a hardship for her."

No, it didn't look as if it had been. Even in the mirror photos there was no sense of doubt. People love each other for the strangest of reasons. Seven years ago she had been obsessed by a man simply because she couldn't have him. There had almost been no cure for that one, either. She noticed he had moved, that he was leaning back against the workbench now, his arms crossed. If you didn't know better you might say he was a man at ease with himself. The cleansing power of confession.

"But it didn't last," she said quietly, because of course how could it have?

He gave a little shrug. "Even money is boring when you have too much of it. I knew that long before she did."

"She left you?"

His head moved down a little. It was possible to read the gesture as a nod.

"She left you and you followed her. Those were the pictures I saw in the living room, weren't they? The ones with the other people cut out?"

"It was for her own good. With money and her looks. Men smell that kind of thing. She didn't realize it. She didn't know how strong the smell was. She thought they liked her. She couldn't tell when they didn't. She would have got hurt."

"So you brought her home again." She paused, thinking it through. "Like you brought me."

He didn't speak. He didn't move. But he didn't deny it, either.

"And then she . . . died." Still he said nothing. It didn't matter. They both knew it, anyway. It was why they were here in this basement, now, together. "Did you kill her, Andreas?"

"No." And the word, the same in both languages, shot out in echo around the room. "No, I didn't kill her. I would never kill her. She did it to herself. If she hadn't gone so crazy in the car . . ."

She waited but no more words came. The car. "Was it the drug?" she said, remembering that moment in the night, the fear of flying and the terrible sense of falling. "The drug you gave her?"

He closed his eyes, hugging his arms tighter around his body, as if to give himself the comfort that no one else could. "I got the dose wrong. I gave her too little. She came awake in the car too soon. We were on the road to Casentino, up in the hills, drops everywhere. She went crazy. She would have crashed us both. So I gave her more—the whole syringe I had in the glove compartment. It was hard to judge because she was fighting me. . . ." He paused. "Then she stopped fighting and went to sleep. When we got back I carried her to the room. I sat with her every moment. But she didn't wake up."

God, how pleased he must have been to see me upright that next morning, she thought. "What does it do, this drug?" she said quietly.

He sighed. "It stops your muscles working. A kind of paralysis. You don't feel anything. Until it wears off."

She took another sip of the water. How much had he given her? How much did it take to kill her? What good would it do him if he did?

"I didn't mean to hurt you," he said, his eyes on the floor. "I only wanted to have you here with me for a while. I thought you would make things better. I knew it couldn't be the same. But while I was watching you in Florence you seemed like . . . well, you seemed like you were looking for something—something different, something new. I don't know." He paused. "I didn't know you had a child."

And the way he said it caught her attention. She remembered his surprise that first evening in the car when she had told him about Lily. It had thrown him then, just as it still threw him now. She took another sip of the water and pulled herself upright. The flesh around her eye where he had hit her felt huge and spongy. It might leave a scar, but it wouldn't kill her. Not on its own. Lily. Her absence filled the room. Lily. The reason she couldn't indulge him with her death, however tired she might feel.

"Yes, I have a child," she said slowly, and this time she spoke in English because there could be no room for mistakes now and because she needed him to be able to tell the difference between a dead wife and a living stranger. "I don't know if I can explain to you what that means. You don't love children in the same way you love adults. It's a passion, yes, even an obsession, but it's a benign one. One that brings out the best in you rather than the worst." She paused. The distance between him and her seemed so immense, too great for words to bridge. But they were all she had. "My daughter is more beautiful than any lover I ever had. She's more innocent, more knowing, more spiritual, more physical, more greedy, more giving, more loving, more manipulative than anyone I've ever known. She can't help it. It's just who she is. It's as if there's a light in her which she hasn't found the control switch for yet, an energy which pulses out across other weaker signals, pulling them into her orbit. She's not afraid of anything or anyone and I love her so much for that. In some way I've helped her to be that. My spirit, my courage. I think she drank it out of me when she was born. I didn't used to mind. I assumed that it was just what happened, whether it should or not. But there have been times recently when I have wondered if there is anything of me left. Anything not connected with her."

She stopped. He was not looking at her. She had no idea whether he was even listening. It didn't matter.

"I think that's why I came to Florence in the first place. To find out who I was without her. *If* I was without her. To see if I could do it alone. Maybe that's what you smelled in me that day in the café: a woman worn out by worship. Just as you are worn out by worshiping her."

From the clothesline behind his head, one of the prints broke free from its peg and flapped its way down to the floor near his feet. He stared at it, his fingers flexing automatically out toward it. A dead woman, still dictating his every move. No. He wasn't listening anymore. But she would say it anyway. For herself, if not for him.

"That's why I have to go home, you see. Because I understand it so much better now. I understand that I love her, but I also love myself, and that I can't live my life through another person, however magnificent or overwhelming they may be." She sighed. "And that's also why you have to let me go. So you can do the same thing for yourself, can start your life again without *her*, just as you are letting me start mine."

While she was talking he had picked up the print and was holding it in one hand, staring down at it. He can't do it, she thought. He can't let her go. Because if he did there'd be nothing left. Poor guy. She watched his right hand reach out for something on the desk nearby and in the glow of the safe light she caught the glint on the point of a needle.

He put down the photograph carefully and walked over to her, the syringe held down behind his back as if he was genuinely embarrassed by it.

She didn't move. There was nowhere to go.

He stopped in front of her. "I'm not going to hurt you," he said, in Italian. "That was never what I wanted to do."

"No," she said. "I know."

As he lifted the syringe upward she noticed it was full.

Away—Sunday P.M.

SHE DIDN'T WAKE, AND HE DIDN'T WAKE HER. WHEN SHE FINALLY opened her eyes the shutters were drawn and her watch read 3:40 P.M. As she pulled herself up in surprise she realized that the room felt different in other ways too: neater, the surfaces less filled with clutter. She went into the bathroom. By the side of the basin there was only her wash bag and her toothbrush. In the wardrobe her trousers hung next to a rail of empty hangers; by the door her new suitcase sat alone. She stood next to it for a moment, not quite able to take in what she was being told.

When she called downstairs, Reception told her he had booked out this morning, but that the room was paid for till tomorrow. She didn't find the envelope until she put down the receiver. It was propped at the back of the table lamp, her name on the front in capital letters.

The letter was in black fountain pen. She couldn't remember if she had ever seen his handwriting before, but as soon as she unfolded the page she knew it was his: big and bold with a touch of the italic about it. It reminded her of an architect lover she had once had, someone for whom the visual construction of the words was almost as important as their meaning. Both of them were men who aspired to beauty, in art, if not in life. I have absolutely no idea what you are going to say to me, she thought, as she started to read. Well done, Samuel/Marcus. You remain a surprise, right to the end.

Sunday 9:35 A.M.

Dear Anna,

I have been wandering the streets for the last hour wondering what to do. I called home this morning (there was something I had to check) and a neighbor answered the phone. She told me that my wife had been taken to hospital. It happened late last night. She had taken an overdose. The hospital says her condition is stable and she is out of danger but obviously I have to go to her. There is a plane at 12:30 from Florence airport. I can catch it if I leave now.

I don't know what to say. I can't lie to you and I don't know how to tell the truth. There were things I didn't tell you; about her, about our relationship, because they were too difficult, and if I had—well, anyway, it's not the time to start now. I'm sorry. You will think me a total bastard and that wouldn't be far from the truth, though there are mitigating circumstances, but once again, this isn't the time for them. I thought about waking you up to tell you all this, but I suppose I didn't have the courage to face your reaction. So much for what you once called my monstrous confidence, eh?

I've taken the car because it's in my name and I have to return it and because it's the quickest way for me to get to the airport. The hotel manager tells me there is a train from a nearby station back to Florence through Arezzo and from there to Pisa and he has promised me that he will get you to the right place at the right time to catch it. Your ticket will be waiting at the British Airways desk in the name of Anna Revell. The flight leaves at 7:45 tomorrow morning, BA 145.

I want to say that I'll call you in London as soon as you get back, but right at this moment I don't know that I can promise anything, since I don't know what will greet me on my return. Knowing what you know about me now, you probably wouldn't feel like answering the call anyway. I don't quite understand what happened between us last night, and this isn't the time to ask. I'll leave it a while before I get in touch, so you can think about how you feel. You can always put the phone down on me. I wouldn't be surprised.

Forgive me, Anna. I want you to know that I didn't lie about everything, only the things I couldn't handle. I shall miss you in more ways than I can say. If I say more, I risk you not believing me, and I'm already feeling guilty about too many things as it is. Yes me, guilty. Who would have believed it?

Yours, with love,
Samuel

It was a good letter, even down to its apparent spontaneity, with the odd words scored out or overwritten in haste or uncertainty. As a way of ending an affair it delivered all the right romantic ingredients: guilt, passion, confession, and the sense of being overwhelmed by circumstance, the stuff of melodrama. Nevertheless, by the time she'd finished reading it the words left echoing in her ears were not his, but Sophie Wagner's: "Very emotionally articulate for an Englishman."

Articulate, though not at all like the calculated vivisection that Ms. Wagner had found herself subjected to. Was there a different method for every woman, a kind of matchmaking of gain to pain? Or had her abrasiveness the night before made him rethink his plans, decide on a swifter exit, one in which he didn't lose the initiative? So was this about a scam complete or a scam aborted? She realized that she

still had no idea. She was not, however, entirely without ways of finding out.

The two most used numbers from his mobile had Geneva prefixes.
That much the operator confirmed. She dialed the first and waited.
After a while an answering machine kicked in. The message was in English, then in French, the woman's tone, with its American accent,
smooth and businesslike, no sex in it this time. "You've gotten through
to the Matterman Gallery. There is no one here to take your call.
Please leave your name and number and we will get back to you." The
second number (home?) was another answering machine. Different
message, same voice. "Anthony and Jacqueline are out at present.
Leave a message after the beep. Or if it's urgent call the mobile at . . ."
She articulated the numbers with singular efficiency. Not a voice with
an affinity to anything as unproductive as overdoses.

She had had time to jot down just two more, but the pencil had
been smudging and she couldn't be sure of the numbers. The first
turned out to be Russian, a district on the outskirts of St. Petersburg.
It rang six times and a man answered. Just as he picked up she realized
she had no idea what she was going to say. The voice answered in Russian.

"Hello. Do you speak English?"

"Yes, I do." And it was clear from the accent that he also did it
well.

"I'm calling from the Matterman Gallery in Geneva. I've had a
query about a painting that I think you may have helped us with earlier this year. February, I think it was."

There was a pause. Either his English had got suddenly worse or
he hadn't liked what he heard. "Who is this calling?"

"Er . . . the Matterman Gallery. In Geneva, Switzerland."

"Is Tony there?"

"No. No. Tony and Jacqueline are away. But—"

"I'm sorry. You must have the wrong number. I can't help you."

The line went dead. She put down the receiver. The phone rang
immediately.

What if it's him, she caught herself thinking as her hand reached

out for it, ringing to see if I'm okay? But she knew it wasn't, even before she heard the manager's voice, efficient, ever eager to help. Mr.
Taylor had said that she would be wanting to catch an evening train
for Arezzo in order to get herself to Florence that night. The 7:20 was
the last through train, and the station was thirty or so kilometers away.
In Sunday evening summer traffic it might take a while. He had taken
the precaution of ordering a taxi, which was downstairs waiting, but if
she had changed her mind he could cancel it again. . . .

It struck her that she should call the airport now to book another
seat. The final irony was that the ticket he had bought her was, of
course, not in her own name, and she might find herself having to
fund her own way home. But the number, when she got through, was
engaged and she didn't want to miss the train. Instead, she got the
hotel owner to cash the rest of her English money in case she should
need to buy another ticket. As he waved her good-bye on the steps he
was, she felt, relieved to see her go. By the end of the season he would
have processed the "Taylors" into an exotic story of domestic violence
and desertion. Even that wouldn't be as colorful as the truth, whatever
that was.

The journey to Arezzo took almost an hour. She sat watching the
landscape turn from forest to scrubland dotted with olive groves and
vineyards as the train moved south down from the hills and into the
valley. Leaving Casentino. She remembered the morning they had
driven out of Florence (was it really only yesterday?), the sun in her
eyes and romantic tales of fates and furies in her head. It was not as
yet clear how close she, too, had come to losing her soul. For now,
against the odds, she was all right, a woman cruising on a high-octane
fuel of curiosity and outrage.

She pulled her eyes in from the window. The leather suitcase was
perched on the seat opposite, like some old-fashioned traveling companion. It was so stylish and perfect that it was hard to see it as a gift,
rather than a token of his self-esteem. Add it to the list of things that
didn't make sense. If this was a scam about fleecing lovers, why waste
good money on rich gifts? Somehow they must be part of the deal.

Fuck 'em stupid and leave them with something to remember you by. But the puzzle remained: Why spend so much on someone you were planning to steal from later?

Unless you knew you were going to get it back. Of course—if you were going to burgle them, it didn't matter how much the gift cost. They wouldn't get to keep it anyway. Had Sophie Wagner's Russian presents walked out of the apartment with her antique rugs and jewelry? Was that what would happen to her—she'd come home to find the suitcase gone along with the stereo and the computer? God knows it was probably worth more than most of the other things in her house.

The thought lit up like an electric light in her head. Of course. The most expensive object was the present that he stole back. That would explain why he had waited till Sophie Wagner got home. If all he wanted was her valuables he could have sent someone in while he was bedding her in another country. But he waited. Presumably because whatever he had given her in St. Petersburg was more important than anything that was already there.

She pulled the case over onto her lap. She was struck again by the extraordinary quality of the work; the suppleness of the leather, the perfection of the stitching. She slid her fingers over its soft sides. Touching skin. It was what this story was about. Think about it, Anna. One more time.

She and Sophie Wagner had met a stranger from the want ads who claimed to be an art consultant, but who in fact made his money through scams.

She opened it up and felt inside. Even the invisible bits were beautifully sewn, a veritable miracle of craftsmanship in an age of cheap disposable luggage.

Scams. The art of theft. Taking what didn't belong to you and making money out of it.

She plunged her fingers farther down, feeling her way past the carefully wrapped wooden horse right to the bottom of the case. Its leather base was solid, and a substantial size too, though still acceptable for hand luggage.

The art of theft. Or, to be more accurate, the theft of art. Two love affairs, two different places. St. Petersburg and Tuscany: the first a city groaning with art and run by new bad boys willing to flog Mother Russia's heritage to the highest bidder, the second a region so stuffed with historical treasures that it was virtually impossible to even document, let alone protect them all. It was just a question of match-making: find the right collector and the right price, and the only prob-lem is how to lift it off the walls or out of the vaults and get it safely out of the country.

She felt the weight of the bag on her knees. She remembered her-self sitting in the taxi that first afternoon from Florence to Fiesole, her old nylon holdall on her lap, the heat sticking her clothes to the seat underneath. It was cooler now, but this case still felt heavier than the other one. Yet she had added nothing since then. Nothing, that is, but the bag itself. It was so simple it was almost an insult. Like giving a present in order to take it away again.

The engine had started to slow down and the voice over the speakers told her they were approaching Arezzo. She hauled herself out of the seat, the bag gripped tight to her chest, and they spilled out together onto the platform, her head spinning. She had just under forty minutes to make the Florence connection. How long did it take to skin a pig a second time?

In the end she went to a hotel at the corner of the station piazza, because the loos were too small, the station waiting room too public, and she couldn't think of anywhere else where she wouldn't be dis-turbed. She took a room for the night. She explained that she had had her wallet stolen, losing everything but the hundred-thousand-lire note she had just put on the counter, but that fortunately she had an emergency stash of British money sewn into the bottom of her suit-case. All she needed was a knife or scissors to cut it out with. He may or may not have believed her. She flashed her wrists to show there was no previous history of self-mutilation. No doubt he had seen and heard weirder in his time. She took the bag and the knife upstairs and started cutting up pigskin.

Home—Sunday P.M.

PAUL LEFT IN MIDAFTERNOON, DROPPING US AT THE TUBE ON our way into town. It seemed better that way, rather than having to negotiate another full-blown set of good-byes. He had told Lily about the meeting and promised he'd be back by Monday night at the latest. He put a lot of energy into emphasizing that fact. I don't know what she made of it, but she hugged him over the backseat anyway and wished him luck.

We got off at Westminster and walked along the embankment to the Tate Gallery. Outside it was hot and sticky and London was full of tourists, people like Anna, clutching guidebooks and money belts, searching for culture with a secret hankering after life. The Tate was already crowded with Sunday art lovers, but Lily was a regular, and she had a plan. She made a beeline for the Kids' Cart set up like a colorful tea trolley in the Atrium. From there, clutching a plastic tray full of scissors, instructions, and sticky bits, we sallied forth to track down the right painting with which to inspire our own collage.

She read the gallery map better than I did and, cutting a swath through the various isms of late nineteenth- and twentieth-century art, we ended up in England circa 1780, in front of a selection of George Stubbs horse paintings, which we then proceeded to re-create with the help of large expanses of sticky colored paper on white card.

I did what I was told. Lily was at her most imperious—concentration like a force field around her. As I sat in the corner cutting out bits of horse anatomy according to her orders, I kept thinking about how my father and I had spent the weekends after my mother's death. I was too old for do-it-yourself art and too young for Certificate 15 movies; it had been a sorry couple of years. Train journeys were out of the question, of course. I don't think my father traveled by train for years after her death. Too afraid of running her over on the line, I expect. Fortunately I didn't absorb that particular fear. Maybe, after all, it's better not to see the body.

For the record, I don't really believe my mother was leaving us for anyone else. I think she just made a mistake. Spent too long somewhere and in her hurry to get back to the station disobeyed the notices and crossed against the barrier. You never think it'll happen to you, anyway. Statistics are only numbers until you become one of them.

No. I don't think there was any subtext—any other man, or the search for another life, any story at all really. I think she was an ordinary woman who loved her family, and that what happened to her was simply an accident.

I feel safer that way.

Lily was staring up at the painting, her nose wrinkled up in deepest thought. "Problem?" I said, ruffling her hair, which I know she hates but sometimes lets me do anyway.

"He's got the back legs wrong, they're too spindly. And look at that tree over there. It's all furry."

It had to be said she had a point. "Fried parsley," I said.

"What?" she giggled.

"That's what one of his fellow painters called Thomas Gainsborough's trees."

"They didn't," she said, evidently delighted.

I shrugged knowingly.

"Really. Who told you that?"

"Can't remember. Must have been something I learned at school," I said. "Where do you want to put this wavy bit?"

"The mane you mean." She snatched it from me, insulted. "Honestly, Stel, you don't know anything about horses."

"No," I said. "Me and George Stubbs."

She rode the rest of the afternoon in equine triumph, but when we got back, tired and hot from the journey, and went into the house, its very emptiness set us both on edge. In the hall the light was flashing on the answering machine. I saw it as soon as we got in and was desperate to answer it, but not in her presence. I needn't have bothered. She marched straight up to it, flicking all the right buttons like some kindergarten pinball wizard. The tape buzzed back and I found myself picking her up in my arms to listen to it, just for protection.

First the beep, then Patricia's voice, dancing down the line, calling to see how we all were and whether Mum had managed to get home as yet, and that she would call again this evening sometime. Patricia, of course, would know that her charge was a dab hand at the answering machine, and mediate her words accordingly. I glanced at Lily's face. The light from the horses had gone out of her now and I could feel what I thought was a growing fragility.

I did what I could. We made supper together, spaghetti carbonara, her sounding out the words in the recipe book while I did the business, bringing her in for the beating of the eggs and the tossing in the pan. We ate it at the kitchen table with Parmesan and tomato salad. It was quarter to seven. The evening stretched ahead like wild unmapped territory, the howl of the wolves getting louder in my imagination.

The phone rang twice between the washing up and the bath. I tried not to run to pick it up. Mike calling from the theater to see how we were. Lily joined in on the extension and he saved the best bits for her, stories of lights that made a snowstorm on the stage, and stars in the sky. Maybe after school tomorrow she would like to pop in and see it.

"Thanks," she said. Then, "But I can't tomorrow. Mum's coming home."

No sooner had we put it down than Patricia called again. Lily chattered to her while I finished running the bath; then I put her into it and took the call alone in Anna's study.

". . . That's grand news. When did she call?"

I took a sigh. "It's not that simple, Patricia. It's a long story."

"Oh," she said, after I had told it. "Oh dear. And I was sure from the way Lily . . ."

She broke off and I realized she was near to tears. Family occasions. They bring out the sentiment in all of us. I cleared my throat and told her we'd speak again tomorrow as soon as she got home. All this and I still had Paul's late-night call to look forward to.

As I put down the receiver I heard the crash from the bathroom. My heart went crazy. I was there almost before she hit the floor. Only the scream told me I'd missed it. She had been climbing out of the bath, foamy dolphin-fat body on slippery feet, and had missed her footing. As she fell the back of her head had slammed into one of the cupboards. When I finally got to look at it, the skin wasn't broken and the bump was no big deal at all, but that wasn't the point. The point was that she was hurt and scared and her mum wasn't there to make it better. Maybe she'd been looking for a reason to cry. I know I had.

Once the tears started they wouldn't stop. I wrapped her in a big towel and clutched her to me, letting the sobs flow. As she cried I talked to her: "You're all right, darling. Stupid bath, poor Lily. Nothing broken," half-repeated phrases, silly mantras of comfort, while I carried her down to the kitchen where I fixed a poultice of ice to stop the swelling.

She sat on my lap, holding it to her head, as I hugged her tight. To my surprise my calm was as great as her distress, and after a while she seemed to take comfort from it, allowing herself to be stilled and quietened. The tears subsided, then finally stopped altogether. We sat in silence, her body hot and clammy in mine. Eventually curiosity got the better of her and she put up a hand to feel the lump.

"What d'you think?" I said. "Egg or billiard ball?"

She made a clucking noise with her teeth. "Mum always says it hurt the cupboard more than it did me."

"Oh, I see. You hit it regularly, do you?"

"Steeellla," she complained, then relaxed back against me. We stayed like that for a few moments. We were, I realized, both so tired.

I put her in her pajamas and brushed out her hair carefully so it wouldn't hurt the bump while we sat together watching a rerun of *Honey, I Shrunk the Kids* on the television. While she seemed fine now I was the one with the jitters. I found the scene of the attack by the giant predatory insects unbearably tense.

After it was over we made hot chocolate and went up to Anna's bed. It wasn't yet nine o'clock, and outside summer was still strutting its stuff. I closed the curtains on an outrageously pink sky. I could barely keep my eyes open. Downstairs the answering machine would talk to Paul. If I didn't pick up his call he would know that was because there was nothing to tell. I could hear about the hotel décor tomorrow morning. I needed to be fresh and early to cope with the school run.

We played Twenty Questions in the gloom for a while, then fell silent. She snuggled into my crook. She felt comfortable there. So did I. You did all right, Stella, a tiny voice said in the back of my skull. I really think you did all right.

"Mummy's back tomorrow, isn't she?" she asked, maybe as much as ten minutes later, when I was sure she was already asleep.

"Probably, darling," I said. "We'll have to wait and see."

Away—Sunday P.M.

HE PLACED HER OUTSIDE IN THE SUNSHINE, AWAY FROM THE FUMES and the chemicals and the dark, in the meadow down by the lake where he had offered to take her that very first day when he had asked her to stay on as his guest and she had refused.

Despite the altitude and the lateness of the hour it was still hot, that blissful un-English heat that drains both energy and tension equally, leaving one listless and sublime. He had chosen somewhere with a tree roof of shade, but of course the shade had traveled with the passage of the sun and by late afternoon she was directly in its glare, the heat soaking into her body, the light poking its way under her eyelids. It was the first thing she became aware of—a shower of shining golden needles raining down on her, trying to get in through the lids.

She opened her eyes and the intensity was so fierce that she had to shut them immediately. She felt sick and heavy, as if she could never get up out of the chair. That was partly to do with the weight upon her. There was something lying across her lap, pinning her to the seat. She opened her eyes again and this time forced herself to look at it. It was a cardboard box, shaped like a shoebox, only much bigger, for boots maybe. Paola's boots.

She was alive and lying in the garden with Paola's boots on her lap. The thought got her halfway to her feet. But the deck chair was low to the ground and her balance still so far from perfect that she fell forward, the box tumbling off her lap and spewing open on the grass, its contents scattering all around.

She found herself on her hands and knees amid a storm of pictures of herself: glossy black-and-white prints of all sizes and shapes, taken in cafés, in mirrors, in bed, drugged and awake, happy and scared, wounded and whole. So many of them. All of them, surely.

Nearby lay two large envelopes. Ripping open the first she loosed a shower of negatives into the air, dark secret strips of frozen moments, the footnotes from a history of obsession, now complete. In the other envelope she found her own wallet, soft with a padding of extra notes. She checked the denominations. Fifty thousand lire. Enough to buy whatever was needed in the way of return tickets, on land and in air. And there, at the very bottom, her passport.

She lay back in the grass clutching it to her chest, her fingers curling themselves in and around its pages, as if by feeling her way through it she somehow became herself again: Anna Franklin, thirty-nine-year-old British tourist on a summer break in Italy, now heading for home.

The sunshine poured over her, heavy and sweet like running honey. It stuck to her skin and her clothes, making her want to give in and relax. She could do that now. She could stay and rest or get up and go. She felt sick and exhausted, but she would cope. He had not killed her. He had set her free. She closed her eyes again and for a while let the sunshine dance across her eyelids.

When she felt she could manage it, she pulled herself to her feet and gathered the contents of the box back into it again. Only now did she notice the plastic bag, which had fallen behind her. In it were a clean set of clothes: trousers, T-shirt, top, and shoes, Paola's designer wardrobe at its most casual, and—in tissue paper—the wooden horse, its hind leg half-severed halfway up. She held it for a moment, then rewrapped it carefully and put it back in the bag.

She changed her clothes in the forest, rolling the crushed red silk into a tight little bundle and slipping it next to the photographs. Then, tucking the box underneath her arm, she set off along a half-obscured path that snaked its way through the trees. She had been walking for less than a minute when she caught sight of the house ahead in the distance. She stopped, old fear curdling her stomach juices anew. From afar it seemed so benign, emerging out of the forest landscape like an advertisement for summer lets, a beautiful old Tuscan building, proud of its ability to withstand weather and history. The sun was behind her, blowing hot breaths across her shoulders and the back of her neck, teasing her with its warmth. She stood for a long time watching it, wondering if in turn it might be watching her. But she could feel no malevolence. She took a few steps closer.

She realized now that the house was closed up, its shutters drawn tight against the insistent attention of the sun, as if the building too was resting afterward, protecting itself against any further madness of its occupant. She could make out the front gravel drive, and as she did so she could hear again the sound of his feet as he pulled her from the car, the beautiful nausea of the evening sky. But there was no car there now. He had gone. Had he followed his wife into that last good night or simply locked the door on the past and walked away?

As she thought this she realized with a shock that she was no longer so afraid of him. It was as if her freedom and his absence allowed almost an acceptance of him; the way you might feel toward a companion with whom you've shared a terrible journey; someone you have disliked, even hated and despised at times, but someone with whom you have seen it through, have come out the other end.

She slipped back into the trees, negotiating her own track through the forest in the direction of the road. She took it slowly, aware of the aftereffects of the drug still washing through her. The sweet, almost familiar sickness played at the edges of her brain, making every step intense, concentrated, so that it took her a long time to cover the couple of miles to the main road, guided onward by the growing sounds of car engines and a haze of sunlight.

Once there, she could probably have got a lift immediately if she'd stuck out her thumb. But the summer traffic that passed her was mainly small cars full of families, and she knew that she couldn't be close to any child but Lily right now; so instead she stayed parallel to the road, hidden in the forest, and walked on alone. The land continued to climb steeply, the low sun fracturing in between the tall towering trunks of the trees, like the pillars of some vast Gothic cathedral suffused with light. At an intersection half a mile on, the forest began to die away and she saw a sign to the Monastery of the Stigmata of St. Francis of Assisi, an austere chapel perched high on a spectacular outcrop of rock to her right, with its adjacent long white buildings seeming to sprout straight out of the stone. St. Francis. There was a man who knew a thing or two about trials and tribulations. The people who visited his shrine would be the sort to help a woman in need without asking too many questions.

After all, she had perfected her Italian now.

One way or another she would get herself a lift, if not to Florence then to Arezzo. If not in time for tonight's flight then in time for tomorrow morning's. It was over. She was going home.

Away—Sunday P.M.

THE WOMAN WAS LOVELIER THAN SHE HAD REMEMBERED HER FROM the church. But then they hadn't been this close to each other before.

She was sitting in the middle of an Italian landscape in high summer, cypress trees and dusty roads, with her son's body draped like a monstrously heavy bolt of cloth across her lap, her crisp blue skirts crushed under the bulk of dead flesh.

Yet despite her body's complaint, her expression was serene. She was beautiful, younger than she ought to have been given her son's age and her own suffering, an almost teenage plumpness to her features, a peach-blossom sheen in the brushstrokes of her skin. Her eyes were cast down as befitting her grief and modesty, yet the overall impact was more human than ethereal. She looked more like someone's daughter or sister than the Mother of God. Take away her awful burden and she would, you might think, have the inclination to go dancing. It was that earthy quality that made her the more arresting, marking her out from a hundred other Madonnas as loving but less alive than her.

Her. The pronoun stuck like a fly in syrup, impossible to miss once you had heard its panic buzzing. "Her." Of course. This was the "her" in the message on the mobile phone; the "her" that had to make all the right connections, the "her" they had to get back as planned because the client was waiting. The Madonna of Bottoni's pietà, plucked from a rural Casentino church and spirited away at the bottom of a lover's gift.

But how and when had she got here? When you are learning to read, you can only get to understand the big words by sounding out all the syllables. She started with what she knew.

Yesterday morning she had stood in front of a tabernacle pietà in a Casentino village, transfixed while a rheumy-eyed old man had waxed lyrical about the minor masterpiece the work had almost been. What was it he had said about it? That there had been a rumor that it might be a work of the eighteenth-century painter Pompea Bottoni: a gift made to a nearby religious house celebrating the entrance of a young woman into their order, a young woman who some believed to be nearer in kin to the painter than would, at the time, have been considered respectable.

Whatever the truth of the story, had the work actually proved to be a Bottoni it would have been of considerable worth. Not simply because it was unusual for a court painter to execute a religious painting, but because the face of the Virgin reflected his talent for portraiture, especially when it came to capturing the features of a daughter he loved but could never acknowledge. All in all, a tasty item for the right collector. If, that is, the Church had been willing to sell it. Which it almost certainly would not.

But as it turned out the Church had never had to make the decision, because the act of restoration had revealed not an original Bottoni but an anonymous nineteenth-century painting, nice enough for a Romanesque altar, but no more than that. A lost opportunity, for both art and Mammon. Cause for disappointment, certainly, but hardly for accusations of fraud, fakery, or theft.

Except that all of those things had, in fact, taken place. The original Bottoni would have been copied while it was in the restorer's hands. It was the perfect opportunity: restoration was a painstaking and transforming process (as was copying; the same man might well be adept at both), and the painting that came out of the studio would, by definition, not look the same as the one that went in. Since its authenticity had always been conjecture rather than fact, restoration would simply have cleared up the matter in a way which, presumably, even experts would accept.

So the Casentino church would get back a pietà that they could accept and love for what it was—not the real thing—while the actual painting would be on its journey to its new owner. And to keep the operation anonymous, they had selected the perfect courier: an innocent tourist with no connection to the art world and no earthly reason to arouse the attention of Her Majesty's customs officials in London. Thus Our Lady and her dead son would travel from a Florentine studio to a safe house in West London, from where they could be picked up and delivered by the people who were selling them. No wonder he had been so eager for them to visit the church. What job satisfaction he must have got from seeing the fake successfully installed, while the original was sitting outside in the boot of his car.

So clever, so simple. And so cheap. What had her art lover said the real painting would have been worth? Upwards of three hundred thousand on the open market. And when the market was closed and this was a onetime special, the chance to own something unique, something that no longer even officially existed? Presumably, if that was what turned you on, then you would pay whatever it took to get it. Even with expenses the profit margin would be considerable. Take away the price of a good faker, the services of a talented leather merchant, and the time it took to wind the right woman around your little finger, and you had—what? Two hundred thousand pounds? Probably more. The last item of cost would hardly register anyway. Even drug barons pay their carriers for the stomachaches they cause. Diseases of the heart, however, do not qualify for compensation. All in all, a highly profitable venture.

But only if you got the product home safely. If something went wrong in transit, if the luggage got damaged or mislaid, then all that handsome profit would turn into loss, and the reputation of the supplier would become as dingy and cracked as the paint on an unrestored old master. Not to mention the damage it would do to their monstrous confidence.

She slipped the plump young Madonna back into her firm leather binding, sealing her off from the immorality of the world around her, then made her way back to the station, where, before catching the night train to Florence, she did what had to be done with left luggage.

When the train got in she grabbed a few hours' sleep on a bench in Santa Maria Novella station, then rang him as early as she dared before she left for the airport: 5:35 A.M. European time. It rang a long time. Where would he be now, this man with his mobile life and phone? At another airport? Reading another set of want ads? Or at the end of a homecoming night with a partner in crime? Ah well, time to wake up now . . .

"Hello, Samuel," she said, standing by the bank of phones, a tower of coins on the top.

"Who is this?" he said, perplexed rather than sleepy.

"What, forgotten me so soon?"

"Anna?" And to her satisfaction, his astonishment was impossible to miss. "Anna—is that you?"

"Yeah," she said gaily. "The same. How are you?"

"I'm okay. My God, how incredible to hear your voice. How did you—"

"I got your letter. It was . . . it was very moving. How is she?"

"She's . . . she's, er . . . going to be fine. Listen, er . . . I can't really talk to you now. I'm, er . . . well, I'm still at the hospital, actually. Why don't you give me your number and I'll call you back in a bit."

"Oh, I'm sorry. I can't do that. I'm in Florence, about to get on a train to the airport. I wanted to tell you about your suitcase, but we can leave it if you like."

"The suitcase? Listen, just hold on for a sec, will you?" The line went quieter, as if he had put a hand over the mouthpiece. She stood and waited, shoving in a few more of her fast-diminishing five-hundred-lire stash. Money-hungry things, mobiles, rather like their owners. Where are you really? she wondered. Hard to tell with a man whose skill was to be close even when he was far away. "Hi. Hi, I'm back."

"Good. She's okay, then?"

"Um . . . she's off the danger list. They can't tell me any more yet. So what did you want to tell me about the suitcase?"

"It's just I can't take it with me. Home, I mean."

"Why not?" And you could hear that he really wanted to know the answer.

"I . . . I had an accident getting onto the train at Arezzo station yesterday evening. I fell and did my back in. I think I might have strained something. Anyway, I couldn't carry it anymore. I had to transfer my stuff to my old holdall. It's got a shoulder strap and I can manage that better."

There was a pause. He would be thinking very fast now, a dozen roads leading away from a single fact. He would be good at that, presumably. "So what did you do with the bag?"

"I put it in left luggage at Arezzo station. I mean, it was too beautiful just to leave. I thought you'd probably come this way for work sometime, and maybe you could pick it up then. If you give me your address I'll send you the left luggage receipt when I get home."

The pause lengthened. Damage limitation. Isn't that what they call it in flash companies? However good you are, it's not going to be good enough, she thought sweetly. "Anna. Listen, it's great to hear from you. Really. I . . . I mean tell me, how on earth did you track me down?"

"Your mobile number, you mean? Oh, I forgot to tell you. While you were in the restaurant last night it rang. I found the receiver in your jacket pocket. The number was in the system and I jotted it down. You were always saying you'd give it to me, remember, but you never got around to it."

"You took a call for me last night?"

"No. I just heard the phone ring. I didn't get to it in time. I presume they left a message." She paused. "Though after I'd read your letter I did wonder if it might have been your wife." He didn't say anything. She fed four more coins into the silence. The line flickered.

"You still there?" he said quickly.

"Yes, I'm here. It wasn't her, was it, Samuel?"

"Er, no . . . no. It was business. Listen, about the case?"

"Yes?"

"I'm probably going to have to be back in Florence sometime in the next week. I could go and pick it up then. If you gave me the details over the phone now—"

"Okay. If you tell me when, I can call the office. Apparently, if you don't have the ticket you have to give them a name and a time of collection." She paused. "You know Italian bureaucracy."

"Er . . . How about Thursday morning?"

"So soon?" she said, because anyone would have been surprised in the circumstances.

"Yeah, I know . . . er . . . I have to be in Rome for a meeting later but I could stop off en route." The pay phone beeped again; only two more coins left. Couldn't stop now. "Anna, Anna, you there?" he barked, definitely a little panicky this time.

She let him sweat for a few seconds, then read the details down the phone. He repeated each digit back to her. No room for a mistake here. A small silence followed. "So," she said, "I hope things work out for you, Samuel. Sounds like you're going to have a lot on your plate for a while."

"Yeah, it seems so. But listen, I'll send on the suitcase to you next week sometime. I've got your address, haven't I?"

"Probably," she said gaily. "If not I'm in the directory."

There was a pause. "Is that under Revell or Franklin?"

She took in a sharp breath. Well, it was only fitting that she shouldn't have it all her own way. She laughed. "Now, how did you know that?"

"I saw your passport in the bedroom. Why, is it important?"

"No. No, not at all."

"Okay. Anyway—listen, I . . . er . . . I'll call you when things calm down, yes?"

"No, you won't," she said softly. "But it's just as well, really, because I wouldn't answer it anyway."

Disappointed in love, disappointed in business. It was going to be a bad week for Samuel Taylor, or whoever he was. Down the other end of the phone he laughed uncomfortably. "Okay. If that's how you feel. I don't know quite what to say."

"How about 'I'm going to miss you'?"

"Yeah, well, you know, that might even be—"

The phone beeped again, then a long beep, like the siren wail of a cardiac machine when the patient is declared dead.

"The truth?" she said as she put the receiver down. "Somehow I doubt that. Bye, Tony."

But he was already gone. She looked up at the board. The 5:47 to Ligorno via Pisa Central was leaving in five minutes. On her way to the train she added the word "Thursday" to the letter and dropped it into the postbox on the main concourse. The church custodian would get it tomorrow morning. She would have liked to see his face as he read the words that told him where, when, and in whose hands his precious Bottoni could be found.

Transit—Monday A.M.

SEVEN-TEN A.M. PISA AIRPORT. THE CONCOURSE BUILDING STARTS where the railway track ends, but, alas, there are no direct trains this early, and passengers from Florence have to go to Pisa Central and take a taxi from there to the outskirts of the town. Seven-forty-five is a crazy hour for a flight to London anyway, but this way the aircraft can make the most of a commercial day, zipping to and fro and getting back into Pisa in time for late evening and a cheaper night stopover than Gatwick would ever allow.

The terminal doesn't exactly rise to the occasion. The one duty-free shop is elegant enough, but closed, the café open but ordinary. Most people don't have time for it, anyway. The flight is already boarding, though the desk is still besieged, a mixture of foreign travelers and Italian businessmen with briefcases heavy with spreadsheets and ambition. The woman at the end of the queue fits in neither camp. Though she has just come out from the bathroom, she looks disheveled. Maybe it's her face. Impossible to ignore the thick purple bruise disfiguring her right eyebrow, or the exhaustion in her eyes, not to mention the large plastic bag that seems to constitute her entire luggage.

Although no one is consciously looking at her she is well aware of the impression she must make, and the fact that when it comes to her turn at the desk it will put her at a distinct disadvantage with the ground staff.

As it does. The man on the desk tries not to look at her face as he scrolls down the computer lists shaking his head all the time. "I'm sorry, madam. We are absolutely full," he says in admirably plain English. "And as you see, there is a waiting list."

She takes a breath. "But you don't understand. I have to get home. My child is waiting for me. I've been trying to get out of Florence for the last three days. The British Airways office in town—they told me this flight would be the one. They told me to come here and try."

He frowns. "They had no right to tell you that, madam. As you can see, we are very busy. This is the high season, and all the planes are full, with people waiting. I'm sorry, but all I can do is to put you on the standby list."

But she knows this isn't the whole truth. She has friends who fly with silver cards and business accounts. She understands that planes are only full to the wrong people, and that depending on who you are or what you are willing to do you can always find one seat.

He is waiting for her to move, but she stands her ground. Then she begins to cry. Quietly at first, then louder, wilder sobs and clutching of breath as if her very heart might break open on the airport concourse and he, the desk clerk, will be the one who has to pick up the pieces. He watches her with growing apprehension. It is altogether too early for hysteria, and in his experience, despite their phlegmatic reputation, the English have a peculiar talent for it. Around her people are beginning to fidget and look anxious. There is no supervisor on site this early and the flight is due to take off in fifteen minutes. He runs his cursor down the computer lists again, then checks the waiting list and the clock.

"All right," he says. And she calms down with impressive speed.

"... World Traveller is completely full. I can't do anything there. But it looks as if we will have one club seat free. There's a waiting list on it, but since this is an emergency and a question of children ... Of course, the seat is more expensive." And he looks up, obviously hoping this will change her mind.

"How much?"

He pushes a few buttons and comes up with a sum that would have taken her to New York and back by most carriers. She doesn't blink an eye, just digs out her wallet and lays the cash on the table, a mixture of English and Italian notes and finally, when that isn't quite enough, the last ten thousand lire in change.

By the time he completes the paperwork and hands her the boarding pass the flight is already flashing last call. At the bank of phones at the back of the concourse she rummages frantically through her plastic bag, pulling out clothes and packages in search of any overlooked currency, adding a few further coins to the pile of lire stacked near the receiver. She takes all the money and shoves it into the slot, then dials. At the other end the message is short and to the point.

"Anna and Lily are not in at the moment. If you want to send a fax please dial—"

She gets ready to speak. . . .

Home—Monday A.M.

I HAD SET THE ALARM FOR 7:30, SCARED THAT WE MIGHT SOMEHOW oversleep and she would miss school, but of course I was awake long before that, lying with her by my side, imagining the rest of my life as a working mother. I had drafted out my resignation letter to the firm and put the apartment on the market. I had yet to find the right job in London—part-time in corporate law is something of a contradiction in terms—but I was far from exhausting the possibilities. As I went through all this, I didn't think about Anna. It was almost as if she were in cold storage somewhere, suspended in Dante's Purgatory, somewhere between the living and the dead. "Due home any time," it read on her label, "contingency plans being made meanwhile."

I had got as far as next year's summer holiday visiting my father in New South Wales when the telephone rang. I looked at my watch. It was 6:37. Too early for Paul.

But an hour later in Italy.

"—not in at the moment. If you want to send a fax—"

Who else could it be but her?

"—leave a message after the beep."

As I hurtled my way down the stairs to switch off the machine I thought of Lily and my mother and all the ways in which you can never, never predict what is going to happen next. Thank God.

"Thank you for call—"

I had it in my hand. I pressed the Off switch and brought it to my ear.

The line was loud and alive with what could have been the sound of a voice, and then, equally suddenly, it was dead.

"Anna," I said softly into the receiver. "Anna." Because in that split second I was absolutely sure that it was indeed she, and that the tunnel of madness we had been pulled through, the fantasies with which we had been torturing ourselves, were about to end.

At the top of the stairs Lily, the telephone ghost, was standing waiting, drawn by the echo of the ring.

I grinned up at her. "I think that was your mum," I said.

And in the joy of her returning smile I saw myself flinging open the windows of my apartment, lighting a joint, watching the smoke curl through my fingertips as I sat contentedly alone.

Three days away can be a long time.

Transit—Monday A.M.

THE LINE IS DEAD, THE MONEY FINISHED. SHE SLAPS THE PHONE angrily, then, grabbing her bag, turns and starts to run toward the departure gate. The concourse is almost empty now; any remaining would-be travelers have dropped off the end of the waiting list and have either left or are settling in for the day.

She is the last through Passport Control, the last through the security check. She smiles her apologies. She is eager to be gone. Glancing into the departure lounge ahead, she sees it is empty apart from the ground staff at the gate, checking the lists in front of them. They won't go without her. Not a club-class passenger. Surely.

As she scoops up her bag at the end of the X-ray machine the top layer comes loose, spewing clothing onto the rollers. She stuffs it back in, and as she does she realizes something is missing. She plunges her fingers down deep into the bag, feeling for the wrapping paper, searching for the weight of heavy wood and the sharp ridge of horse legs. But it's not there. Lily's present: she must have taken it out when she was going through her bag for extra coins to make the call, must have left it at the telephones. She can see it in her mind's eye, discarded on the floor, waiting for her to come back for it. The wooden horse. Maybe the only thing from this whole wild, vicious journey worth keeping. She glances quickly back from where she has come, but the concourse is already a foreign country (separated by customs and Passport Control). And the flight is leaving. . . .

Her hesitation lasts barely a second before she hauls up her bag and moves swiftly toward the gate.

The departure lounge stretches out in front of Anna like the future. On the other side of the barrier the rest of her life is waiting, and she is aching to walk into it. She will be different now, she knows, though in what ways it is, as yet, impossible to tell. She can already imagine her arrival: the sound of the key in the lock, the force of Lily's body as she flings herself up and into her arms, their joint voices exploding into laughter. With each step she feels lighter, carefree, made almost younger by the sense of anticipation.

Anna is coming home.

Meanwhile, behind her a man walks across the airport concourse to a bank of telephones and, reaching down, lifts up a small brown package, before continuing on his way.

About the Type

This book was set in Centaur, a typeface designed by the American typographer Bruce Rogers in 1929. Rogers adapted Centaur from the fifteenth-century type of Nicholas Jenson and modified it in 1948 for a cutting by the Monotype Corporation.